She heard him drawn in a ragged breath. Seconds ticked by.

"And," she continued, "it wasn't what I thought it would be. Or hoped it would be. The admiral was . . . well, now I smell wretched."

She watched as his free arm reached for a bloom on the white rosebush beside them. He crushed the flower and his hand came away with petals.

Slowly, gently, he brought the petals to her shoulder and eased them along the curve to her neck. Soft like velvet, the bloom's sweet fragrance washed away the other scent.

He had never been so close to her before.

Without thinking, she raised her arms and wound them around his neck. She gazed into his dark, mysterious eyes, staring intently back into hers, and neither of them breathed.

It was the most exquisite moment of her life.

Until the next instant . . . when he released the petals and harshly drew her into his embrace. His firm mouth found hers and she could not stop a rush of wildness flowing through her, making her shiver.

By Sophia Nash

THE ONCE AND FUTURE DUCHESS
THE DUKE DIARIES
THE ART OF DUKE HUNTING
BETWEEN THE DUKE AND THE DEEP BLUE SEA
SECRETS OF A SCANDALOUS BRIDE
LOVE WITH THE PERFECT SCOUNDREL
THE KISS
A DANGEROUS BEAUTY

Sophia Nash

THE
ONCE AND FUTURE
Duchess

AVON

An Imprint of HarperCollinsPublishers

AVON BOOKS
An Imprint of HarperCollins*Publishers*
195 Broadway
New York, New York 10007

Copyright © 2014 by Sophia Nash
Excerpt from *Between the Duke and the Deep Blue Sea* copyright © 2012 by Sophia Nash
ISBN 978-0-06-227363-5
www.avonromance.com

First Avon Books mass market printing: June 2014

Avon Trademark Reg. U.S. Pat. Off. and in Other Countries, Marca Registrada, Hecho en U.S.A.
HarperCollins® is a registered trademark of HarperCollins Publishers.

Printed in the U.S.A.

10 9 8 7 6 5 4 3 2 1

To
Carrie Feron
Thank you for your belief in me.
And to
Michel, a true gentleman through and through.

Chapter 1

There comes a time in a lady's life when she must lace up her stiffest corset and face what she fears above all else. It's called a day of reckoning in polite circles. But in the privacy of her mind, Isabelle Tremont, the Duchess of March, preferred language far less refined. Base, in fact. Yes, this promised to be a rotter of a day full of sodding answers. Yet she had little choice but to harness pluck and see it through. And so she would wrestle through a forest of indignities to avoid future brambles of regret. Cowardice was just not to be borne. Her father, the Duke of March, had often told her that before he died three years ago, leaving her a duchess in her own right. A rare creature to be sure.

She only prayed God would not smite her when she did not fully own up to her true sentiments. It was one thing to take on the enemy, or rather . . . the gentleman who owned her heart. It was altogether another to bare her sensibilities. Pride was natural. Indeed, it protected one's dignity. And one's dignity protected the soul. And one's soul . . . Oh, for the love of God, there was no time for pastoral ruminations. Endless speculation was mere procrastination. Procrastination was worse than waiting for *someone else* to come to *his* senses.

And so, at precisely three o'clock in the afternoon, deep in Mayfair on a brilliant, cloudless late summer day, which did not match her mood, the petite duchess descended the stone steps of March House toward her destiny. At least no one else could fathom her inner tumult. Her maid, who not only excelled at pulling corset stays tighter than a French straitjacket, but also kept calm in the presence of silent madness, trailed her steps toward the carriage.

And then Isabelle saw an excellent sign.

A single crow alit on the roof of the family's crested, gilded, well-lacquered barouche. The onyx-colored bird appeared disoriented and lost; his murder—why a flock of crows was called a *murder* she would never understand—had forsaken him. Whoever said crows were vile knew nothing of the matter. They provided the finest quills, laid beautiful blue splotched eggs, and were the single most intelligent bird on the Continent. He squawked and flapped his wings with displeasure. She knew just how he felt. But he would soon learn that independence was a lovely thing . . . once you got used to it. The crow flew off, and so would she.

Yes, a crow was a very good sign.

She was sure.

The liveried footman opened the barouche's door, and as she reached for the servant's outstretched hand to aid her, she froze.

Calliope. Perfect hell. Her younger cousin was inside.

"'Morning, Isabelle," Calliope chirped. Her cousin's spectacles caught the sunlight and her eyes were hidden. Calliope glanced toward the maid. "'Morning, Lily."

The maid dipped a small curtsy.

"Dearest," Isabelle began. "Whatever are you doing here? Surely Mr. Malforte is waiting for you in the ballroom."

"He left. I don't think he's coming back."

"And why is that?"

"I told him gentlemen look like wounded partridges bowing and hopping on pointed toes. A jig is all right, I suppose, but the minuet?" She pulled a face. "He didn't seem to care for my observations."

The waiting footman cleared his throat to cover the sound of a snort.

Isabelle suppressed a sigh. "Calliope?"

"Yes?"

"Dearest, we'll discuss this later. Will you not wait for me in the library until then?"

Calliope studied her with eyes magnified twice their size and then turned her attention to the maid. "Lily, Her Grace and I need a moment of privacy please. We've a matter of some importance to discuss." She glared at the vastly entertained footman. "You, too."

Isabelle ground her teeth. She would be lucky not to spend an hour with the tooth-drawer if her cousin remained in March House a full year as agreed. "Calliope shall accompany me, Lily." Lord, she could not be late on this day of all days.

"Of course, Your Grace." Her maid's passive expression gave nothing away. Isabelle knew that every last one of the servants were wagering on how long Calliope would last before being sent back to Portsmouth, where Isabelle's poor maternal aunt lived with a huge brood.

She stepped into the barouche and the carriage door closed. Calliope opened her mouth, but Isabelle raised her hand. "Dearest, not now. I need a quarter hour of quiet. On the return you can tell me everything."

Calliope closed the blue velvet carriage curtains with a peevish willfulness that only the very young or very old dared to do with genuine flare.

Isabelle, in the darkness, was silent. She had but

one last quarter hour to reconsider. Ill-ease clogged her throat. She arched her back, exhaled, and attempted to regain the quiet dignity her father had tried to instill in her. No success. She might be able to hide her sensibilities, but the other was another matter. In fact, the only time she achieved stateliness was on cloudy days with the letter P in them.

Her young cousin pretended to study a random page in the slender volume she held in her lap, and said idly, "I suppose you would prefer the curtains open."

Isabelle bit back the truth. "Actually, I find I can't deny you the bliss of reading in the dark. One of life's little joys, I always say." Living with a cousin of four and ten who had mastered the art of a contrary contrarian five times her age was illuminating. Had she herself been like this a mere four years ago? Impossible. She had never thought she would have sympathy for Miss Hackett, her ancient ape-leader of a governess who had ruled with ill humor and iron discipline.

Calliope trained her attention on Isabelle, her book forgotten.

Isabelle gave up any notion of reflection, quiet or otherwise. "Now would be the time for you to say, 'But Isabelle, I know you'd prefer to take in the beauty of the day.'"

"Why would I suggest such a thing?" Calliope said. "Then you'd agree and I'd be forced to open the curtains. Where's the fun in that?" Her cousin pursed her lips like a dowager with a secret. "Very well. I can take a hint. I'll read while you pretend this is an ordinary day."

How was she to have a chance of success with the notorious Duke of Candover if she couldn't manage an adolescent? At least now she had a moment to think. Isabelle resisted the urge to relax her spine against the well-cushioned squabs.

Flashes of him fluttered in her mind's eye. His powerful stature and his harshly chiseled features declared him a noble of the highest distinction. "Austere" was the word most used to describe him out of his hearing. And it had been that mysterious asceticism in his dark eyes that untethered the first romantic yearnings of Isabelle's young heart six years ago. The depth of his character and the sheer raw masculinity he exuded had left her reeling, a sensation hitherto foreign to her.

He was a paradox—inspiring such warring emotions within her—confidence, and yet vulnerability, which she deplored. From the start he was her champion and the man she most admired. And yet, she secretly feared she would never truly earn his esteem. Hell, she didn't just want his good opinion. That was all good and well.

She wanted his *love*.

And she just knew—knew without the merest wisp of doubt—she had not a prayer of a chance. He was not attracted to her in the least. He thought her a child. A capable, willful, very young duchess, whose father had the misfortune of having a daughter instead of a proper son to leave his duchy.

It was not like her to be such a pessimist.

Yes, indeed, James Fitzroy could very well condescend to make her the happiest of women. The premier duke in England, infamous for cool reserve, might just scoop her off her feet, twirl her about like the foppish dance master, and unfetter his secret years of grand passion for her. And then they could feed each other chocolates and take turns reading aloud love sonnets until dawn.

Right.

Calliope, without gloves as usual, was inelegantly biting a thumbnail, her attention glued to Isabella.

Isabelle cleared her throat. "So is the book Edgeworth or Byron, dearest?"

"Not telling," Calliope replied, not meeting her gaze.

"Not telling?"

"No," Calliope replied. "Unless you tell me what the visit is all about."

"I've a better idea," Isabelle replied archly. "I shall tell you why I'm *not* going to Fitzroy House and you will tell me what you're *not* reading."

A little smile finally appeared beneath the brim of Calliope's countrified straw bonnet. "Guess."

"Lady Caroline Lamb's lurid stew," Isabelle said, referring to Calliope's tract, meanwhile resisting the urge to straighten the sagging haystack resting on her cousin's small head. She would drag her to Bond Street tomorrow without fail. Honestly, what creature of the fairer sex did not like shopping for hats?

The creature known as Calliope.

Her cousin pursed her lips. "You know nothing of it." She paused, and raised her pointed chin. *"Johnson's Sermons,"* she continued, well-pleased. "Fascinating, actually." She turned a page. "All about pride versus duty. And dignity and the soul."

She started. God was smiting her already by granting Calliope the ability to read minds. "Liar."

The imp giggled. "Killjoy."

Isabelle finally allowed herself to laugh. There was a reason she had arranged with her unfortunate aunt to have one of her cousins come to live with her. She was tired of living without any family. At first when she dismissed Miss Hackett and her father's disapproving, unimaginative advisors the day after attaining her majority, she had reveled in her hard-won freedom. But freedom did not prevent loneliness. She needed companionship, and her aunt's family needed one less mouth to feed.

She was certain Calliope would not agree. Her cousin's father might have been a poor man, but the huge family had always been jovial—until he died, leaving them very short on funds.

Just when Isabelle discarded her last hope for a few more moments of peace, Calliope lowered her head and began to read in earnest. The barouche drew ever closer to St. James Square.

Isabelle was prepared. She had rebuttals to every possible argument James might wield. And she could retrench using the element of surprise.

The surprise was in her pocket.

There was but one thing she could not do—retreat. Apprehension knitted her mind to the nth degree. The sensation had become all too familiar the last three years. Death in a family tended to do that.

Something beyond the carriage window snagged her attention. A flower girl hawked her posies on a corner. Isabelle grasped the ivory handle of her father's old cane, forever resting in its place within, and rapped on the roof. The barouche swayed to a stop and she quickly lowered the door's brass lever before a groom could descend. A hand clenching a large bunch of violets appeared as Isabelle withdrew tuppence from her beaded reticule.

"Thanky kindly, yer ladyship," the girl said before she backed away in awe. A moment later the carriage drove on.

"Calliope?"

"Yes?" Her cousin's eyes danced. "I thought you wanted me to keep to myself."

Isabelle was learning the patience of all the saints in heaven. And she was certain her father and governess would agree it was justice due, given the silent, deadly looks of disapproval they had worn ninety-eight percent of the time. The other two percent of the day Miss Pickering had mysteriously smiled, which was fairly difficult to distinguish from a frown.

Isabelle offered the enormous posy to her companion. "For you, dearest. Don't pretend you don't like them."

Her cousin's brown eyes softened. "For me?"

"They compliment your eyes," Isabelle lied.

"What are you up to?"

"Why on earth do you insist something is afoot?"

"Because you have that look."

"What 'look'?"

"That look that says you're trying to hide something."

"I haven't the foggiest idea what you're talking about," Isabelle replied.

"Yes, you do," Calliope insisted. "You look like those statues in front of March House." Calliope paused, considering. "Not the one with the spear in his ribs, dying in misery. But the others—all deathly pale and frozen. Like you now. "

"Did your mother teach you any manners at all?"

She tilted her head. "Whatever do you mean?"

There was no need to reply.

Calliope pulled a face. "Everyone knows honesty is always the best course, especially with family."

"Since when does honesty have anything to do with manners?"

"According to Papa . . . since the day I was born."

"Your father was a brilliant man."

"I know," the younger lady replied, her smile slowly disappearing.

"I'm sorry, Calliope. He was a wonderful father." She wished she could say the same. "You were very lucky to have him."

"I know that." Calliope ducked her head, fishing a sweetmeat from her pocket to hide her expression.

Isabelle instinctively felt for the folded note in her own pocket. The barouche swayed as it rounded a corner and she glanced out the carriage's small window. In the distance, the chimneys of Candover's magnificent townhouse rose above all others. Isabelle forced her attention back to her cousin.

Calliope sucked on her candy. "Are you ever going to tell me why we are visiting Old Sobersides?"

" 'We' are not paying a call on Old Sober—" She closed her eyes for a moment to regain her composure. "I mean, His Grace. I've a rendezvous to discuss a matter of importance, and you will wait for me in one of the salons."

"The salon with nothing of interest, or the salon with the odd artifacts? Or perhaps the chamber with the caged military spoils?"

She sighed. "I don't know."

Calliope blinked her large eyes. "Well, don't they keep some sort of schedule at Candover's pile?"

"Schedule?" she asked faintly.

"Of course. He should not bore his visitors to pieces by storing them in the same old chamber they've seen again and again."

"Any other complaints?"

"Yes. He's extremely irritating."

"Why would you say that?"

"Because he's self-righteous, top lofty, stuffy beyond reason, and refuses to be provoked."

Isabelle bit back a smile. "A challenge to be sure."

"How can you enjoy the company of someone so unfeeling and heartless?"

"He has a heart."

The girl's eyes challenged her. "Have you ever managed to quarrel with him?"

"No." She feared that might change today.

Calliope muttered, "Why would anyone want to spend time with someone who looks like he has an icicle stuck in his—"

"Calliope!"

"—throat."

Isabelle prayed to a saint known for patience.

Calliope let out a long-suffering sigh like a master. "Honestly, have you not ever wondered what is going on in that colossal skull of his?"

Forever. "You know, Calliope, for one who claims not to esteem the man, you can't seem to stop talking about him. One might think you actually like him."

"I refuse to like someone who always makes us wait forever and a day until His Highness decides he will condescend to give a person fifteen minutes of his time. And not a minute more, by the by." She smiled. "I've timed it."

"Calliope?"

"Yes?"

"I realize you've never been more than a dozen miles from Portsmouth, but do you think you could make more of an effort to embrace the ways of Town?"

"Does it include kowtowing?"

"Yes."

"Are you going to send me home if I don't?"

"Yes."

"Liar," her cousin retorted with a mischievous gleam.

Isabelle stuck out her tongue. She knew how to lance a Parthian shot with the best of them.

Calliope nearly choked with laughter.

Lord, she hadn't stuck out her tongue since the day old Hacksaw—uh, Miss Hackett—had nearly yanked it out of her mouth.

Calliope removed her spectacles and wiped her eyes with her hands before Isabelle could remind her to use her handkerchief. At least her expression had softened.

"So why must you see him by yourself? My mother explicitly told me my main duty was that I'm never to leave you alone with any gentleman. Mama puckered like she'd swallowed a peeled lime when I asked why."

Isabelle smiled despite herself.

Calliope looked at her with knowing eyes. "You're not going to set his servants to gossiping, are you? I do have a reputation to maintain."

"Do you now?"

"Yes. If I'm to be your companion, at least I want to be an excellent one." She paused. "Isabelle?"

"Yes, dearest?"

"I know more than you think."

"Really?" Isabelle smoothed the folds of the elegant patent net over the pale blue gown trimmed with jonquille ribbon. She pleated her stiff hands, the picture of everything proper. "And what, pray tell, do you know?"

"I know that nothing good will come of your visit with the Duke of Candover. And I know something is brewing, otherwise you would not have that look." She handed Isabelle the book of sermons. "Here, you need this more than I."

Isabelle glanced down, only to find it was, indeed, that bit of nauseating fluff by Lady Lamb. She opened it. Out of the corner of her eye she could see Calliope part her lips to speak, but she interrupted. "I'm reading, Calliope. As *you* suggested." She was abashed to descend to her cousin's level.

Calliope snapped her mouth closed and appeared to turn her attention to the world outside their conveyance. Isabelle had all of thirty seconds before her cousin rattled her cage again. She trained her unseeing eyes on the page.

Dear God, she could not lose her resolve. Yet suddenly she could not remember how she was to say it. She had overprepared last evening. Twenty-three times repeating the same outrageous question would make anyone feel like a fool. But perhaps he would see the practical brilliance of the idea. Two birds . . . one stone. Two dozen words . . . one idiot. Two friends . . . one soon to be former friend. Then again, could gentlemen and ladies really be just friends? Lady Lamb's ridiculous tract showed every evidence of the impossibility of it. *Johnson's Sermons* warned against it at every opportunity. And her estate library's section on animal husbandry never mentioned friendship between the sexes.

But could she go through with it? Even if her pride screamed no, every particle of her heart insisted on it. He was the gentleman meant for her. She had known it since she was thirteen and he arrived on the vernal equinox during one of his twice yearly visits to her father. That visit, James had insisted she learn how to use a pistol, one of the endless number of skills he said she must acquire. It had been unsaid that she would soon be alone in the world when her father died.

He had shown her how to prime and load a dueling pistol, and when she proved a miserable shot after watching his demonstration, he stood behind her, wrapped his arms about her, and suggested she inhale and exhale with him to steady her breathing. When he placed his warm, strong hands over hers to show her how to take proper aim, his jaw had rested on her temple, and his masculine scent invaded her senses. It had been a miracle she hit the target at all.

But that had been nothing compared to what he said six months later as her father lay on his deathbed. She'd overheard them speaking about her. Her father was worried, as always, about the duchy and her questionable abilities. James's words were seared in her memory. "To be sure, she is young. But she is courageous, and intelligent, and a born leader. She will do you proud. Of that, I promise you." She had tiptoed away when she heard the butler's footsteps. But she had held tight to James's words during the weeks and months of difficulties after her father died. James never lied, and if he believed in her abilities, so could she.

The barouche again swayed as they turned yet another corner. Isabelle's gaze darted to the window where St. James Square's well-manicured central garden loomed. She watched the town houses of the Allens, the Pickerings, and the widowed adventurer Mr. Lyerley slip beyond view. As the carriage horses slowed on the approach to 9 St. James Street, she glanced toward the imposing gray stone town house endowed to the Candover duchy.

Her stomach lurched and she finally slumped against the carriage seat. Well, "slumped" was not entirely the right word, considering the torture device under her gown. She felt more like the library's enormous atlas leaning against a shelf.

And for the first time ever, she spied anxiety in Calliope's face. Indeed, if her cousin's expression was any indication, she had not a prayer of a chance at this game. Not that she ever truly thought she did.

But by God, at eighteen she was a fully grown

woman, a duchess in her own right, who very capably oversaw three estates with a myriad of details, and she knew the value of occasional risk and opportunity.

And so she would play her cards.

For everyone knew you had to play if you wanted to win—no matter the odds. And Isabelle Tremont very much wanted to win.

Chapter 2

James Fitzroy, the Duke of Candover, replaced his perfectly trimmed goose quill in the stand and studied the letter to his steward in Derbyshire. It was the last of seven letters to seven stewards in seven counties. Sanding it, and then pushing it aside, he exhaled deeply and allowed his tired eyes to roam. Dark portraits of ancestors and pastoral landscapes intermixed with scenes of ancient naval battles won and lost decorated the vast length of this favored chamber. High above him, haloed angels, gods, and their cherubs surveyed all with arrows and pitchforks at the ready. In front of him, a bronze compass, sextant, and other military artifacts rested on ebony and gold Egyptian tables sitting on a vast sea of crimson carpet. There was a peaceful stillness to the great room. Indeed, it was the only place in all of his vast splendor of estates where James enjoyed any real sense of privacy. His servants knew better than to ever disturb him here. Yes, James knew every square inch of this gilded prison.

And he liked it.

His hand rose to touch the intricate world globe his mother had specifically bequeathed to him. He traced a journey he would never make to mysterious lands filled with fascinating flora and fauna he would never see, as he had far too many other more important affairs to oversee. At his feet, under the magnificent Roman scrolled desk, the slender, elegant head of his greyhound, Syn, lay on outstretched paws. On James's other side, Syn's twin, Tax, raised his head and emitted a soft woof.

James removed his pocket watch and glanced at the hour. She was on time. That was to be expected. It was only too bad she did not always do the expected. Then again, a duchess in her own right could do whatever she damned well pleased. Just like him . . . as long as he remained in this chamber. Outside, servants, royals, and everyone in between observed his every waking movement. His life was lived in an opulent fishbowl awash with other creatures who were either awed, overly effusive, or silent with fear, indeed never at their ease.

There were exceptions, of course. He steepled his hands and stared sightlessly at the dust motes glistening in the shafts of sunlight from the windows. His fellow members of the royal entourage, that band of dukes, who preferred each others' company if only for the fact that there was no fawning or falseness between them. But now, because of his own damnable mistake, something in which James rarely indulged (mistakes, that is), the Prince Regent's posse of favored bachelor dukes was dwindling in number. It was all due to the future king's newfound love of marriage, not that the royal's own union could be considered anything but a debacle.

A debauched night of events, which had led to James's bride cooling her heels at the altar the next morning, had incited the disenchanted masses *à la française*. The Prince Regent's ire had reached new heights, even if he'd been glued to their sides all night. Indeed, the next king of England was accountable for more than his fair share of the well-documented mayhem. James only wished he could remember the half of it.

It had been all well and good until the prince decreed that the most efficient way to quell the masses' fury was aristocratic reform. This was to be achieved via the time-honored tradition of leg shackling.

But James himself was finished. Two matrimonial attempts in one lifetime were more than enough for any nobleman. And that was why, at the advanced age of nearly one and thirty, he would damn well do what he pleased, marry when and if he pleased, and even how he pleased—Prinny be damned. He allowed himself no reprieve from a dutiful life, apart from this one exception.

Perhaps a decade ago—before his first fiancée's death—he had dared to think that love and marriage could go hand in hand. Later, his father, and his godfather, each in very different marriages, had explained the truth about *wedded bliss*. It was simple. Marriage was a contract and was to be entered into with a clear head and with the sole reason to produce the next generation. Succumbing to the illusion of romantic love only led to disaster. But if one was very lucky, then detached contentment would rule the union, and not indifference or worse. And passion? As described by the great poets? James was made to understand it was an absurd notion that had only ever led to weakness of character. Wildly unguarded happiness was not part of the strict life of the premier duke of England.

And a third attempt to wed was not something to contemplate until later. Much later. Until . . . he could stomach the entire affair one last time.

He glanced once more at his pocket watch and rose to his feet in one elegant economy of motion. He would not keep the Duchess of March waiting beyond the usual prerequisite of seven minutes. His dogs silently padding along on either side of him, he crossed the

large space opposite the carved oak door and emerged;
two footmen guarded the chamber just as their ancestors had guarded his forefathers.

His butler, Wharton bowed. "Her Grace, the Duchess of March, and Miss Little are arrived, Your Grace."

James curtly nodded and turned on his heel toward
the blue salon fronting the town house.

Wharton cleared his throat.

This was never a good sign. "Yes?" James said,
facing the acre of black and white checkered marble
that separated him from the visitors.

"The young ladies are not in the blue salon, Your
Grace."

James allowed a moment of silence to reign before
he turned to face his butler. "And why is that, Wharton?"

"Her Grace was content with the choice, but her
companion"—Wharton's sour expression spoke
volumes—"suggested that yellow was a much more
suitable color for a Wednesday, and—"

James felt the old tic in his eye flare. "Where is she?"

"In the *rose* salon, Your Grace."

He waited.

The man cleared his throat. "I understood from the
last visit that Your Grace would prefer not to encourage
Miss Little."

Without another word, James headed in the opposite
direction, toward the rose room.

Wharton's cough stopped him cold. This was grave. Even Syn whined. "Yes?"

"Miss *Little* is in the rose salon, Your Grace. Her Grace awaits you in the garden."

"The garden?"

"Yes, Your Grace."

What in hell was going on? Wharton had not disobeyed an order since half past never. "I see." James turned around yet again, his dogs at his heels and all of them feeling somewhat like idiots. He knew this because Syn and Tax yelped. Wharton did not emit one last bloody sound to stop him.

He strode down four corridors and two staircases before coming to a halt in front of the French doors leading to the garden behind the great house. Not fifty yards beyond the window she stood in profile beside the small fountain.

While she was petite in stature, she was perfectly formed. Before he could rein in his thoughts, he imagined tossing her hat in the hydrangeas and letting loose that heavy coil of lush hair she now always pinned under a hat very properly. And then he would— For Christsakes . . . only the worst sort of bastard would continue thusly. He ruthlessly censored his thoughts as he narrowed his eyes.

Her regal posture bespoke of education and station in life. She was a lady of great standing, and breeding. The fifth largest duchy and fortune in England rested on her shoulders—a formidable thing for a very young innocent lady. She did remarkably well, considering. Actually, she was better than most of the other dukes of the realm. What she lacked in experience she made up in determination and sense of duty.

It was a moment before he realized he was smiling, an action in which he rarely indulged. He frowned and nodded to the footman to open the terrace door.

The duchess turned toward him, her delicate oval face pale but her expression neutral.

James snapped his fingers and his dogs obeyed the signal to investigate the garden at large. He closed the distance to her and brought the back of her hand, gloved in yellow kid, to his lips. The fine scent of jasmine rose from her fine-boned wrist and met his nostrils. It was such a poignant old-fashioned perfume. He knew no one else who wore it. It unleashed the familiar wave of the potent attraction before he harnessed the desire he took extreme measures to ignore.

"James," she said with a small curtsy.

"Isabelle," he replied solemnly. "To what do I owe the pleasure?"

"Such a delightful fountain," she noted with a forced smile. "I've never really noticed it before."

"It's been here for six generations."

"Of course. And what is it made of?"

"Common marble."

"I see."

She studied the simple fountain and he studied her. Her large, intelligent eyes, the intriguing color of the finest whiskey, had not witnessed enough of life. She was just beginning to bloom, her adolescent coltishness giving way to feminine mystique. Wings of silky light brown hair framed her face, which when animated was quite beautiful. Indeed, sometimes it hurt the eye to see such uninhibited exuberance. Yet today there was not an ounce of liveliness to her remote countenance, now hiding below the brim of her elegant bonnet. He tried to turn his attention from her plush, rosy lips, which promised utterly forbidden sweetness for which he would give his fortune to taste.

"What brings you, Isabelle?" He spoke evenly, without showing a hint of the worry her blank expression now inspired in him.

She glanced toward the French doors and returned her gaze to his face. Her unusual golden eyes gave nothing away.

"Well, you see, the thing of it is . . . we've both of us a dilemma." She paused.

"Are you referring to your cousin? I'm afraid she's a problem of your own making. She will not do as a companion. You need someone of age who can attend societal functions."

"This has nothing to do with Calliope," she insisted. "I don't know why the two of you do not get on."

"I do," he replied.

She looked at him expectantly.

"She's the devil."

Her lips trembled with amusement. "Don't I know it."

He relaxed his guard. This was the young duchess he knew. A breeze rustled the leaves in the trees and dislodged a lock of her hair from her coiffure. Instinctively, he reached forward and brushed the curl away from her lovely face. He could feel the warmth of her face through his glove, and he longed to lean in and catch her scent again. These tortuous emotions were getting completely out of hand with each passing month.

Her expression returned to ill-ease, and she picked at the tip of one of her kid gloves when he refused to fill the lengthening silence.

"Did you not receive a letter from the Prince Regent?"

"I did." He made it a point to never answer more than what was asked.

She pressed. "Well . . . mine contained a royal command to marry. Prinny mentioned that you and also Barry were to follow suit."

"Hmmm." A word, or rather a sound, that suited every occasion.

"So what do you plan to do about it?"

Ah, the quandary of the decade. "I think it unnecessary. The recent sacrificial lambs of our circle have appeased the zealots."

"I don't think the prince shares your view," she retorted, darting a glance to her pale kid boots.

"Of course he does," he replied. "He's just using the occasion to ensure the rest of us are as miserable as he."

"Perhaps," she said, the hint of a smile curling her lips, "but we've always been very frank, have we not?"

"Speak, Isabelle."

"Well, I hope you'll pardon me for reminding you that the prince considers you the prime instigator of the current state of affairs."

"I was, indeed, to blame for that night of—"

"We both know it wasn't your fault. It was Kress's," she insisted. "None of us could have known the potency of that French absinthe. It was revolting and—"

He interrupted. "*You* tried it?"

She avoided his gaze. "Perhaps. What did you expect? You left your sister, me, and—"

"*My sister* drank that frog water?"

"I beg your pardon," she said, not begging his pardon at all. "You are not one to read me a lecture. You were forty-seven sheets to the wind along with the rest of our friends. You missed your own wedding!"

He ignored her. "You can be certain I'll have a word with Verity's abigail about this. Today."

"Amelia Primrose is here?"

"She returned from Scotland last evening."

"It was not Amelia's fault. You can blame it all on me if you must." Isabelle excelled at that guileless expression of hers. She forged on before he could speak. "But seriously, you didn't think we would pluck harp strings or embroider while the rest of you were cavorting about London to celebrate what turned out to be *not* your last night of bachelorhood?"

"I suppose improving the mind by reading would have been out of the question . . . Virgil, Homer, Epictetus are always excellent, or perhaps even *Johnson's Sermons* in a pinch."

She rolled her eyes. "No one reads *Johnson's Sermons.*"

"Really? That will be news to his publisher, I'm certain," he replied, hiding his amusement. He was so happy she was back to rolling her eyes. "I know you prefer Epictetus." He relished the rare occasions he managed to lead her off course.

She wrinkled her nose. "Well, Virgil's epics are epically boring and no one will say it. And Homer—" She stopped.

"Yes?"

"Look, I'm not here to debate philosophers. Now, what are you going to do about Prinny's demand?"

"Take a decision." He halted. "Eventually."

"When?" Only this particular young lady would dare to press him.

"When I'm ready." He stopped himself from folding his arms over his chest.

"I see."

She didn't appear to see beyond the end of her nose.

"Well, I choose not to try our sovereign's patience," she continued stiffly. "I don't avoid decisions." Her lips pursed for a moment before relaxing. She tilted her chin.

He studied the determined look in her eyes. "But sometimes to act without full consideration can lead to regret."

"Is that all you have to say on the matter?"

"Is something more required?"

"Yes," she said.

He was far better than she at ignoring bait.

"Well," she continued, her face becoming more pale by the second, "I shall dare to suggest the obvious if you will not."

A small breeze passed through the branches of the trees in the garden, casting a play of shadow and light over her face. He could see flecks of gold near her irises. She had been headstrong during her girlhood. But willfulness often went hand in hand with courage. The latter she had in abundance. What was the matter with her today? He'd never seen her so ill at ease, so—

"James—" She abruptly stopped.

The hairs on the back of his neck rose. Why on earth

would she use his given name? Few had ever used that name except—

"I realize you've little interest in contemplating another trip to the altar, given your past failed attempt, or rather, *attempts*, but . . . Well, the thing of it is . . ." Her eyes held steady on his but her voice had become reed thin. "Yes . . . indeed"—she finally careened toward a conclusion—"the reason for my visit is to propose a union."

He blinked. "You're here to suggest a bride for me?" He'd never been hoarse in his life. "Isabelle, I've always condescended to allow you a far greater amount of informality of manner than I should. I do it because of your connection to the royal entourage and because your father was a great friend. But there is a limit, and you've reached it." He should tell her to mind her own bloody disasters. No one told him what to do—not even the Prince Regent.

Time seemed to slow as he watched her raise her hand to brush something from the lapel of his blue superfine coat. She was staring at her fingers, and a bee buzzed near a spray of flowers on the side of her elegant bonnet. He was suddenly caught between opposing desires to grasp her still, small hand and pull her into his arms—the army of servants beyond the windows be damned—and yet he also knew he should push her fingers away and end this disastrous interview.

"James Fitzroy, will you do me the honor of becoming my husband?" Her voice was now clear and steady. "Or not?"

He went still. "I beg your pardon?"

She removed her stiff hand from his lapel. "It's simple enough, isn't it? You and I have been ordered by the Prince Regent to find spouses, and I am asking if you would like to marry"—she lowered her voice—"me."

His mind restarted.

She rushed on. "It would solve so many problems, no? Kill two crows with one—oh, never mind the analogy." She stopped. "So shall we . . . ?"

He stared at her.

"Marry?" Her voice was now a whisper.

"My dear, why ever would you choose someone twice your age? Why, I could be your father."

Her faced flushed. "You were *twelve* when I was born. I highly doubt you could sire children at that age."

He said not a word. The sounds of a summer reigned. Birds sang in the sky, crickets sawed in the grass, horses whinnied in the mews, and he could not form a reply to save his life.

Her voice rose an octave. "Father might have been your *friend* in the latter part of his life, but he was also your godfather the earlier part. Do you have a better argument against a union?"

She knew nothing of the world. Nothing of life. She might have learned the vast array of intricacies involved with running estates with her quickness of mind, but she was not ready for the restraints and certain disappointments of tying herself to someone for the next half century or more. But she was unlikely to acknowledge this truth. Part of being young and innocent was not accepting that one was young and innocent.

"I will call off Prinny," he said quietly. "There's no need for you to marry yet. You were never part of the equation that night. And you should enjoy a few more years of freedom—freedom to live your life, oversee March property the way a Tremont would see fit, before you tie yourself to a gentleman, who will try to put his own stamp on *your* lands." He could not stop himself now. "By God, Isabelle, pay homage to your forebearers who were determined not to let a future generation's failure to produce male progeny be the end of the duchy."

"You're worried about the original Duke of March's wishes? He's been dead for three hundred years."

Words failed him once again. If he had not been a gentleman, he would have shaken her. If only to stop himself from giving in to temptation to do something far more wicked. God, what had he done to deserve such wretchedness?

"Do you want to marry me or not?" She studied her gloves once more. "Or do you have more arguments to—"

"I do," he replied quietly.

She hesitated, dark hope clouding her expression. "You 'do' what? You accept my offer or you have further excuses?"

"Enough," he insisted. He resisted the urge to loosen the damned knot of his neck cloth that was strangling him.

Her expression was odd. "And that is your answer?"

He stared at the innocence of her face and hated himself as it withered.

"Damn you," she finally whispered.

His dogs appeared on either side of him and sat at attention. "Isabelle . . . my dearest—"

"I am not *your dearest anything*. You might be the premier duke of England, but I am your equal in rank. Do not condescend to me. I'm the bloody Duchess of March."

He bowed slightly. "Indeed, you are."

She labored on, her chin rising with each word. "I'd hoped you'd at least consider the offer. Have you not always insisted that reason and duty should be behind every vital decision? Is not marriage of primary importance?"

"You are correct."

She waited a beat. "Well?"

"I can find no pleasant way to tell you." He continued tonelessly, "I will not do myself the great honor of accepting your proposal. I am sorry. I'm not the man for you. I'm far too—"

"Don't say—" she interrupted.

"—old and we would not suit. Trust me, Isabelle."

"You once told me never to trust anyone."

"Except me."

"Precisely," she replied. "And yet you will not show me the same courtesy. Why won't you trust my instincts?"

"Because it's impossible."

"Hang it," she choked, "We suit each other very well."

"No," he said with a finality she could not misunderstand.

He just had a moment to see her audacious grit failing before she looked away. God, he had no stomach for disappointing any female, but most especially her. *Bloody hell and damnation.*

He would give his last farthing to dislodge himself from this sodding mess. Sadness lanced his gut. She was the last person he wanted to hurt in any way. She was courageous, and good, fresh-faced, intelligent, and kind in every way. And he was ancient compared to her. She had no idea of the impossibility of an alliance between them. More so, flirting with a disaster known as matrimony, pushing aside the past, and filling the Fitzroy nursery with squalling infants was not a priority.

And it would not be for a very long time.

Men were known to sire heirs at eighty. He would not tempt fate. He'd do it before seventy-five, which gave him another four plus decades of relative peace . . . aside from managing the lives of *five* sisters, three aunts, and one great-aunt—each more time-consuming than the next. Yes, he was damn well drowning in females, and he would not take on another.

He could only see the top of her bronze silk bonnet, trimmed with flowers, as she suddenly kneeled to pet Syn. The dog whined before James snapped his fingers. Syn instantly stopped and looked at him with adoration.

At least there were two females who obeyed him. The human variety was altogether another story—especially if they were related to him or about to become related to him. Ladies were complicated, always had to discuss every last notion ad infinitum, and their minds were not well regulated on the idea of a simple fix to any given conundrum. They were also prone to histrionics—right now being a prime example. And when it came to engagements and marriage—the first had never guaranteed the second in his godforsaken life. Most females, in his estimation (and that of every gentleman he knew), did not know what they wanted, or remained as mysterious as sphinxes if they did. His past was littered with evidence in every direction.

Yes, of course, he was at fault for leaving Lady Margaret Spencer at the altar during this last ruinous brush with matrimony, but he very much doubted she regretted it. His gold guineas, yes. His person, no. In the end when she married someone else, his former fiancée would profusely thank him. There was no one more eligible and less suited for marriage than he.

Isabelle Tremont did not want a remote, impersonal marriage of convenience to a man who could be, at the very least, a young uncle, who she would end up nursing half her life. No, he would never agree to it. And his kindhearted, devoted godfather, more a father to him than his own sire, would thank him and expect it of him.

Of that there was not a single doubt.

He looked down at her now bowed head. She loosened her elegant bonnet and allowed it to fall down her back—at the end of its tied ribbons. The shiny brown coils of her luxurious hair gleamed in the rays of sunlight. Without thinking, James silently removed one glove and reached toward the crown of her head. His fingers, a hairbreadth away from her sleek head, stopped. He could feel warmth radiating from her—so close yet so far.

And in that moment he imagined the beauty of the

life he would have if he had been allowed to close the distance between them. He willed her to glance up at him, but she did not.

The shadow of a raven passed overhead and cawed its displeasure.

He returned his hand to its proper place by his side.

Chapter 3

Isabelle could not feel her feet or hands. She had dropped to her knees, ostensibly to pet the refined head of one of James's greyhounds, but really to recoup her composure. She bit down on her tongue, a trick her beautiful mother taught her many years ago—before she left and never returned. Her mother had said it made one see stars, but it was guaranteed to reverse the course of waterworks. She only wished Mama had told her how to stop the pain in her chest.

While looking into the warmth of Syn's watchful eyes, Isabelle acknowledged her grave mistake to herself. She had not kept hope at bay. With sudden clarity, she realized that hope was nothing more than an optimist's crutch.

He would never want her.

He would never love her.

He was nothing more than an advisor and friend. No, worse—he probably considered her nothing more than his friend's *daughter*. Just a young, foolish female. *Another responsibility*. She knew that behind the two-inch-thick door to her father's private chambers, James and the eighth Duke of March had often discussed her future.

"Pardon me for one moment," he said in his deep baritone voice.

Out of the corner of her eye Isabelle saw James cross the lawn toward his butler, who descended a few stairs from the town house. She exhaled roughly.

The other greyhound nudged her hand for attention and she complied, grateful for the companionship of his faithful dogs. She wanted to flee to her barouche. And yet, there she would be forced to endure the weight of Calliope's boundless curiosity.

And so she remained rooted to the spot. In truth, she knew she had no choice. She had to plod on, undeterred from her well-planned course of action. He would not be able to deny her second point now that he had rejected her.

This would be her way of recouping dignity, and she would not let it slip away, discomposure be damned. But also, if she did not move forward, she feared she might be haunted by James for decades. She was a realist just like he. But sometimes, just sometimes, one had to dream.

She had allowed today to be that day. She had dreamed large and lost quite famously. But as long as not a single tear appeared, her pride would remain intact. She had only to endure a bit more and then she could escape to the confines of her bedchambers at March House, and then lock her door against the rest of the world. She had no taste for false good humor. But right now she had no choice but to wear the proverbial horsehair shirt of her own making. It was the only way to save face and tend her bruised psyche.

Isabelle scratched the ear of the fawn-colored greyhound one last time and forced herself to rise when she spied him dismissing his butler and crossing back toward her. James Fitzroy's coffee-colored eyes met hers as he approached. He had that heavy-lidded look, as always, and she suddenly wondered if it was because she was so much shorter than he. The top of her head barely reached his shoulders. She refused to think of them as broad. Just like how she now refused to think him handsome at this moment—although he was, if one liked large beaks for noses; wide, firm lips for kisses one would never receive; and a large forehead to house an obstinate brain filled with stupid ideas about three-hundred-year-old ancestors that were not even his.

Annoyed and hurt were far too tame descriptors for her current state of mind. Well, she had her answer, and she knew what must be done. Waiting about was not in her makeup. Besides, she might be a duchess in her own right, but she knew very well that she must procreate and marry . . . not in that order, of course.

He stopped in front of her. "It was very good of you to call," James said stiffly.

"I'm sorry to overstay," she replied, pride coloring her words. She reaffixed her bonnet atop her head and tied the ribbons tightly in place. "I'm certain you wish this visit to be over as much as I, but—"

"That's untrue. It's always a delight to see you." His manner and expression were as impossible to fathom as ever. "It is good we spoke. You can be sure I shall remind His Majesty that not a word of the reports of the debacle marred your good name. I won't allow the prince to trump up a reason for you to be married off in haste. It's indecent to—"

"I'm sorry," she said as sweetly as she could manage, "but I must stop you. You misunderstand. Perhaps *you* do not wish to marry, but *I* do. And now is as good a time as any."

He raised his quizzing glass to his eye.

"Don't you dare look at me with that. I'm not an insect whose legs need to be counted."

"I beg your pardon," he said as he allowed his quizzing glass to fall on its ribbon. "I had no intention of examining anyone's, uh—" He stopped abruptly, for once taken off guard.

"And don't worry, I've no intention of renewing my suit toward you." She forced a casual smile to her lips.

"But there is no need to rush into marriage."

"Of course there's a need. As you so brilliantly suggested, one cannot let down three hundred years of ancestors who are depending on my womb to produce the ninth Duke of March. And," she cleared her throat, "it might take time. Look at poor Lady Carlyle. She's been married for a decade and still has not provided the earl with an infant."

James coughed and appeared vastly ill at ease.

She soldiered on. "And this"—she withdrew the note from her voluminous pocket and carefully unfolded it—"is how I shall go about it."

Not a muscle on his person moved. "And what, may I ask, is that?"

"A list."

"Of?"

"Eligible parties."

A tic in the hollow of his right cheek made an appearance.

She glanced down at the list, unseeing. She soldiered onward. Her wounded pride she wore like a suit of mail to protect her against further injury. "Prinny was kind enough to forward names to consider . . . yours was the first among them, hence my visit, of course . . . and I added a half dozen more.

By the by, do you think it too lowering to consider a French émigré?"

"A Frenchman," he echoed, struck off balance.

"Yes," she continued, "he's quite lovely, actually. Brilliant mind, sterling wit, very pleasing to the eye, of course. He even taught Calliope how to manage a kite near the Thames last Saturday."

"And who is this paragon?"

"Le Comte de Villeneuve."

He was very good, she had to admit. He showed not a whisker of emotion.

"Isabelle?"

"Yes?"

"You know as well as I that Villeneuve's pockets"—his tone froze by ten degrees—"as well as his stockings, breeches and shirts . . . in fact, every last one of the wrinkles in his overly frilled articles of Gallic clothing are to let."

She lifted her chin a degree and formed a smile on her lips. "Are you suggesting that he's courting me for something other than my charm?"

"I do not make a habit of insulting ladies."

"Good. Because we both know that gentlemen and ladies often marry to refill their family coffers. In fact, it's something of a tradition, in case you haven't noticed." She tried very hard to keep the sarcasm from her voice. It was obvious she was no good at it.

James narrowed his eyes. "Villeneuve wagered away

every last sou of the meager fortune he smuggled from France. You cannot marry an inveterate gambler, Isabelle."

She smiled inwardly.

"Who else is on that list?" His jaw was set so firmly that his lips barely moved when he spoke.

She made a show of scanning the names. "Too many to say. In any case, I've kept you far longer than I ought. It's nearly four. I'm certain you've better things to do. And I know I do, too. I've the ledgers from three stewards to review and—"

"May I see it?" he interrupted.

"No," she replied. "But . . ."

"Yes?"

"We could discuss *your* list."

She knew she had gone too far when two veins on his forehead became visible. They resembled twin bolts of lightning, joined in the middle, only to dissipate near one brow. Then again it was good he was angry. She had planned for this. She'd never seen him this way and had hoped this depth of feeling was inside him. Somehow, it made him more human, more like the rest of mankind. And any emotion was better than the bland condescension he'd shown her in the past.

She was not one of his sisters, for the love of God.

"You are too kind," he said, as stiff as the uncracked spines of half her tomes by Virgil. "But, I fear you have overstepped your—"

A commotion on the terrace drew their attention. Lord above, it was Calliope and Wharton. The duke's housekeeper was also involved. Her cousin was in fine form—hands on hips, chin thrust out, and her voice particularly insistent.

"I will not wait another moment," Calliope said sharply. "There are four reasons. One"—she held up her index finger—"it's been twenty seven minutes—well beyond protocol. Two"—up went a second digit—"she's not supposed to be alone with any man unless they are engaged. Even then it's not allowed, although many companions just look the other way. I'm not one of those." She took a breath and held up the third finger. "Three, I want to know what's going on. I'd wager it's no good. And lastly, no one should be made to sit in a chamber without a single thing to do or see." She stared daggers at the butler. "I told you I preferred a room with curiosities."

Isabelle poked him once on the arm. "I'm taking my leave."

His countenance was unreadable. "You're certain you cannot send her back to Portsmouth?"

"Why would I want to do that? I prefer bluntness. And she appears to be the only one here who is not afraid to do or say exactly what she wants."

A small vee appeared between his eyebrows. "What are you suggesting?"

"Nothing. Absolutely nothing at all."

A dozen or more crows descended from the sky to roost in James's oaks. Their caws mimicked laughter, mocking her. Suddenly, a "murder of crows" seemed apt. All the sooner to force James Fitzroy, the infuriating, powerful, stoic, pigheaded Duke of Candover, to eat crow. God help her, but she would do it. Sometimes a lady had to take the lead, and this was one of those times.

And she had learned all about leading from the master.

An unusual tide of fatigue engulfed him as he went through the practiced motions of an evening alone in the town house in which every generation of Fitzroys had lived and died. He could not remember the last time he had dined alone amid the gilded, polished splendor of the dining hall. A brief respite was needed, after all. His four unmarried sisters had decided to forgo the upcoming Little Season in town—in favor of the pastoral beauty of the family seat in Derbyshire. His fifth and middle sister Verity was recently married to another member of the royal entourage, the Duke of Abshire. Neither of them had been particularly good at forwarding news since retiring to Abshire's neighboring estate in the Peak District.

He had no appetite despite the usual excellent dinner fare produced by his cook and the bevy of staff in the kitchens belowstairs. James casually placed his fork and knife parallel to each other on the gold and ivory

Wedgwood plate. Instantly, one of four liveried servants appeared at his side.

"I'm for the library, Thomas."

The man removed the dish full of half-eaten fare. "Will His Grace take coffee there?"

"And brandy."

His servant showed no emotion. It was a prerequisite of employment at Candover House. But surely the man was surprised. James had not partaken in spirits since the debacle. He learned from his mistakes, unlike most.

He walked the great expanse of wide checkered marble corridors toward the library, the favored place of his academic-minded sisters. His mother, a famed naturalist during her lifetime, had filled the vast chamber with glass cases of birds' nests and eggs, rare dried flowers, and artifacts of all kinds.

He had deeply shared his mother's passion for nature in his youth. She had filled his dreams with sea voyages to exotic lands filled with birds that laid eggs the size of his fist, and fascinating plants that ate insects. But they had been merely dreams of youth.

His father had coldly insisted to him alone that preoccupation in the mysteries of the earth was unproductive and a waste of time, especially for the future premier duke of the realm. Publicly, the former duke had benevolently encouraged his wife and daughters to pursue their interests to keep them out from under foot, James finally understood.

Indeed, his father had been a great actor on the stage of life. No one had ever guessed the inner turmoil of the former duke—except James. And he had only been taken into his father's complete confidence at the very end. Yes, playing the role of premier duke of Christendom entailed duty above all else. There was no time for private dreams of exploration, passion, and curiosity for all things in nature, and certainly nothing but heartache to be gained by foolish love. James's first fiancée, Catharine Talmadge, had proved his father's sage advice on every level. Indeed, there was no time or good reason for any of it. And a mountain of duties—familial or public—was excellent at drumming out interests of no value that leeched away one's days.

It was a privilege to be the premier duke. And he should take pride and show gratitude for this privilege by fulfilling the duties of his position. Everything else was a goddamned waste of time and a sign of laziness.

As he approached the end of the long hall, he forced his mind away from the fresh memory of Isabelle's lovely, vibrant eyes that brimmed with honesty and everything innocent and good. She reminded him too much of the days of his youth, when life had been carefree and filled with wonder and joy. There was a time and a place for every emotion.

Tomorrow he must return to his private great room to study plans for the improvement of the tenant cottages in Suffolk. But tonight he settled into a polished brown leather armchair before a fire, chasing away the first chill of late summer. The unseasoned wood hissed and smoked. On either side of him, his two greyhounds slid their slender noses between their outstretched paws.

He could not push the events of the afternoon from his mind, though he took pride in usually being free of distraction. Isabelle's face and impossibly naïve proposal returned again and again to the forefront of his thoughts.

Oh, he'd always known she had an innocent fondness for him that bordered on the sort of girlhood infatuations that tended to fade over time and change course on a whim.

He knew all about that.

Syn's velvet muzzle nudged his hand, and he absently stroked his beloved dog's head. She placed one slim paw on his knee and he scratched the back of one of her ears as she looked at him with unconditional devotion.

"I know, old girl, I know. You want a good run in the country."

His faithful dog raised her head, and her twin rose up on his haunches for attention, too.

"I would like it as well," he said simply, returning his gaze to the fire as more memories burned within him.

Isabelle's father, the Duke of March, had extracted a promise from him before he'd died. James was to advise her on estate matters if needed and, most importantly, make certain that Isabelle selected a suitable husband. The old duke had been very precise on the latter subject. James had agreed to his godfather's deathbed requests. How could he not? March had guided him when his own father had died and he'd taken on the dukedom's responsibilities.

He stared into the flames, flickering and illuminating a portion of the library. Perhaps he should return to Derbyshire. Or tour the family estates. None of it held any appeal, and yet he did not want to remain in Town. There was no reason to be here. The Little Season promised to be flat, and he was not needed until Parliament was in session. His closest friends, his fellow dukes in the royal entourage, were either newly married—due to the prince's demands—or scattered God knew where. The last time he'd seen Sussex, the overly charming member of the entourage he watched like a hawk, he'd disappeared from Kress's absurd house party in Cornwall with nary a word of explanation. And the Duke of Barry was likely entrenched somewhere to avoid the Prince Regent's notice. The vast majority of other gentlemen James held in high regard were in Brighton, Bath, or partaking of the fine weather to shoot as many feathered and furred creatures as they could find in the countryside.

There were any number of invitations he could accept.

A knock sounded on the solid oak frame of the library's door. His dogs raised their heads. Miss Amelia Primrose, his sister's abigail, appeared, carrying a tray. She exchanged a word with the footman trailing her and the man disappeared.

"Your coffee," she said with a tone that belied the firm taskmaster she was.

"Where is Thomas?"

"I told him I would deliver the tray. I wanted to select a book, Your Grace."

"Very good," he replied.

She settled the tray on the low table beside him. There was not a drop of brandy in sight. He did not say a word.

"Would you care to join me?" He nodded toward the other leather chair. She was one of the rare ladies of his acquaintance to whom he would make such an offer. She was a terrifying young woman of substance, with a delicate beauty that hid a will of iron. He had employed her a dozen years ago despite her youth and inexperience. She had been the last resort, and over the years, she'd overseen a miracle—the miracle of transforming his most challenging sister, Verity, into a proper lady. His other four sisters, Faith, Hope, Charity, and Chastity, had never truly given him a moment's unease, even if he suggested otherwise. Their noses were mired too deep in scientific journals or mathematics to consider the joys of mischief.

"Thank you, Your Grace. I will," she replied as she

poured the dark brew into a delicate cup. "I've actually a matter to discuss, if I may disturb you? It could wait if Your Grace would prefer."

"Not at all," he replied. "I trust this has something to do with your recent impromptu visit to your family in Scotland."

She poured a second cup and took her place on the other side of the low table. "Indeed." Miss Primrose bowed her head. "It's what I wanted to discuss. I've decided to give my notice. I must return to Scotland."

He studied her. "Is a family member ill, or in need?"

"No, Your Grace," she said simply.

"I have four sisters who depend on you, Miss Primrose."

"Pardon my impertinence, sir, but that is not true. Since the day Verity married the Duke of Abshire, my job was done. Your other sisters have no need of governing. They have always governed themselves."

He raised the cup of coffee to his lips and savored the bitter taste. His senses picked up something amiss. And yet, as always, Amelia Primrose had not a blond hair out of place in her strict coiffure, and she sat perched on the edge of the seat, her back arched, as proper as you please. He was ever grateful she never deviated from formality.

Formality was the mask they both wore to ignore the ugly familial truth to which she had borne witness many years ago. But he would dare to cross the line, as he could not rest if someone who had done so much was in trouble. She was a lady to whom he owed eternal gratitude.

"May I ask you a question of a personal nature, Miss Primrose?"

"Of course, Your Grace. I will do my best to honor you with a reply."

"What was the true reason for your recent journey to Scotland? You left with such urgency," he said. "And you never mentioned any family in all the years you have lived with us."

Her eyes never wavered from his. "Why do you ask?"

"Because I want to assure myself that nothing is troubling you, Miss Primrose."

"I am perfectly fine, Your Grace."

He could not make out if she was telling the truth. Then again, he doubted anyone could see beyond her halo. Syn made a quiet whimper beside him and he dropped his hand to her velvety head to calm her. "You would tell me, Miss Primrose, if you needed my aid?"

"Perhaps," she replied. "But more likely, no. Everyone must carry their own burdens in life, Your Grace. You of all people realize that."

She had never remotely referred to those difficult moments of long ago.

"True. But I would hope you would come to me if you were ever in distress. I will not have it. But if you insist on leaving my employ," he said as he returned the cup to the saucer and placed it on the tray, "you cannot and will not deprive me a show of gratitude by bestowing a generous pension on you."

She bowed her blond head.

He could feel her indecision. Most would not offer a pension to a woman who had so many obvious years ahead of her in which to work. "May I inquire if you intend to seek other employment?" he asked softly.

"I will," she said. "I was not meant to be idle."

"Must it be in Scotland?" He noticed that she was clutching her delicate hands so tightly in front of her that he could see the white points of her knuckles. He would get to the bottom of this before he'd let this paragon set one foot outside Mayfair.

"Yes, I am almost decided to return. But, why do you ask, Your Grace?"

Ah. Again deflection via this particular question. Everyone in the family knew her favored trick. "Because, the Duchess of March is in dire need of your services."

Understanding bloomed on her face. "One of Verity's letters mentioned that Her Grace had invited her young cousin to stay. A Miss Calliope Little, no?"

"Precisely, Miss Primrose. Although I would ask

that you not tell Her Grace that I suggested you enter into her employ."

"And why is that?"

He gave her an arch look.

"Pardon me, Your Grace. I should not have asked."

"By the by, Miss Primrose, is it true you allowed my sister to drink absinthe?"

She studied her fingernails in the firelight. "Yes."

"Do you really think that was a good idea? I've never heard of an abigail who would condone such outrageousness."

It was her turn to arch a brow. "Perhaps Your Grace is correct. However, Verity is happily married to the Duke of Abshire as a result, is she not? I do hope Your Grace will pardon the great liberties I'm taking in talking so freely, but . . . well, in the end, I think it was an excellent decision for Verity, at least"—her voice lowered and he had to lean closer to hear her—"if not for the rest of us."

And suddenly James came to a decision without his customary period of reflection. "Miss Primrose?"

"Yes, Your Grace?" Her head was bowed again.

"You are aware that my other sisters will eventually retire to a large unentailed estate in the North if they do not choose to marry."

"Yes."

"I will arrange for you to have the use of the dowager cottage there during your lifetime along with a significant pension. It is your due, whether you do me the great favor of reforming Miss Calliope Little or not."

She opened her mouth to speak but he would not let her.

"No, I will brook no argument," he said, and added dryly, "If you take on Miss Little, I assure you that you will need three decades of staring at the beauty of the lakes to recover."

Much but not all of her anxiety seeped away. Slowly, a genuine smile made an appearance. "We shall see, Your Grace. I shall try, but I'm not altogether certain I will remain in England. But I thank you for your generous offer."

It was one of the few times in their long acquaintance that he witnessed a hint of true happiness on her face. There had been times during which neither had reason to smile. Deep mortification tended to do that.

At least he had managed to bring a measure of joy to one person today. He only feared it was not the person who most required his aid.

Then again, Isabelle Tremont would not now seek out his help if she was stranded on an island and within shouting distance of him on a vessel. After today's disastrous conversation, he rather doubted she would ever seek him out again. Just the thought of her disappointed expression she had tried valiantly to hide on her lovely face made his gut tighten. He had to stop thinking about her—and her impossible proposal.

Miss Primrose abruptly stood, returned the delicate cup and saucer to its place, and then picked up the crested silver tray. The Duke of Candover stood as well.

She was the single most trustworthy person in his employ on all his entailed estates. And she was about to face a challenge.

Chapter 4

The Pickerings' box at the Drury Lane theatre was one of the best, as it had not only an excellent view of the stage, but also offered others an excellent view of the box, which was the reason the Pickerings always reserved it. And while Isabelle attended the theatre because of her true passion for the art, tonight she also attended to practice a different sort of art—the art of flirtation, something at which she had never excelled. A tendency toward forthright honesty always hampered her efforts. But now that she had the answer she'd sought and feared for so long, she knew she had better learn how to attract a gentleman of the first order. She refused to dwell on disappointment. There was nothing to do but go on.

She had promised the Prince Regent she would marry. And she would see through her plan.

The great Edmund Kean was on the playbill tonight, and so the house was filled to the rafters. He did not disappoint. Isabelle only wished she could have said the same.

Seated in the box, the eight guests of Lord and Lady Pickering chatted during the long intermission.

"I daresay Kean is the greatest actor of our generation," Lord Amsley commented, his monocle trained on the sea of theatregoers below them.

"Indeed," she replied. The earl's moustache was very prominent and bushy. She feared it would not be pleasant to endure such whiskers during a kiss. Not that she knew a single thing about kisses. But she could imagine it—although she'd certainly never envisaged something quite like that. How would one find his lips? Perhaps one could angle the head from below. Or discreetly part the wings of whiskers. How on earth did one go about it?

And why had no one ever been moved to even try to kiss her? She greatly feared it had to do with her outspoken nature.

Certainly she was the last female her age to be unkissed. To be fair, her position and title intimidated many gentlemen. As for the bachelor lords who might have been more willing to steal a kiss, the phalanx of dukes in the royal entourage, as well as her servants, and now even Calliope, all presented a daunting front.

But she had no intention of reaching her next birthday in the same state. All the same, Lord Amsley would not do.

"Would you care to take a turn, Your Grace," he asked gravely. "Perhaps you require refreshments."

"Thank you, but no, sir. I think I'll remain here. But please don't let me keep you from joining the others." The Pickerings and their guests were filing out to stretch their limbs during the break. Isabelle did not want to be tied to the earl's side. He bowed and joined the others.

She turned to the man still seated on her other side. Mr. Thomas Knowles was a handsome gentleman from a very old family. His fortune was lamentable, but his easy wit renowned. He was her age and she had put him on her list.

He leaned toward her. "I've been watching you, Your Grace," he said for her ears only.

She pulled back. "Have you, sir? Whatever for?"

"I understand it's your turn."

She smiled. "My turn? At what?"

"At the game of the ages," he said with a glint of humor in his green eyes.

"I can't imagine to what you refer," she said, plying her fan to cool herself. It was very warm.

"The game of marriage, Your Grace."

She snapped her fan shut and tapped him on the shoulder. "Where did you hear such nonsense?"

"It's true, is it not?"

She could not take offense. He pressed her with such charm and good humor. "And why would I want for a husband, Mr. Knowles? He might very well muck up my life. I already have a duchy and why would I want to answer to anyone?"

"All true," he retorted, "but you don't look the sort who would let anyone muck up your life and"—he winked at her—"why would you chance the grave risk of going mad living all alone during those terrifyingly long winters in the north regions?"

She liked his humor very much. She smiled.

"I only ask," he continued as he casually surveyed the masses below milling about, "as I might like to make a play for you myself if it's true."

She had no idea how to reply. "I see," she said stupidly.

He turned his gaze on her once more. "But I've been asking myself why go to all the effort if it is for naught?"

"Is the effort to spend time in a lady's company so trying, Mr. Knowles?"

"Ah. Not if it's the right lady, of course. But one can never know if she is the right one soon enough to spare one the endless trips to the florist, hours trapped in a carriage during Hyde Park's afternoon spectacle, and so forth and so on. And ninety-nine percent of the time it leads to nothing."

"You speak as a man of experience," she said, laughing.

"No. I speak as a man with a mother determined to hold her own against her circle of friends whose only topics of conversation appear to be marriages and christenings."

Mr. Knowles was extraordinarily easy to talk to. She relaxed. "Perhaps you should consider introducing your mother to a new set of friends."

He smiled right back at her. His teeth were even and very white. "A capital idea. Except that I do believe she is the ringleader." He paused, studying her. "So is the rumor true?"

"Which rumor is that?"

"That you are the next member of the royal entourage the Prince Regent is determined to marry off."

She froze.

"I thought so," he said a bit smugly. "Oh, don't be offended, Your Grace. I've already told you my miserable predicament. There's no difference between us, really, if you examine it closely . . . My mother. Prinny. Demands. An ocean of ladies, or in your case gentlemen, eyeing the possibilities. I say, let's tackle them together in this marriage expedition. And who knows . . ."

"Who knows what?"

"We might like each other in the end."

"Don't count on it," she retorted. "You don't know me yet."

He threw back his head and laughed. "I fear it's too late, Your Grace. I like you already. I will not be put off. I'm determined that you will fancy me, too."

"How provoking."

"You're never going to attract anyone with that sort of air. Don't you know how to flirt?"

"No."

His raven hair shined in the darkness as his face drew closer to hers. "I might be able to teach you," he said wickedly. "I shall drive you about Hyde Park to-morrow afternoon for a start." He winked slyly.

"I have another commitment," she replied. He was a bit improper and bold, but then again, it was lovely to have a gentleman seek her company so ardently.

"Cancel it."

She had not noticed that someone entered the rear of the box until a familiar, authoritative voice spoke. "Her Grace does not enjoy anyone telling her what to do." James emerged from the shadows and stood next to her. "And you should not be with Her Grace unchaperoned and on display before everyone below."

Mr. Knowles jumped to his feet, his famous wit evaporating. "Your Grace . . . I—I am certain—"

James cut him off. "You shall apologize to her. Now."

"That is entirely unnecessary," Isabelle insisted, standing, too.

James ignored her, his countenance reaching glacial proportions. "Mr. Knowles?"

Flustered, and not nearly so sure of himself, Mr. Knowles bowed to her. "Please accept my deepest apologies, Your Grace, for any harm I might have caused you."

She did not trust herself to look in James's direction. She was too annoyed. "I'm certain you meant nothing by it, sir."

Mr. Knowles glanced at James and then at her. He bowed. "I shall take my leave. I fear the Pickerings might be expecting me below." He departed with alacrity.

She wished James would leave as well. She had no desire to exchange words with him. A hot flood of embarrassment filled her just thinking about yesterday. She trained her eyes on the people below the box. A few were looking in her direction. She knew without glancing that James was still standing beside her.

"I'm thirsty," she announced, without thought.

"Would you care to descend for lemonade?"

His low, commanding voice had always attracted her. But now it only served to infuriate.

"No, thank you."

"Would you like me to bring it to you here?" He would not be put off.

"Thank you, but no."

Awkwardness hung in the air. And still she would not meet his eye.

"Are you angry, Isabelle?"

"Yes."

"I shall have another word with Knowles. He won't dare address you so improperly ever again. Indeed, I promise you he will not dare approach you after tonight."

She had always deferred to him in the past. But everything was different now. "I will thank you to not interfere in my affairs. They do not concern you any longer." She knew she appeared peevish but she just didn't care. She had nothing to lose anymore.

"Isabelle?"

"Yes?"

"Will you not look at me?"

She slowly turned and looked up at him standing so tall above her.

"I apologize," he said, his voice deep and slow.

"For what?"

"For disappointing you." He paused. "Yesterday."

"You did not disappoint me," she lied.

He searched her face for the truth. "Good. Because I never want to disappoint you."

"I must ask you to stop overseeing my life," she said quietly.

"Knowles is trouble," he insisted. "He should not be on your list."

"I'm not an idiot. I was in the process of figuring that out all by myself when you interrupted us." She surveyed the crowd once more and exhibited a false smile to ward off rumors. "Almost no one—most of all you—trusts me to do or learn a damned thing on my own."

"This has nothing to do with trust and everything to do with protecting your good name," he said quietly.

"Whatever do you mean? I would never—"

"You know what I mean," he interrupted.

"I do not."

"You've spent most of your life in the country. This is the first year you are in Town and essentially alone—a state of affairs rife for disaster. Eyes will be on you wherever you go."

"I've done nothing untoward."

"Of course you haven't. That's not the point."

"Then spit out what you mean."

He sighed. "Members of the haut ton can be vicious toward one of their own. Especially in London. The entertainments breathe on gossip and innuendo. It's far too easy to become fodder."

"Says the gentleman of the hour."

He paled. "I will clarify, much as it pains me and will infuriate you."

She was too annoyed to speak.

"The word has got out. I wouldn't be surprised if it was not the Prince Regent's own doing. Already the betting book at White's is filled with wagers on who will win your hand."

"That's ridiculous."

"It's as I told you, Isabelle, there are no secrets here."

"Well, in a way that makes my task easier."

He had that austere look plastered to every particle of his being. "You're not actually going to continue with that list idea of yours, are you?"

"Of course I am. And you would do well to do the same, if only to choose a lady before the betting book at White's begins to feature *your* future wife's name."

"There is not a chance of that." The sudden fierceness in his eyes left no doubt. "Who are you truly considering, Isabelle?"

"I do not have to answer that."

"But if you are insisting on this mad scheme, I should see the candidates. You are new to Town and do not know anyone's true character as I do. You need counsel."

"I've seen to that, thank you. Today I received a letter from Kent. From Lady Mary Haverty, who has accepted my invitation to stay for the Little Season. She's a veteran of the marriage *wars* here and since I know you *esteem* her greatly, as do your sisters, even you cannot find fault with my choice."

"Mary is a lady of unparalleled good sense," he agreed. "But no lady knows the secrets between gentlemen."

"Look, whatever responsibilities you feel toward me due to you being my father's godson, I relieve you of them. I gave you a chance to have a say in my life and you declined. Thus, I'm no longer your concern. I sacked all three of the advisors I inherited from my father. And you will be next, unless . . ." She let the word hang in the air.

"Unless?" His voice and manner were stiff.

"Unless sometime in future you allow yourself to become *my* concern."

Those entwined bolts of lightning appeared on his forehead again. "I cannot fathom what you mean."

"Since you are so fond of telling me what to do—although you appear to have a supreme dislike of others attempting the same—Mr. Knowles being the most recent example—then I should be allowed the same privilege."

She held up her hand when he attempted to argue. "So if you want to advise me on my quest to find a husband, then you must stop procrastinating, stop thinking an heir will magically appear without a wife to plague you, and allow *me* to help *you*. In other words . . ." She fished a piece of paper with a list of names out of her black-beaded reticule. "You may take this brilliant list of suitable ladies I created for you, after which you may supply me with a list of gentlemen of good character, intelligence, wit, and charm." She kept going before he could answer. "You know, I have the oddest notion you believe you can hold off siring an heir until you are eighty."

His expression took on the glint of a man who had just tasted the truth and didn't care for it. At all.

She relaxed and allowed a smile. She was making progress. "Your sisters are worried. They don't like your heir. Neither do your servants and tenants in Derbyshire. I was given hints when I visited last summer."

"Did I really suggest that society in Town ruled the gossip world instead of sisters in the country?"

"You did," she replied.

"There is nothing wrong with Frontine Fitzroy, by the by. He is a model gentleman and heir."

"Perhaps I should add him to my list, then."

He started. "He is but fifteen."

"Too old—too young," she said airily. "I must start somewhere. And so should you."

"Why are you so determined to see to my future?" he asked.

"Because it is so wholly unlike you to avoid a task."

He slowly moved his quizzing glass toward his eye.

"You see me perfectly well, James Fitzroy. Put that down." When had she gained such nerve, calling out a giant of a man capable of reducing most gentlemen to blithering idiots? "You are the one who taught me duty is everything and must come first. So do right by your sisters and everyone else who depends on you and get on with it."

His eyes became as hard and cold as marble. "All are fully provided for—especially my sisters."

"Of course they are. But they also want to see you settled. And the duchy secured."

He refused to say another word.

"Look, there's no need to argue the point. So what is it to be? Are we to compare notes on the marriage mart? Help each other as equals? Or do we part ways here?"

"Are you attempting to blackmail me?"

"Is that what you call friends looking out for each other?"

"Yes."

"It's your choice," she retorted.

"So as I understand it, you will allow me to guide you, offer you advice on potential husbands, which I still maintain you do not have to find for several years at the very least, and in return for making certain you do not make the mistake of the century, I must suffer," he continued with distaste, "the company of ladies I have no desire to endure."

"Exactly," she said sweetly.

His expression darkened. "You've been spending too much time with Calliope."

She knew when to back off. Victory was in the air if he was turning the subject. "I intend to change that very shortly thanks to you, by the by. A most fortuitous event occurred this morning. Amelia Primrose came to March House to return a book. She managed to fascinate and control Calliope in an astounding fashion. Most impressive. I am guessing you put her up to it."

"And why would you think that?"

"Because I never lent her any book."

He studied her silently. Not a hair of emotion crossed his inscrutable face.

"She has agreed to postpone her return to Scotland, remain at March House, and teach Calliope a few finer points during a prolonged stay."

"I would offer my view on your good fortune, but I do believe you would prefer I remain silent," he replied.

"I'm indebted to you. But it is the very last time unless you take this list and do what needs to be done. If only for your sisters." She held out the note.

She felt an arctic blast of disapproval radiating from him.

She refused to lower the list.

A thousand thoughts raced through her in mere seconds. She could not explain why she felt the way she did, but James Fitzroy drove her to distraction. She had the strongest urge to jump on the unsteady chair and kiss him. Tonight he had displayed more emotion—none of it warm, unfortunately—than she'd ever seen on his countenance.

And it made her want to run her fingers through his perfectly cut short dark brown hair and muss it. And she wanted to tug on one end of his starched neck cloth tied in that formal fashion and untie it. But most of all she wanted to shout at him, provoke him to quarrel with her, if only to wipe clean the now stark indifference from his expression.

Just once she wished . . . just once she wanted him to kiss her. She did not want to kiss Lord Whiskers or Mr. Cocksure. She wanted to look into the depths of this man's mysterious brown eyes and share something wicked and intimate. And she wanted desperately for him to know her. As a woman, and not as the child he thought she still was.

He finally grasped the paper, his lips pressed in a thin line of distaste.

She released the breath she had not even realized she'd been holding.

"Come along . . . You wanted lemonade," he said quietly.

"I'm not thirsty anymore."

"Well, I am."

"All right," she acquiesced. "We can discuss which events we should attend."

He groaned.

And that is when she knew. She was going to have to do something outrageous before this would be over between them.

Letter from HRH, The Prince Regent

My dear Duchess,

One can hope the second half of the play last eve was more engrossing than the first. I shall never know (unless you undertake the chore of informing me) since my usual tittle-tattlers failed to remain awake.

If you do not reply to this royal letter—despite my command to do so—I shall not only be gravely disappointed, but I shall also assume that 1. Knowles is the delightful syco-phant I suspect him to be, 2. Amsley is too old for you, and 3. Candover is too . . . too . . . alors, as the Frogs would say, un peu de trop. Yes, a bit too much. Too much to take on for any female.

But I am counting on you. And if you will not

*take a crack at him, I assure you one of the ladies
on the list I gave you will.*

> *Your Faithful, Fearless Sovereign from the
> House of Hanover,*

> *G.*

Isabelle lowered the royal letter into the candle's
flame. Being the Prince Regent's favored secret cor-
respondent had its benefits and its price. Unfortunately,
usually the price was double the benefits. And if she
did not keep a good sense of humor firmly in place,
humiliation was sure to result.

She reached for one of the quills from the stand on
her escritoire and absently brushed the small raven
feather under her chin before dashing off a response.

Thankfully, the rest of the morning's correspon-
dence, ledgers, and daily household reports and decisions to be taken were far less intriguing.

The afternoon was just the opposite.

Hyde Park was the inferno of the equestrian world
during the Season. Landaus vied with cabriolets, and
curricles sidled up to phaetons while solitary riders
negotiated the vast squeeze of vehicles circling the
popular venue. During the Little Season, when the
summer leaves began to turn and wither, one could

breathe a bit more, for only the most determined resided in Town.

But this afternoon it was hot.

No matter, Isabelle was determined to escape March House and the worries that plagued her. And so she had her stable master bring 'round the well-sprung landau and the matched grays. She, Amelia Primrose, and Calliope would go for a drive during the fashionable hour of the unfashionable season.

Tonight she was attending a ball given by Lord and Lady Allen for their daughter, who was recently affianced to their future son-in-law. She had no doubt that James would make a rare appearance, for the Allens were his neighbors. And their families had been friends for longer than France had fought England. There was also the matter of his promise after he had accepted the list from her hand. James was a gentleman who lived up to his word. She only hoped someone else from her own list would also decide to attend.

"Why can't I go?" Calliope's face was hot with frustration.

"Because you don't like to dance," Isabelle replied with a shrewd smile.

"But I'm your companion. I must go."

"Companions do not decide these things," Amelia Primrose informed.

"They do sometimes. And you're going. I can't see why I may not, especially—"

Amelia interrupted. "I thought you wanted to see the curiosities at the Egyptian Hall in Piccadilly with me tomorrow."

"What has that to do with it?" Calliope crossed her arms, defiant. "I can do both, don't you know. As I see it, the only benefit of being fourteen is I have more energy than older people. Don't you agree, Isabelle?"

"Indeed," she replied, determined to hide her amusement, "I assure you that four years from now, your joints will be stiff in the morning, and gout will soon follow." She looked toward Amelia for support.

Amelia cleared her throat. "Of course you can do both, Calliope, but you promised to finish the painting you started for your cousin, and you also promised the housekeeper that you would help organize the baskets for the orphanage. If you do not keep promises to others, how can you expect others to keep their promises to you?"

"A fine one to talk," a masculine voice ground out nearby.

A shadow had fallen across Isabelle and Amelia, who sat side by side, facing Calliope.

"Sussex!" Isabelle exclaimed, delighted. "How lovely to see you."

His bay horse drew parallel with them and Isabelle's

carriage driver took her signal to veer to a shaded area for a moment's conversation.

"The feeling is entirely mutual, Isabelle," said the most charming of all the dukes of the royal entourage.

"It's been an age," she continued. "The last time I saw you, you were escaping Kress's interminable house party without even a by your leave. Why did you depart so suddenly?"

His famously green eyes, the color of jade, were focused solely on Amelia Primrose. "Why, I loathe the countryside of Cornwall, don't you know," he replied with a false smile. He finally glanced at Isabelle. "Far too many goats."

"Goats?" Isabelle echoed, suppressing a grin.

"And cows, and chickens," he continued. "But most of all there were too many dukes."

Calliope giggled. "There can never be too many dukes."

Amelia nudged her new charge's foot to silence her.

"There was a rumor that you disappeared because you took offense to the notion that the Sussex cow, Sussex chicken, and Sussex goat were inferior breeds," Isabelle said finally allowing a hint of amusement to color her words.

"There is no such thing as a Sussex goat," he retorted dryly. Disgust marred his handsome face.

"There should be," Amelia whispered so quickly that Isabelle barely caught it.

"I'm sorry," Sussex intoned, narrowing his eyes in Amelia's direction. "Did *you* say something?"

"Nothing at all, Your Grace," Amelia replied.

"I heard her say something," Calliope piped up.

"What did she say, my sweet?"

Isabelle felt a very odd frisson of fury radiating from Sussex, while Amelia's face was as white as parchment. Isabelle gave her cousin a look, to no avail.

"She said, 'There should—'" Calliope suddenly stopped when her eyes finally lit on Isabelle's. "Uh . . . she suggested how fitting your title would be for a—" Calliope blinked, "—goat."

"That's what I thought," Edward Godwin, the third Duke of Sussex commented, his easy expression hiding something more.

Amelia avoided his glare. "Do you know this person, Calliope?"

"No."

"Perhaps a lady *might* wait until she is properly presented before she speaks to a strange gentlemen."

"And perhaps," Sussex inserted, "a lady *should* wait until a strange gentleman has regained his wits before she has the audacity to—"

Amelia cut him off. "Perhaps if a gentleman did not

imbibe strange spirits, they would not lose the wits they have in short supply."

What on earth? Isabelle's neck hurt from whipping it between the two. "Sussex?" she inserted, in an attempt to detour the two combatants, "may I present to you my cousin, Miss Calliope Little?"

"Delighted to meet you, Miss Little."

"Calliope," Isabelle continued, "His Grace, Edward Godwin, Duke of Sussex."

"Ohhh," Calliope breathed, "you're the one."

"The one?" Sussex's horse pawed the ground, impatient to move forward. He steadied him with an easy hand.

"Yes," Calliope continued. "The one all the ladies swoon over."

He burst out laughing.

Amelia pursed her lips.

"Not that I've witnessed it, to be sure. Some people"—Calliope glanced at Isabelle and Amelia under her lashes—"insist fourteen is too young to be out. What do you think, Your Grace?" Calliope blinked once.

Edward Godwin, the Charmer, smiled shrewdly. "I think all the young gentlemen I know are going to need at least two more years practice to match wits with you, my dear."

Calliope wrinkled her nose and then giggled. "Everyone knows that young boys are useless."

His Grace threw back his head and laughed again.

Isabelle rushed in while he was distracted. "Now that I think of it, Sussex," she shaded her eyes against the glare of the sun, "I have a favor to ask."

He looked at Isabelle with kindness. "Of course, my dear. Anything for you. Anything at all."

"All this talk of presentations has me thinking." She paused. "I would be most grateful if you would escort us to the Allens tonight. And perhaps . . ."

"Yes?"

"You would be kind enough to present several gentlemen to me from a list I possess." She knew she could not count on James.

He shook his head. "So Prinny has turned his royal glare in your direction now?"

Calliope's eyes were as round and as wide as an owl's peepers at midnight. She opened her mouth, but Amelia shook her head and Calliope closed it again.

"I wish I could deny it," Isabelle replied, "but I cannot. So, will you do me the honor?"

He nodded to Amelia without looking at her. "Is she going?"

It was the height of rudeness. So very unlike Sussex. And it flustered her.

"Yes," Isabelle replied, simply.

"No," Amelia Primrose said softly, " 'she' is not."

"I thought Isabelle said you were going," Calliope

piped up innocently. "Don't you remember? You said companions do not get to choose. Surely, you don't get to choose either."

"How ridiculous, Calliope. Of course Amelia gets to choose," Isabelle said with ill ease. "She is my guest at March House."

Calliope sighed. "I do believe we can all stop pretending she is not there to reform me."

"I prefer the title of abigail, dearest," inserted Amelia.

"All right," Calliope agreed. "But surely abigails fall under the same category as companions in that they must pretend that their employer's wishes are their own."

"Precisely," Sussex said, an odd smile twisting his mouth. "Companions must do the bidding of their superiors. Sort of like wives, who must obey their husbands in all things."

Amelia's beautiful eyes narrowed. "True, Your Grace. However, companions, abigails, or wives do not have to pay homage to goats."

Isabelle observed the two of them with fascination. She had never seen Sussex even mildly irritated by any female. And she would wager her very last farthing that rudeness of any sort had never crossed Amelia's lips until now.

Watching the battle of wits between these two

beautiful creatures was sort of like witnessing an ancient, formal duel between two well-matched opponents. And she was certain the reason Sussex was so infuriated was that he feared he might very well lose.

Chapter 5

James Fitzroy knew he was in too deep the moment he grasped his ivory-handled walking stick from Wharton and struck out for the Allens' town house half a block from his residence. A crush of waiting carriages stretched all around the square. Horses whinnied and stamped their hooves, drivers muttered oaths, and the high-spirited giggles of hopeful young ladies permeated the air along with the scent of ripe manure. The latter was far more enticing than the former, he thought with customary displeasure.

He wanted no part of this. The last time he'd accepted an invitation to a ball devised solely for the purpose of leg-shackling in the guise of celebrating an upcoming leg-shackle had been in the Year of our Lord Who Knows When. He'd sworn then, before all five of his sisters, that the next time he attended such frivolity it would be only to mark one of their weddings. He was grateful Verity's union had been a very private affair not requiring a ball. Then again, after her brush with near ruin, he guessed she did not want to cause him any more headaches. His other four sisters would never marry despite their great fortunes. They were far too interested in their mathematical and scientific pursuits to allow the possibility of husbands dictating their lives.

He could not have been more delighted. It was their choice, and his preference. One brother-in-law was enough. Abshire he could tolerate.

Now.

But it had not always been so.

Twelve years ago James had watched Abshire cross a field toward him—the limp body of *his* dead fiancée in Abshire's arms. James had understood then that Catharine Talmadge had never loved him. Never wanted him—only his title and his family's position in society. She had loved Abshire, his best friend, who'd had nothing to his name in his youth.

Abshire had duped him, and Catharine had too. Or so he had assumed. He had been cut off at the knees by the two people he trusted above all others.

It was not until recently that the full story had emerged. Abshire had loved and secretly won the heart of Catharine well before James had courted the beauty. But Abshire had had pockets to let in his youth, a most unappealing state. And Catharine, fickle and with a mother who insisted a premier duke with a grand fortune trumped love with a penniless lord, secured James's affections and eventual proposal of marriage. That did not, however, stop her from eventually throwing herself at Abshire. It all ended during a wildly impetuous attempt to impress Abshire by galloping a horse to a massive stonewall, and breaking her neck in the process.

Both had been scarred and scorched to their cores. And it was only now, upon Abshire's recent marriage to Verity, that each man had come to terms with the past.

Almost.

Abshire had come to terms with the past. James had come to terms with Abshire's blamelessness. He understood ladies in their youth were often fickle.

He was not the first man to learn this.

Isabelle's father, his godfather, had learned it before him. And had suffered greatly due to it.

The worst and most prolific cases always involved a young lady with an older gentleman. Not that he blamed them, no. Ladies in their prime should not have to spoon-feed porridge to toothless old codgers.

It was the reason he had stopped going to balls, entertainments in which ladies just out of the schoolroom were often thrust under the noses of much older gentlemen by order of fortune and rank. He had them both in abundance.

Initially, he had followed society's rules, chosen the brightest flower, seen her dead in another man's arms, and had a host of new blooms thrust under his nose within a sennight; all offered to soothe his disappointment. They knew nothing about him.

No one did. He did not want to reopen the cage to his heart. It was far easier to perform the duties of the role he was tasked to play from birth, enjoy family intellectual pursuits in private, and go on with life.

Very soon thereafter, he lost all interest in blooms, and flowers, and young ladies with marriage on their mothers' minds.

And yet here he was again. In a moment of dizzying déjà vu he was taking the stone stairs two at a time up to the entrance of a town house near his own. Just beyond the polished mahogany doors, footmen silently accepted his walking stick, his hat, and his second pair of stark white gloves. In this inner sanctum of future doomed engagements, the hum of more than one hundred guests could be heard. He nodded to the footman outside the ballroom doors and they were opened for him.

The buzz of the crowd quieted and half the room

looked toward him. And then the hum redoubled its original sound.

He was back.

And with a damned list this time.

Isabelle had given up hope. He was not coming after all. Despite his promise. Despite her list. Despite everything. He was not coming. It was not like him to break his promise to anyone.

The ball had begun, and Sussex had done his part admirably. The dance card tied to her wrist with gray ribbon over her long white kid gloves was full. He'd introduced her to three of the aristocrats on Prinny's list, and then three more who were not. The latter were far more intriguing. Oh, who was she kidding? There was really only one interesting gentleman, a rear admiral of the Royal Navy, splendidly impressive with his strict posture, military dark blue coat with gold epaulets, and an economy of words. What was it about the silent, proper ones that aroused interest? Why couldn't she be attracted to the charming, vociferous gentlemen who complimented and smiled with ease?

And so she danced. She danced the opening set with Lord Allen. She danced the second with Lord Pierson. The third was reserved for Sussex, who did little to satisfy Isabelle's curiosity concerning his un-

characteristic ill-humor with Amelia Primrose. He
often glanced toward the abigail, sitting with a group
of matrons.

Halfway through the supper dance with Rear Admiral Sir Peter Baird, the hum of the guests intensified
and Isabelle glanced toward the door.

He had arrived.

James was taller and broader of shoulder than
all the other gentlemen in the ballroom. Or perhaps
it was his stature and bearing that gave the impres-
sion of great height. He raised his quizzing glass to
his eye and surveyed the room. Oh, he was the only
man Isabelle knew who could do that without looking like a portentous nonesuch with an icicle stuck in
his, ahem, throat. She smiled to herself. She had not
allowed anyone to claim the second to last set on her
dance card.

It was hard to extinguish hope.

The music from the small orchestra situated on the
long side of the ballroom came to a conclusion.

"Your Grace," the rear admiral said quietly, "shall
we go in search of supper? Would you prefer to dine
inside or out?"

"Oh, the terrace would be preferable, don't you
think? It's so warm inside." She spied James still sur-
veying the ballroom. Every person in the gilded chamber had stood a little straighter when he entered. The

premier duke had condescended to attend, and no one would miss an opportunity to be noticed by him.

"Indeed," the rear admiral replied, his pale blue eyes twinkling. "The stars are always preferable to candle-light."

He offered his arm and she grasped it as he guided her toward the opposite chamber filled with fare for the most discriminating palate. After offering her the choicest morsels from the silver service, he guided her beyond the French doors to the tables arranged on the latticed terrace overlooking one of the largest, most beautiful private gardens in London. Torches and potted palms dotted the railing, while a handful of lanterns set off pretty patterns in the leaves of the trees for those who ventured beyond the terrace.

"How long have you been a member of the Royal Navy, sir?" Isabelle lowered herself onto one of the exotic Chinese dining chairs as the officer did the same across from her. So far no one else had chosen to dine outside.

"Since I was a boy of eleven, Your Grace," he replied.

"Were you acquainted with Admiral Nelson?"

"Indeed," he replied with a kind smile, "I was a lucky fellow. My father was a distant relation and I was volunteered to serve him."

"It must have been very difficult to go to sea so young."

He studied her. "As one who had to undertake grave

responsibilities at a young age, Her Grace must understand very well."

Baird's face was rugged from years on deck, and his pale eyes seemed weary despite his smile.

"Did you always serve under Nelson?"

"Until he died. I had the privilege of his patronage, serving as a midshipman at fifteen and passing the examination for lieutenant at twenty."

"And then?"

"Am I not boring you, Your Grace?"

"Of course not. And I should be delighted if you address me less formally. Isabelle, will do."

He nodded, and she could not help but notice a few gray strands threading his pitch-black hair, shiny and tied back in a severe queue. It was hard to guess his age. Perhaps thirtyish?

"What more can I relate to you? Are stories of pirates or are French naval tactics more to your taste?"

"Actually, more of your life."

He carefully ate every last pea on his plate. "Not as interesting."

"What sort of ship did you first command? Was it unrated or were you a post captain?"

"A sixth-rater first, then a frigate, before a hundred-gun ship of the line." He raised a brow. "Since when does a young lady know of such things?"

"Since the day I decided to read every book, including the annual news registers, in my family's library."

"And what provoked such a feat?"

"I showed very little aptitude in the arts. My water-colors were always muddy, my voice likened to a dying warbler, and my embroidery resembled a barn cat's scratching post. Reading is my only forte."

His eyes crinkled at the corners when he laughed.

She refused to tell him that she had once overheard her father inform her very reserved mother that he feared their daughter was so ordinary and untalented that she would never attract a superior husband who could oversee the estates; only fortune hunters would seek her hand. He also suggested Isabelle had the most uninformed, uncultivated mind in three counties. The first complaint she could do nothing to correct. The second was altogether possible to change—if she read everything in sight. At least she naturally excelled in numbers.

"So," she continued, "were you on the *Victory* at Trafalgar?"

He exhaled slowly. "I was."

"Is it true about Admiral Nelson's last words?"

"You are not like other young ladies, Isabelle."

"How so, Admiral?"

"Peter."

"Peter," she noted. "Like the saint."

"I am no saint, my dear."

"And how am I not like other ladies?"

"Most prefer to talk about pirates." His smile was uneven; one corner rose while the other descended.

She was enjoying herself very much. "Did Nelson really utter, 'Thank God I have done my duty'?"

"I believe that has been well documented," he said, without missing a beat.

"I hope I will have earned the right to say something similar when I depart this mortal coil," she returned.

"It would be a tragedy for England to be deprived of one of its best and brightest hopes."

"Such flattery, sir. I would think the effects of salt air and the company of a ship's crew would not be conductive to such fiddle-faddle."

"Just the opposite, Isabelle," he replied. "Months at sea make one long for the pleasure of gazing at beauty and goodness."

She did not know how to respond. She had never been any good at being on the receiving end of compliments, only the reverse. She was a product of a stern father and a quiet mother, both who despaired at educating a girl to follow in her father's footsteps once it became clear there would be no male child to ascend to the title.

She abruptly stood, and the rear admiral instantly was at her back, easing away her chair.

The night air was warm but not oppressive. She had no desire to return to the stuffy ballroom. She had almost forgotten that James was inside. And she did not want to watch him converse with others. It was stupid, of course. She had instigated this idea of a list, but faced with the reality of a host of eligible females vying for his favor was unpalatable.

"The garden is lovely at night," she said artlessly as they studied the white blossoms piercing the darkness.

"It is," he agreed. "I've never seen anything like it."

"Lady Allen's moon garden is a model of beauty." She had no idea how to excel at inane conversation like other young ladies who could speak of the vagaries of the weather in biblical proportions.

"Would you care to take a turn below, Isabelle?"

She didn't hesitate. "Yes, thank you."

Again he offered his arm, and she placed hers along the length of it. He was a mere inch taller than she, and their strides complimented each other's easily.

But they shared few words between them, each choosing to keep their thoughts private. Only the plaintive call of a nightingale could be heard above the discordant sounds of the stringed instruments being tuned well before the second half of the ball inside the town house.

Isabelle suddenly missed March Hall in the Lake District. She missed the crescendo of the hordes of crickets in late summer, and the grasshopper lark's song all through the night. She missed riding through the fields, examining crops, talking to tenants, poring over accounts, and most of all the cold winds scudding across the lakes as she walked to take in the magnificent views.

She had waited patiently and then ardently for her come-out in society and presentation at court last spring. It was delayed, as she had been in mourning for her father. But now, only a few months later, she was suddenly tired and wanted nothing more than to return home to the Lake District.

But no. She had to find a husband. A palatable second choice. For if she did not produce an heir, the duchy would revert to the Crown, as there were no other Tremonts. No eighteenth cousins twenty-seven times removed.

There was only she.

And the combined weight of three centuries of ancestors bearing down on her, according to James. He was not the only one who had suggested it.

She glanced sideways under her lashes to examine the rear admiral's profile and wondered what it would be like to spend the rest of her life with him.

He appeared to feel her gaze upon him and turned to her. Their eyes locked and he came to a halt behind a tree in the darkest corner of the garden.

And for a fraction of a second before he dared to steal a kiss, she had the oddest thought. She didn't want her first kiss to be such a cliché. She didn't want it to be with a daring stranger behind a tree, during a ball in Mayfair. It sounded common—like something come to life from Lady Caroline Lamb's violent plume. She wanted . . . she wanted something she would secretly smile and cherish in the privacy of her mind for the rest of her life.

But it was too late.

Rear Admiral Sir Peter Baird's face tilted to one side as he closed the slight distance between them. His hands lightly touched her waist and his lips met hers. It was not unpleasant. She felt his mouth moving over her own, and she raised her arms to grasp his shoulders with her hands. Her fingers registered padding under the epaulets. Quite a lot of it. An odd thought intruded. Either he had suffered the effects of naught but wormy biscuits as sea rations, or the rear admiral had performed very little physical labor in his life.

She suddenly remembered to breathe. The pungent scent of seaweed, mildew, and unwashed man registered in her nostrils at the same moment she realized she should not have allowed this to happen.

He moaned slightly and reached for one of her hands on his soft shoulders to move it behind his neck.

She wondered how long a kiss usually lasted.

She hoped it would end soon. Very soon.

He finally released her mouth and then playfully dropped a peck on the end of her nose before pulling her more fully into an embrace. She was now in the awkward position of having encouraged someone she did not know and beside whom she would never be able to spend the rest of her life, let alone the rest of the evening. Once again she would have to learn from her mistakes.

Always the hard way.

"My dearest Isabelle," Peter Baird whispered in the darkness, "I would not for the life of me allow a smidgen of a stain on your good name. I should return to the ballroom before we are discovered missing. You should return a different route. May I call on you tomorrow afternoon, my dearest Isabelle?"

As if she had a choice. She had allowed this to happen. She'd invited him to use her Christian name, agreed to walk in the garden, and now she would suffer his dancing attendance on her for Lord knew how long. "Of course. I shall be delighted," she said, breathing through her mouth to avoid another blinding wave of pungent Eau de Rear Admiral.

He bowed and crept into the night, plotting a course to the extreme port side of the garden.

She breathed in deeply to refill her aching lungs. It had not been all that interesting. And she felt a bit soiled as she pondered her declining admiration for the officer.

She instinctively shook out her skirts and came 'round the opposite side of the tree, only to walk squarely into James Fitzroy. The sound she made on impact was quite inelegant. But it was like walking into a massive wall. His strong hands steadied her before he put space between them.

"What are you doing here, Isabelle?" His voice was as calm and even as always and held not a hint of malice.

How utterly mortifying. Had he witnessed the rear admiral kissing her? She had not a clue, as she could not see his face clearly. The light of a distant lantern was behind him, leaving his face in complete obscurity.

"I'm sorry?" she said, modulating her voice.

"I said, what are you doing?" He paused. "Here."

She would not lie to him, but she could not say the truth, and so she said not a word.

He dropped his hands from her upper arms. "Are you feeling ill?"

"No."

She finally could make out his pupils, which were very dark. And his flesh was the color of gray parchment in the glow of the waxing moon.

"Then why are you out here by yourself?"

"Because I wanted to take the air." She bit her tongue before she could scrape together a ridiculous, defensive lie.

"You must take better care," he said quietly.

"Don't lecture me." Her gloved forefinger tapped his solid chest on its own volition. "And don't spy on me."

She took a step to his side to better see him. He accommodated her.

His features appeared hard, uncompromising even, except for his mouth, which was relaxed. "I would not."

"Yes, you would. I'm tired of everyone watching over me as if I'm incapable of seeing to myself."

His bearing imposing, his mind impenetrable, he stared at her. "I apologize for being concerned." He leaned closer to her, examining her intensely. "You're shivering."

"I am not. It's warm outside."

He was already shrugging out of his corbeau-colored coat. The white of his shirt was startling in the darkness. She had never seen him in his shirtsleeves.

He wrapped his coat about her shoulders despite her protests. And then he stilled.

He was so very close. For the love of God, this could not be happening. Was he about to kiss her? She had waited eighteen years for one kiss and now she was about to receive two in one night? And now from the man that she—

He leaned in closer, sniffed her and quickly drew back. "What is that god-awful smell?"

"I can't imagine," she said faintly.

He leaned his face down again, nudged aside his coat and breathed in.

"You smell like a dog who's rolled in dead bird."

"I think you mean seaweed and," she winced, "mildew. Perhaps there's even a whiff of . . ." She stopped incriminating herself.

Comprehension dawned and James Fitzroy froze. "You dined with Baird."

It was the culmination of all the worst days in her life rolled into one long painful moment.

He jerked back. "Did he . . ." He couldn't seem to form the question.

With potent regret, she slowly removed his coat, still warm with his heat, from her shoulders. She offered it to him but he made no move to accept it from her hands.

"What happened?" he asked urgently. "Tell me."

She had no reason to hide the truth from him now. "He kissed me." She shrugged her shoulders. "I encouraged him."

His eyes narrowed, his pupils constricted, and the hollows in the harsh planes of his cheeks deepened. Without a word he turned on his heel and headed toward the ballroom.

She ran after him, blocking his path halfway back to the terrace. "Wait!"

"Step out of my way, Isabelle."

"It was nothing, James. You must know that."

"Good. Now get the hell out of my way."

"All right," she agreed, not moving. "But tell me just one thing. One little thing. Are you angry at me or are you angry at him? Or both of us?" She paused, her voice rising, "You're not going to challenge him to a duel are you?"

"Of course not," he replied.

She waited.

"I'm simply going to kill him." The tic in his cheek appeared.

"You cannot," she said. "I have very good reasons." Isabelle was amazed he did not ignore her and give over to some mysterious primordial male impulse to pound the ever living brains out of another man.

Instead he waited, his hands clenched at his sides.

"Look, for one it's my fault," she managed. "I gave him leave to use my Christian name. And second, I said I preferred dining on the terrace and he probably misunderstood my praise of the garden. Really, any man worth his salt would have— Oh, James, please don't. It will only cause gossip. And everyone will guess that . . ." She could not go on. She knew the tone of her sadness was probably the only thing that caused him to stay to listen to her.

He finally grasped one of her gloved forearms gently and led her to the shadows of the terrace near the roses in bloom. The potted palms above cast a shadow over them.

"First, you did not lead Baird on," he insisted. "I know you and you do not employ those sorts of feminine arts. Second, it is perfectly acceptable to dine outside, and to admire the garden. Perhaps you should not have given him permission to use your Christian name, but I doubt you'll do that twice. You never repeat mistakes."

She was light-headed from his words. "You're not angry?"

"Not with you," he replied stiffly. "Admiral Birdbrain is another matter."

She knew jealousy was not part of his nature. He had too much control over his sensibilities to allow something so base to rule him. He was simply acting in the misguided role of a guardian, annoyed he had not protected her from an unsavory kiss.

And then she realized that she wanted to tell him everything. There was no one else to whom she could speak about this in London. Calliope was too young. Amelia was in her employment. She would never dare to sully the ears of James's sisters. There was no one to whom she could confide.

"Please don't bother with the admiral. He's harmless, I promise you."

"You don't know most men's natures, Isabelle."

"I might not," she agreed, "but I'm only flustered because . . ."

"Because why?"

He had not eased back into his dark coat. It was slung over one of his shoulders, and she had never seen him so casual in his dress.

"Because . . . it was the first time anyone has ever kissed me."

She heard him draw in a ragged breath. Seconds ticked by.

"And," she continued, "it wasn't what I thought it would be. Or hoped it would be. And now . . . I smell wretched."

His face was granite-like in the light of the moon. He was so still she did not know whether she should go on. After a few moments of indecision, she decided she would not. He didn't want her to confide in him. He was disgusted by the entire affair. And now she was, too.

She watched as his free arm reached for a bloom on the white rosebush beside them. He crushed the flower and his hand came away with petals.

Slowly, gently, he brought the petals to her shoulder and eased them along the curve to her neck. Soft like velvet, the bloom's sweet fragrance washed away the other scent. She watched his dark coat fall to the ground as he crushed another bloom and brought it to her other shoulder.

The first notes of the music commencing from the Allens' ballroom faded into the night as his warm breath fell on her cheek. He had never been so close to her before.

Without thinking, she raised her arms and wound them around his neck. She gazed into his dark, mysterious eyes, staring intently back into hers, and neither of them breathed.

It was the most exquisite moment of her life.

Until the next instant . . . when he released the petals and harshly drew her into his embrace. His firm mouth found hers and she could not stop a rush of wildness flowing though her, making her shiver.

He pulled her ever closer to the warmth of his powerful hard frame and she could not stop the small sound which escaped from her throat. He was all heat and restrained strength. His striated muscles rolling under the fine layer of shirt linen made her feel faint with pleasure. It was so much more than she had ever imagined.

And then she dared to breathe the taut flesh of the hollow of his cheek. The same wildly potent scents she remembered so well for so long rushed through her senses, leaving her flush with wanting. He smelled of shaving soap, and starch, and new leather—all indefinably masculine and deadly potent.

There was nothing on this earth that could move her as much as his evocative scent. It was the essence of a true gentleman through and through—powerful, irresistible, honest, and never to be forgotten. He smelled of chivalry and deep mystery mixed with raw male.

He kissed her again and again, playing with her mouth until he urged her lips apart and twined his tongue with her own. He nipped at her lips and played with the edges of her teeth. She thought she might swoon from the intimacy of it. His iron-like arms pulled her deeper into his embrace and she felt her legs parted by one of his own as she gave up every effort to remain balanced on her toes. The soft rustling of her gown mingled with their hot breath as he crushed her to him. Her breasts ached and sparks ignited along every inch of her that touched him.

A suddenly deep desire flooded her, spiraling downward to her core, where one day her child would be nurtured—in her womb.

The intense, white-hot craving flowed ever lower to settle between her legs, where his thigh was wedged. Every nerve pulsed to the beat of her heart.

So this was passion . . .

She was lost in the moment, lost in his unyielding arms, and giving herself to him in the maelstrom of emotions coursing through her like the wind rushing through the acres and acres of woods, then swirling down to chafe the lake's surface before eddying in the cattails and giving wing to the heavens before settling at the home of her heart.

She could feel tears forming in her eyes and tried desperately to regain control. She breathed raggedly as he eased away from her. His dark silent eyes studied her. She swallowed awkwardly against a ball of emotion lodged deep in the back of her throat.

She knew without a single doubt that she was hanging onto her last shred of a nerve and it was wavering.

For what she saw reflected in his stark expression was not passion. It was certainly not love.

It was something that could not be forgiven.

It was regret.

Chapter 6

Amelia Primrose stood in the shadows at the farthest edge of the Allens' terrace. A good abigail knew how to be unobserved. She had secretly watched Isabelle tour the garden with the rear admiral. She did so to make certain no one else witnessed the encounter. She knew how to intercept disaster.

She finally relaxed her guard when she saw the Duke of Candover go after the duchess. As soon as he did, she retreated to the remote place on the other side of the terrace. She did not want to be seen or found by anyone. Especially not *him*.

She took care not to lean against the rough stone of the building for it would snag her dark blue gown—the only gown she had for evening affairs. It was long in practicality and short in elegance. But she had never sought elegance. She never wanted to attract discomfiting situations involving gentlemen of the nonchivalrous kind. It was the reason she took care to never ease her reserve, to dress her pale blond hair severely, and to dress her person even more severely. The rest she could do nothing about.

In the past she had been lucky. Her previous charges had not liked entertainments such as these. The Fitzroy females had preferred lectures, plays, the theatre, and nature walks. Lots of nature walks. Which had suited Amelia Primrose perfectly.

It had been a quiet life—one she enjoyed immensely. She deeply loved the Fitzroy family. They had saved her, really. She'd had no references (had never worked, in fact) and been in desperate need of employment when her parents suddenly died of lung fever one harsh winter. Amelia had replied to a newspaper request for applicants to fill the post of governess for the Duke of Candover's sister.

She could not remember what she wrote, but something must have appealed for she was invited to present herself. From the highlands of Scotland, she had taken off on foot, then by dog cart, when a kind vicar offered her passage. The last stage, she had ridden in a milk cart driven by a farmer and his team of oxen. She'd helped the man deliver milk to seven inns before arriving in Derbyshire.

Lost in the reverie of her past, looking at the stars in

the clear night sky, she did not see the Duke of Sussex's approach.

"I searched half of Scotland trying to run you to ground," he growled softly.

She turned to face him. "Why would you do that?"

"I've been asking myself the same question for the last six weeks."

"And what did you determine?"

"I'm an idiot to have wasted half the summer trying to corner a female who is running away from me."

"It must have been a novelty for you, at least."

His lips were thin with anger. "To be sure."

"Then why didn't you stop looking?"

"Well, one tends to keep going when one is in search of one's *wife*."

She clenched her hands at her sides. "I shall have it annulled."

"I have only one question," he pressed.

"Don't hesitate," she replied.

"Why?"

"Why what?"

"Don't play that game with me. For the love of God, I am your husband. *Your master.* Answer me. Why did you get the archbishop, corked to the ears along with me, to marry us the night before Candover's botched wedding? In the dozen years I've witnessed you coaxing Verity Fitzroy into something resembling a lady, there was never a hint of your now apparent calculating nature."

"I assume Verity was the one who informed you," she said, unable to meet his eyes.

"Of course she told me. She whispered to me that I was married to you, 'due to special circumstances,' and then she was packed off to Derbyshire by her dear brother before she could explain the nature of those 'special' circumstances. Care to explain, *wife*?"

"I'm certain," she said quietly, "it's neither valid nor recorded. There was no license, special or otherwise, and obviously no banns. I doubt the archbishop even remembers the event. If it has any validity, I assure you it will be annulled. Very, very soon."

"Really? And how do you plan to go about it?"

"I've requested an audience with the archbishop."

"He won't see you," Sussex said acidly. "I shall have to see to it myself."

She stood straighter. "This was my mistake and I will correct it."

"You still have not told me why you did it."

She would not answer.

He stared at her, furious. He used his finger to emphasize his words. "If you think I won't get a full explanation of this outrageousness before the ink is dry on an annulment, then you don't know me, Miss Amelia Primrose—or do you assume that I will call you 'Your Grace'? And all these years I thought you a lady above reproach. Does Candover know about this?"

She shook her head, unable to speak.

"It's a good thing. It'd break his heart, it would. He always said the sun and moon rose by you. What would he say now?"

"I cannot fathom." Oh, yes, she could. "Promise me you will not say a word to him."

He looked at her shrewdly. "That will be considerably difficult, considering . . ."

"Considering what?" she asked.

"That I'm living under his roof."

"I beg your pardon?"

"As of this afternoon."

She waited for his explanation.

"Because of you, my dearest devoted, saintly wife."

"I cannot imagine why I would be to blame for—"

"I had planned to be hunting grouse with Abshire right now. But as I found it more important to hunt down a certain Scottish madwoman, and your trail led me here, well, here I must stay."

"What of your town house?"

He appeared vastly annoyed. "The knocker is down."

She waited for him to continue.

"I'd arranged for improvements, renovations, re-everything from roof to cellar during my absence." His expression was pained.

"How inconvenient," she said.

"Precisely." His eyes bored into hers.

"And so you have been invited by His Grace to stay at Candover House."

"Well, he had no choice when I went to him after I tracked you down in Hyde Park today. I loathe hotels and he's the only other member of the entourage in Town, and it was *his* damn fault that all these ripples of disaster occurred."

She clenched her hands at her sides. "You know very well he was not to blame." A cold ball of fury formed in her abdomen. "And if you were a gentleman you would not hold another responsible for your own actions."

"Ah, and now I am to feel chastened?" His tone was frozen with disdain.

She held her ground. "Injustice never bodes well. And people who make excuses are intolerable." She paused, gathering wind. "I will not listen to you blaspheme His Grace. And I won't have you say a single word to worry him. I told you I will correct my mistake on my own."

His eyes narrowed with distrust. "Why are you so concerned about Candover?"

"Because . . . because . . . well, just because."

"And you expect me to accept that sort of flimsy explanation?"

"It's the best I can do."

"And you call yourself a governess."

"No, I call myself an abigail."

"Well, I can tell you one thing you will never call yourself."

"And what is that?"

"My duchess!"

The following morning, James Fitzroy descended from his suite of chambers at Candover House to take his breakfast. Six o'clock was his favorite hour of the day, as no one in his family ever descended before eight, Cook prepared predetermined fare, and Wharton always had the newspaper freshly ironed. It was important to start each day with perfect order and calm.

Especially important when the rest of his damned life was going to ruin.

Had he not learned time and again that losing one's head—for even just one moment—was destructive, disastrous, completely irresponsible, and sometimes even fatal, if not always life-changing for the worse?

He had but one mission in life, and that was to do his duty to those who depended on him. There was no room for a grand passion, which only made fools of those who thought it could endure a lifetime or bring lasting happiness. Indeed, allowing extreme desire and impetuous love to ruin one's equilibrium could result in grave consequences. His first fiancée's death had been a prime example.

And had he not learned that being lax in conduct—always—*always*—proved disastrous?

Would there not be one Fitzroy who could do right by the family? Fulfill the role model of strict and correct character for England? Was that not the obligation of the premier duke of Christendom?

Obviously, once again last night, he had failed the test.

What the devil had he been thinking? He could not even blame it on spirits, given the bread-and-water spartan life he'd recently imposed on himself. He damn well was losing his grip. He'd allowed himself to be vulnerable—to give in to momentary desire. And that was unacceptable. It only ever led to loss.

Indeed, allowing another person to see even a glimmer of the true essence beyond the persona society demanded he present to the world was showing weakness.

And that was simply not who he was—who he was mistakenly destined to be. The deep, sonorous voice of the man he had most wanted to please—but always failed—his beloved father, rose from the deepest corner of his mind. He would do his duty. He would not give in to temptation.

Yes, he'd be damned if he'd let things slip further. He had no idea what had possessed him in that blasted garden of the Allens. But she had looked up at him from those fathomless golden eyes of hers, her mouth slightly parted, and then she'd had the audacity to put her beautiful, young arms around him. Those lips of hers had made him want to do unspeakable things. His neck was hot and he hardened just thinking about her. And he had no one to hold responsible but himself.

The entire evening had been a disaster of epic proportions. He'd had to endure an entire herd of innocent ladies fresh out of the school room, and their gushing mothers and peacocking fathers, not to mention assorted blushing aunts and grinning grandmothers who, by the looks of all of them, were considering possible names for an heir. *His* heir. And he'd had to restrain himself from going to the terrace when Isabelle and that bloody rear admiral chose to dine there. And finally he'd had to discreetly remove himself from the ballroom so no one would follow him.

God.

Isabelle . . . just the thought of her. Damn it all. Replaying the night in his mind a thousand times and trying to forget it a thousand times more had only left him more wretched.

There was no escaping it. He would have to own

up to his abominable actions toward her and apologize. Promise it would never, ever occur again. And after, he would restore order to his mind, and attempt to forget the primal, near blinding pleasure that fired his veins and turned his spirit inside out while kissing his friend's daughter, a lady who in all likelihood was younger than any other female present.

The footman opened the door to the dining hall and he stopped dead in his tracks as it silently closed behind him. Obscured by the open pages of *his* newspaper, Edward Godwin, the Duke of Sussex, sat in *his* chair. The other duke lowered *The Morning Post* to reveal three plates bearing a mountainous portion of eggs, toast, herrings, and something that looked like mashed kidneys.

"Shall I have Wharton send in a roast suckling pig and pheasant?" His tone was so dry that a fire could have been started with it.

Sussex ignored him and returned his gaze to the paper. "No, no need, thank you. Two more rashers of bacon should do it. Although it's too bad you don't have liver on the morning menu."

"Ever hear of gout?"

"Pfft," Sussex replied before delicately shoveling an enormous forkful of eggs on toast into his mouth and then elegantly using his napkin. "Jams and jellies always manage to round things out."

"Ever hear of rules and house guests?"

Sussex shrugged. "I'm not a guest. I'm more like a brother, right?"

James's heart stuttered before he regained his composure. He should never have agreed to host Sussex. The sideboard beckoned, and he turned to cross to it. The usual fare lay decimated like the French at Waterloo. Except for an apple. He snatched it, turned, and stared at Sussex sitting at the head of the table.

He had the most absurd desire to take aim at the other's head.

Instead, James sat down to Sussex's left.

"Shouldn't you sit on my right?" Sussex tore off a section from the paper and resumed reading and eating.

With one lightning fast swipe, James snatched *The Morning Post* from Sussex's hands. "And why should I do that?"

Sussex chuckled that way of his—warm and good humored. He was the opposite of James in every way. "Because in the order of precedence the most important female always sits to the right."

"Precisely," James returned, coolly. "That's why you're on *my* right."

Sussex grinned and leaned forward to thump him on the back. "Do you ever smile, man?"

"Are you ever serious?"

It had always been this way between them. They had known each other longer than any of the other dukes. Since infancy, really. They might not have spent much time in each other's company during childhood, but their years together at Eton made up for it. And James had always been careful to keep a hedgerow of casual indifference between them. It was the only way he could tolerate their friendship. There was so much more at stake than the other knew.

Wharton, red-faced, entered the dining hall carrying a large silver platter of eggs, toast, and four rashers of bacon. A footman followed him with more fare. "May I prepare your plate, Your Grace?"

Both gentlemen replied yes at the same moment.

"Sorry," Sussex said, "force of habit."

"How long can we expect the *pleasure* of your habits?" James took a bite from the apple as he waited to be served.

"Just a few weeks, actually. The architect said the upper chambers will be finished in about six weeks."

So would he if he had to endure this that long. Wharton placed James's usual fare in front of him as the other footman plunked down half a side of bacon in front of Sussex.

"His Grace and I require a bit of privacy, Wharton," Sussex said.

What on earth? Now he was to be usurped?

Wharton's face blanched and he turned to James, who nodded his assent.

"By the by," Sussex said, "I saw your beloved abigail nattering with Isabelle in the park and at the ball last night. I understand she's no longer living under your roof."

"Miss Amelia Primrose gave me her notice. She entered Isabelle's employ."

"Hmmm. How odd. Thought you might have sacked her." Sussex stopped eating and was glancing at him with false ease.

Something was off. "Why would I sack her? She's the best abigail in the country."

"I did not know that you condoned females drinking absinthe is all."

James wanted to throttle him. "And why would you suggest the females in Carleton House that night were drinking that damned frog poison?" He might know the truth, but he didn't want anyone else to know.

For a mere second something flashed in Sussex's face. He turned around to make certain the servants had departed. "Well, of course they were. You don't think they were embroidering, do you? And haven't you wondered why they didn't wake you up at the very least?"

"I'd prefer not to say."

"So you know why?"

James slowly raised his quizzing glass to his eye.

"Did you know that makes your eye look twice as big as the other?"

"Sussex?"

"Yes?"

"You have a bit of lard on your chin." James pushed back the legs of the chair and stood up.

"No need to go. You haven't touched your toast, man."

"No appetite."

"Are we not feeling well?" Sussex used that detestable nursemaid voice he did quite well.

"We are feeling perfectly fine."

"May I have your plate, then?"

"Be my guest."

"Such generosity of spirit."

James resisted the urge to yank him out of his chair by his neck cloth. "Just looking out for you. You'll need it."

"Need what?"

"Food for strength."

Sussex's brow furrowed. "I've no idea what you're suggesting."

"Well, if you're going to take on Miss Amelia Primrose, you'll need all the strength you can muster for a man with gout."

"Why on earth would you think I have any interest in that damn female?"

"Careful. You might possess a duchy by happy

circumstance, Sussex, and you may be slightly my elder, but I'm still your superior. And if you cause Amelia Primrose a moment of ill ease, there is no amount of absinthe I won't force down your gullet before I feed you your own kidneys and liver for breakfast."

Sussex narrowed his eyes. "Really?"

"Really."

"All right. But if we are going to descend to that level then perhaps it's only fair I warn you in return that I spied my favorite member of the royal entourage, Isabelle Tremont, running up the Allens' stairs from the garden last night just before you sauntered up those same stairs not two minutes later. And if I ever again see the duchess's face with the sort of expression I witnessed, you'll be substituting apples for grass for breakfast."

James stared at the other man for an age before he spoke. "I'm going to exercise one of my horses on Rotten Row."

"How lovely."

"You are not welcome to join me."

"So glad to be in agreement for once," Sussex said without a hint of malice.

"And remember what I said about Amelia Primrose. Stay away from her."

"I'm not sure why the two of you are so protective of one another," Sussex retorted, "but perhaps you should consider telling *her* to stay the hell away from me."

"Consider it done."

"Good."

"Excellent."

"Are you ever going to take your leave?" Sussex finally had a peevish expression on his face.

"I was about to ask you the same question. Ah, but never mind. My good manners prevent me from disturbing the present distribution of fat to your ankles."

Sussex responded by returning his attention to *The Morning Post* and waving his cup of tea in the air in a regal, "you may go" fashion.

James did not know if he had won this round with Sussex. But then again, he had taken so much from Edward Godwin that it didn't matter.

On the other side of the door, he took Wharton aside before heading to the mews. "I shall take breakfast in future in my private chambers until Sussex departs."

"Yes, Your Grace. We do the same for all the ladies of the house, and—"

"Wharton?"

"Yes, Your Grace?"

"Are you suggesting I am acting like a female?"

"I would not dare, Your Grace."

"Good. And contrary to what the Duke of Sussex

might request in future, only apples will be served in this dining hall in the mornings."

Wharton bowed and backed away. "Of course, Your Grace."

James did not care that he was acting like an ass. He'd never done it before, and it felt good.

Chapter 7

Letter from HRH, The Prince Regent

Dearest Duchess,

I understand the Allens' affair was merely tolerable. A bit too hot given the scarcity of windows, and a bit too dry given the lack of spirits. Why, I ask myself frequently, do hosts not understand that they should double the amount of food and drink, and halve the number of palms, which offer far too much privacy for my lack-wit emissaries to investigate?

Indeed, I require a report on your progress. And that of Candover's usual lack of progress.

Shall we not dispense with beating about the bush (or palm, if you will) and have out with it?

Have you or have you not secured his hand? Or have you decided (quite rightly) that thawing him out will take an Ice Age?

Your most patient (but not forever or for much longer for that matter) Sovereign,

G.

Nota Bene: my dear girl, you were on to something in the Allens' garden. You will melt the most frozen of hearts in this fashion I assure you.

Nota Bene II: avoid naval officers. Their beloved mistress is the sea, which makes their wives remarkably irritated (and often barren). Not for you, my dear. Not at all.

For nearly three days Isabelle stewed. She had stewed so long that she was sure her mind had taken on the gelatinous consistency of the orange marmalade on the supper tray before her in her chambers. A tart bitterness of spirit completed the image.

For the first time in her life, she had lost her appetite. "Lost" was not the correct word. It implied she had left it somewhere on a street corner. But that was not it. Her appetite had evaporated little by little as her anger mounted. Her Italian chef had tried to tease her palate, sending up trays with all manner of foods. Clearly, as she looked at the feast before her, tonight was about coaxing her famous sweet tooth. Four miniature portions of dessert surrounded a plate of boiled eggs, the only dish she had requested. Boiled eggs were remarkably easy to quietly dispose—via reticules or pockets or even open windows. Desserts were far more complicated.

Isabelle used a spoon to toy with the panna cotta and watched it wobble.

When her friend Mary Haverty had not arrived from Kent at the hour she'd suggested in her last letter, Isabelle retired to her chambers. She had not been able to stand another early supper at table with Calliope and Amelia, who pretended not to notice her reticence. Well, Amelia pretended not to notice while Calliope spoke about the importance of food and the unimportance of dukes with the letter C in their name.

At first, anxiety had kept her from sleeping. That and the memory of his kiss ignited her mind hour after hour. The sensation of his arms wrapped around her, of his great strength, and his lips on hers, permeated every fiber of her being. His scent, the play of his muscles beneath the layers of her gloves and his clothes were simply unforgettable. She swallowed. She feared that kiss would haunt her forever and a day. His obvious regret had been an arrow to her heart.

She had been certain James would pay a call on her at March House the next day, during an hour that was unfashionable for other visitors. He would bow and scrape with rigid hauteur and perform the ancient ritual of all false apologies—many perfunctory words and little genuine emotion.

And she in turn would be expected to bestow forgiveness while suggesting that his apology was not necessary, all the while serving him tea—no sugar, no milk—and no biscuits.

But three days of waiting for the charade to unfold, only to have it *not* unfold, had left her so distinctly uncharitable and irritated that she could not stop thinking about him. She contemplated the silver tray of delicacies. Yes, if he dared to show his face now, she would fling this mellifluous panna cotta dripping with raspberry coulis in his face—tea and no biscuits be damned.

She sighed in frustration. All this introspection, intermixed with fuming, had to end. And it would. She had seen to it today. She was now officially older and wiser, and she would get on with the business of selecting a husband.

Tomorrow she would ride in Green Park, visit the lending library and the dressmaker, followed by the joy

she would take watching Calliope try her first ice from
Gunter's. Then Lord Holland's literary salon for dinner
followed by discussion by some of the finest writers
and artists of the era. Two of the eight gentlemen on her
list would be there.

Thank God there was not a hint of a garden attached
to Holland House. And thank God too that James
would not be there. He detested Lord Holland.

He was obviously so put off by events at the Allens'
town house that he could not even face her. She would
do the same. She tried hard to ignore her infantile response but could not quell it.

She knew she had too much pride, but there was no
use trying to change such a deeply entrenched trait.
Pride had been brewing in Tremonts for three hundred
years and it would not dissipate now.

She pushed aside the tray on her canopied bed and
lay down, staring at the intricate pleats above her. Of-
tentimes, she closed the curtains surrounding the bed
and imagined herself far away in one of the foreign
places of which she had read: Egypt, the West Indies,
Peru, the Far East. Closing her eyes now, she tried to
envision the pyramids.

His face stared back at her, hideous regret lurking in
every nuance of his stark features.

It was not to be borne.

She sat up, furious. A change was in order. Tonight.

She would not wait until tomorrow. She nearly knocked the tray off the bed in her urgency to reach the pull. Lily appeared within moments.

"Please tell the housekeeper that I want my father's former chambers reopened and aired." She glanced at the wall clock. It was still early evening.. "Straight away. My affairs can be moved tomorrow, Lily. I will only need fresh linens tonight."

Lily bobbed her head. "Yes, Your Grace."

"Where are Calliope and Miss Primrose? Have they finished dining?"

"Yes, ma'am. They've set up easels in the gallery."

Isabelle glanced at the nearly untouched tray on her bed. "Very good. Um, Lily . . . please tell Chef that his food was exceptional as always. The eggs especially." She quickly took three of the hard boiled eggs and placed them on the table.

The maid gathered the tray without a word.

Isabelle placed her amber-colored shawl around her shoulders and descended to her favorite place at March House—the library. She was glad to find it empty. She preferred to be confounded by philosophers in private.

She should have been born a man, she thought. Lord knew, her father had wished it, had voiced it numerous times. Her mother desired it, too, even if she had not said it outright.

Her mother rarely if ever had said what she thought. Instead, Mama often just gazed out of the bay of south-facing windows at March Hall, wistfulness threading itself in the perfection of her delicate features.

It had always been difficult to tell what her mother was thinking.

And when her mother left the Lake District, leaving the Duke of March behind, as well as her only child, then there had been nothing left to try to know. From then on, Isabelle had no choice but to accept that her beloved mother's actions and ensuing silence spoke more profoundly than any words could have.

Now she wondered if her mother was still staring, unseeing, at the world beyond new windows.

Her mother's silence was the reason Isabelle did not allow herself to fall into bouts of circuitous introspection. Except for today. And yesterday. And damn it, yes, every day since she'd received the letter from the Prince Regent.

But she refused to be like her mother. She was a Tremont through and through. Actually, she was not like her mother, and not like her father either. She was herself. At least that was what she had overheard James insist to her father just before he died. The words were seared in her memory, to be reviewed before each new challenge she faced: *She will excel, right from the start, I assure you, godfather. She's better than all of us. She's somehow managed to retain all the good in us, and avoid all of our faults—except perhaps that stubborn streak that seems to come part and parcel with a duchy.*

She pushed aside the remembrance as her fingers trailed the spines of the books containing the brilliant and not so brilliant minds of great men and women. She walked along the rows of books, uncertain what to choose. Finally giving up, she mounted six steps of the movable ladder, closed her eyes, and selected a volume at random. This method often provided the most interesting results.

A familiar voice floated beyond the library door, and the volume slipped from her hand to crash with a thud on the Aubusson carpet below.

She steadied her hands and turned around on the book stair.

A footman preceded them.

For the love of God . . .

"Her Grace will be informed of your arrival, Your Grace and Lady Haverty," her man said.

"Do please tell Her Grace how sorry I am to arrive at such an hour," Lady Haverty said as she walked into the library ahead of James.

He had come. And now the two of them must play out a charade in the presence of Mary Haverty. Her hands gripped the ladder rail.

"There's . . ." Isabelle rasped, and tried again. "There's no need. I'm right here."

Their faces turned toward her. She trained her eyes on the ladder, which she descended slowly. With her luck, she would stumble.

"Isabelle!" Mary rushed toward her. "Oh, how lovely to see you."

She embraced her friend and finally turned toward the devil, who stood watching. If she could have avoided his touch she would have. But from the time she first met him over a dozen years ago, James had always taken her hand and brushed his lips against the back of it as a mark of deference to the duchess she would one day become.

And so it was now. She would not meet his eyes, but she could not help but glance at the way his dark brown hair feathered on the back of his head as he bowed to press his lips against her ungloved hand. For such a large man, his lips were remarkably soft, and very warm.

"Your Grace," he murmured for her ears only.

She nodded without a word.

"Oh, Isabelle," Mary breathed. "I'm so very sorry to arrive at this late hour. There was a bit of a problem with the carriage. One of its wheels, actually."

"Are you all right?" Isabelle frowned.

"Very well. My only luck was that it happened near St. James Square, and so I enlisted James's help. If a wheel had to break, better there than some-where along the miles and miles of rutted road from Kent." Mary smiled toward him. "James insisted on accompanying me himself. Your chivalry knows no bounds, sir."

"It was nothing, Mary," he said evenly. "I could not allow you to go alone."

"But I have my maid," she replied, laughing.

It had always been this way between Mary and James. The russet-haired beauty of astounding wit and charm was nearly the same age as James, and had spent almost every summer visiting his sisters in Derbyshire. Their friendship had begun nearly a decade before Isa-belle was born.

"You must be hungry, Mary," Isabelle said softly. "Shall I arrange supper for you? And . . . Your Grace?" She had noticed out of the corner of her eye that he was wearing starkly formal evening clothes. His white neck cloth was tied in an intricate fashion, and the stiff brocade collar of his dark coat was so high he might cut his jaw if he turned his head.

"I cannot help but admit I'm starving," Mary said. "The fare at the last inn was so wretched, I could not eat it."

"Let me arrange something, then. I'm so glad you've arrived, Mary."

"Oh, me, too. I miss Town. There is nothing but the sounds of haymaking and crickets in Kent."

Mary's warm, throaty chuckle filled the library. "I cannot tell you how delighted I was by your invitation to stay for the Little Season. We shall have such fun together!"

"It is you who are doing me a great favor, Mary."

James was as silent as a statue.

Mary opened her mouth and then suddenly closed it. She turned to look at James. And then she looked at Isabelle. The silence between them was as awkward as it could be.

"What is going on?" Mary's candor was legendary. Almost as legendary as her green cat-eyed auburn beauty. Indeed, she was so lovely that hostesses with marriageable daughters very often remembered to forget to send her invitations.

Neither responded. Mary looked at both of them again.

"I have no idea what you're talking about," Isabelle finally said.

Mary looked at James.

"I accompanied you here because I require a word with Her Grace," he said, his lips barely moving.

"Since when do you refer to Isabelle as Her Grace in front of me, or any of our friends for that matter?"

His chin rose a fraction of an inch. "Since I owe her an apology."

"His Grace does not owe me anything," Isabelle replied directly to Mary.

"Oh," Mary said, laughing. "And you're so formal, too. This is capital. James, guilty of something? I do believe the last time I heard he did something wrong, there might have been a queen on the throne."

"Indeed," James said, as stiff as a knight in armor.

When he did not continue, Mary did. "So what did you do?"

"I'd prefer not to say," James ground out.

"Well, how will you apologize without retelling it in gory detail?"

She had to stop this. It was like watching some sort of hideous accident about to unfold. "Absolutely nothing happened. I have not a clue to what he is referring."

A pair of green eyes and a pair of brown eyes examined her, but she could stonewall with the best of them.

Mary bit her lips. "Devil take it. This is impossible. How can you expect me to do the proper thing and leave you both to your own devices? You'll surely make a muck of it. I'm an excellent referee." Mary paused. "Truly. And I promise not to laugh again. So James, what did you do to Isabelle? Or not do? No, you never fail to act. So, what did you do? Or was it something you said?"

Isabelle walked to the door as casually as she could manage. "He didn't say or do anything, Mary. Pardon me for a moment," she said as she opened the library door and asked the footman to arrange supper for Mary. She closed the door again and tried to look James in the face but could only train her eyes on his chin. "And whatever you think that you did that might have offended—not that I think or can imagine that you did anything that caused me a moment of concern— please don't burden your conscience any longer." She wondered how many extra degrees of heat would be hers to enjoy in the little corner of Hell she'd occupy for such lies.

Mary's good-humored grin faded.

James's expression was arctic. "Mary, would you be so kind as to allow Her Grace a moment with me? Surely, you have something important to attend to for a quarter hour?"

Mary bit her lip. "I rather think this is going to take longer than a quarter hour, but all right. So, does Signor Benorini still rule your kitchen, Isabelle?"

"Yes," she replied.

"The most enchanting chef. Does he still create those divine desserts?"

"Oh, yes," Isabelle replied. "His panna cotta with raspberry coulis tonight was extraordinary. Indeed, I was imagining how much His Grace would enjoy it not one half hour ago. But I cannot have you dine alone. Come, I'll join you at the table."

James examined her with hooded eyes. "Isabelle?"

"Yes?"

"Will you not honor me for a few minutes? Alone."

She wasn't sure which urge was stronger—the one to grab onto his lapels and kiss him within an inch of his life to make him see what an ass he was, or the one in which a delicious dessert would be wasted. "There's no need, I assure you.

"This is far more serious than I thought," Mary said softly. "Well, I think I shall go. I fear my appetite is in danger of being affected if I stay."

"You're not the only one," Isabelle muttered.

"What did you say?" James's expression darkened.

"Although . . ." Mary said with classic indecision, "we could all have dessert right here."

"No!" both Isabelle and James replied at the same time.

"Finally . . . some agreement," Mary purred. "It's a start. All right, then, since I don't want to become another person who requires an apology, I shall take my leave. For a quarter hour."

As Mary left, the two of them did not move. James was five feet away from her.

"Isabelle," he began, his voice as deep, calm, and even as always, "please forgive me for my momentary lapse in—"

"Don't you dare, James Fitzroy," she interrupted. "If there was something to be said, you should have said it two days ago. Now it's too late." Dear God. She hadn't meant to say what was in her heart now that he had rejected her. She'd meant to attempt what her mother had taught by example—to keep her sensibilities in check.

"I agree."

"And don't you dare do that either," she said peevishly.

"I beg your pardon?"

"That annoying habit of yours."

"Habit?"

"Oh botheration. You know what I'm talking about. You only have one aggravating habit," she said. "Well, maybe two or three at most."

He stared at her.

"The one when you end an argument before it has a chance to bear fruit."

He raised his eyebrows.

She sighed. "When you immediately agree with something provoking."

"So you are trying to provoke me?"

"And now you're changing the topic."

"But you've already said you won't forgive me."

"You are supposed to insist. Or promise something in return."

"Is this in some sort of guide to etiquette?"

"No. It's something one knows innately."

"I see." He didn't appear to see at all.

She glanced at the nearest row of books on the

shelf near her. She felt like a fool, which only made her more annoyed. Perhaps he needed a dose of his own silent-as-the-grave mannerism. No . . . she could not. "Go on, then," she ground out. "What is it you have to say?"

"All right," he said as cool as you please. "Although one can hope you will hear me out without interruption."

Well, at least he could follow instructions. She raised her chin a fraction of an inch and waited.

He took one step closer to her. "I request your forgiveness for taking advantage of your fragile state three nights ago."

"I've never been fragile," she ground out. "And you know it."

Whatever was turning in that great head of his, he managed to hide it as always. "Then I beg your pardon for taking advantage of you, period."

"No one 'takes' anything from me, James Fitzroy," she continued, "that I do not want to give."

He opened his mouth and then closed it.

"Oh, spit it out for God's sake. There's no need to overthink these sorts of things."

"I'm certain guides to good manners advise against epithets."

"Are you daring to correct me?" Yes, she might very well strangle him before this was over. "When you are the one who owes me an apology?"

He replied quickly, "So you admit I owe you an apology."

"Of course you do, you oaf."

His cool expression finally changed. A degree. A degree toward incredulity. She suddenly wondered if the premier duke of England had ever been called an oaf before. Probably not.

"But not for taking advantage—but rather for being momentarily distracted and impudent?" He stopped. There was a strange expression decorating his face. Sort of like if he had taken a bite of something at a dinner party, found it inedible, and could not decide whether to swallow or discreetly search for his napkin.

"Have you ever truly lost your head for even half a moment in your life?" she dared him.

"I'm sure I don't know what you mean," he replied stiffly.

"Have you ever wanted something so passionately that you didn't care if you made an utter idiot of yourself trying to get it?"

He pursed his lips. "In all fairness, perhaps I should point out that you are now exhibiting a less than desirable trait of your own."

"Tell me you are not criticizing me *again* while attempting to apologize?"

He would not take the bait.

"All right." She could not stand not knowing. "Tell me what you find annoying."

"When you phrase something in which neither yes or no will appease or appear to advantage."

"Just answer my damned question."

He exhaled slowly.

Honestly, the man was insufferable in his unflappability.

"Yes," he replied.

"Yes, what?" she encouraged.

"I've made a fool of myself in the past."

"When?"

"Recently," he admitted. "The night before the wedding that did not happen."

"That doesn't count."

"Not according to the Prince Regent."

"Have you or have you not ever felt passion, James Fitzroy?" She waited far too long for his answer.

"What has that to do with anything, Isabelle?"

"I think I'm allowed one answer to any question I choose. Indeed, let's make it part of the penance. So, what is your answer?"

Only his lips, now thin and whiter than usual, gave his ill-ease away. "How do you define passion?"

Would he ever answer? Well . . . she would not let him go now until he did. What was behind that impenetrable veneer of his? Was there yet another layer of ice, or just the reverse, as she had always imagined. She was in it for the duration. "All right," she replied, about as patient as a veteran schoolteacher. "Let's see . . . I would say passion is a deep, near ungovernable emotion. Intense desire to know another person or . . . or something on this green earth—at the deepest level. It even sometimes overrules a regulated mind."

He studied her for a long moment, his eyes hooded. In the lengthening shadows of the remains of the day coming from the windows, he appeared steeped in mystery—a man unused to ever discussing himself or his past.

She wondered if he had ever been innocent and carefree.

He cleared his throat. "But passion's meaning is also rooted in suffering. If that is what you ask, then yes, I have endured passion. I've also witnessed the consequences left in passion's impetuous wake. It always involves loss—of self or of another. But I am a man, and as you know, a gentleman does not dwell on such things. It does no good and is a waste of time. I would hope you are forever spared passion's grip— for it removes balance from most people's lives when they reach for something so bright and impermanent. I will always reject passion for duty—to my sisters, to the people who depend on me, our sovereign, and my position. "

"You are wrong, James," she said quietly. "Passion is not just about suffering. I think it's a gift, whether it's a passion for something or some*one*. It's to be embraced—experienced. To be explored. To be cherished. Sometimes frustrating, sometimes even sad, yes, but still it's too rare to squander. Life is not meant to be lived in muddy grays. Passion in life brings color and vibrancy."

He frowned, his discomfort almost palpable. "Do you come by these notions firsthand or are these ideas you've formed without direct experience?"

"I don't have to experience something or read about it to understand it," she insisted. "I also think passion takes courage. Do you know the root of that word? *Coeur*—or heart in Latin."

"Your memory is astounding," he retorted. "I distinctly remember explaining that notion to you the day you attempted to avoid the tooth-drawer, who wanted to examine your teeth."

"Yes, well if you had heard the scullery maid and footman screaming before you arrived that day, you would have understood."

The barest hint of movement at the corner of his mouth relieved the tension of the moment.

She exhaled. "Well, perhaps you've paid your penance even if we cannot agree on passion or avoiding bloodthirsty tooth-drawers. But now we must determine your offense."

His eyes widened. "That should be obvious, even if you disagree."

"You did not take advantage of me, James." She tried to save her pride and his. "These sorts of things happen all the time. Perhaps it was the champagne, or the music—actually I know it was not the music, as the violinist sounded like a screeching cat. Or perhaps it was the heat of the night—who knows? It doesn't matter." She swallowed against the ache in the back of her throat from telling untruths. But she pushed a small part of her pride aside and said what needed to be said. "I'm only annoyed because I was certain you would call on me the next day. And you did not come. And then the next. And still you did not come. Even if you did not owe me an apology, you should have come. It was the gentlemanly thing to do."

His expression was unreadable. "I hope you will find it within your heart to forgive me for any anxiety I caused you."

Thank God he had chosen not to pick apart her irrational argument.

"So why did you wait?" She continued, "I had something of importance to discuss."

"What is it?"

"No. I want to know why you waited."

"I, er, well . . ."

It was a first. James tongue-tied.

"Yes?" she encouraged sweetly.

"Look, I'm not in the habit of apologizing. To anyone."

She kept her smile in check. "Perfectly understandable."

He examined the back of his gloved hand. "And the matter of that kiss. I would not want you to think—"

"Actually," she interrupted, "I must thank you for it."

He went still. "Thank me?"

"Why, yes. It gave me another perspective of how it might be done. The rear admiral's kiss was not very interesting. The one with you was . . . well, *pleasant*. And now that I know how to go about it, well, I will know what to do the next time I—"

"Isabelle Tremont," he interrupted with a low growl, "you will only invite trouble if you creep about gardens kissing gentlemen with whom you are barely acquainted."

"So it's only acceptable to kiss those with whom I share a long-standing acquaintance?"

"No," he ground out. "That moment with me was an extreme aberration. It's not acceptable for you to kiss anyone."

"Except my future husband?"

"Perhaps once." He coughed. "After one is engaged."

"And you follow these rules?"

"You know very well that each sex has its own rules."

She smiled. "Of course I do. That is why brothels

exist. And light-skirts, mistresses, bits of muslin, high fliers, Cyprians, and—"

"No need to go on," he interrupted. "I won't ask how you've come to know these terms." He looked toward the ceiling as if he would find help there. "I think we've said all that needs to be said."

"Except the matter I wanted to discuss."

"It's not about Calliope, is it? Only Amelia can help you there. And Mary will guide you in all matters of society."

"No. I wanted to ask if you had managed to converse with one or two ladies on the list I gave you." She gazed into his eyes without blinking. "And about that list you were to prepare for me?"

A muscle in the hollow of his cheek clenched and then released. "List?"

She smiled. "Have you forgotten your desire to advise me on a husband?"

His eyes took on a glassy quality.

"The prince requires progress . . . *on my front and yours,*" she said sweetly.

He groaned.

"What?" She shook her head. "This should be easy for you. It's all about duty. Not passion."

Devil take it. Why was she always talking about damned lists? Lists never worked. The Duke of Kress's house party in Cornwall earlier this summer was proof enough of that. An entire herd of well-heeled young ladies approved by the Prince Regent had not appealed to any of the dukes present. Indeed, the combined charms of nearly a dozen daughters of earls, marquises, lords, and barons had not overcome the appeal of a certain Cornish tin man's daughter, who Kress had chosen as his bride.

And her comment regarding his kiss . . . It was just *pleasant*? It was interesting? She was the most confounding lady of his acquaintance. And that was why he—

"So, did you dance with any of them? Lady Susan was in very good looks and she comes from a long line of very fertile ladies who have provided heirs with astounding speed—"

"We will not have this discussion. There is a limit, Isabelle, and discussing if a lady is fruitful is beyond it."

"But it is a top priority. Indeed, your only priority if you were to ask—"

A knock at the door interrupted her. Mary Haverty poked her head inside. "Is everyone still alive in here? Or should I send for a surgeon?"

"Alive, yes," Isabelle chuckled. "Finished, no. But I do believe we might be in need of your opinion now."

"Oh, delighted to help," Mary said, carefully closing

the door quietly behind her. "And by the by, I just made the acquaintance of Calliope Little. Your cousin is such a delight!"

James made a sound that could have been a snort if he were not so refined.

"What can I do to help you both?" Mary's brilliant smile was blinding and it was all for Isabelle. "Did he apologize nicely?"

"He improved as we went along."

"I see I'm no longer needed here," he said dryly. "And I've a rendezvous at White's."

"One moment, if you please, James," Isabelle insisted.

At least she had ended the formality. She placed her hand on his arm, and the hairs on the back of his neck rose. He didn't like it when she touched him. "Of course," he said, his notion of escape cut off.

"Mary," Isabelle said quietly, "I think it important to share a confidence with you."

Mary's merry green eyes showed infinite amusement. "How delightful. I adore confidences. And unlike everyone else, I'm very good at keeping secrets. Except when I choose not to. But yours I will keep most faithfully, I assure you." Mary crossed her heart with her index finger and then dropped it to her side.

"Are your fingers crossed?" He was unable to keep annoyance from his voice.

Mary chuckled and raised her hands. "Absolutely not. Now what is it?"

"James has given me his word that he will choose a wife from a list I gave him of eligible females. The Prince Regent has demanded that we each choose a spouse."

"I did not agree to choose a wife, merely to investigate the possibility," James clarified.

"No," Isabelle inserted. "You agreed to commence the search for a wife when you accepted the list."

He glared at the two women in front of him. One would think he would know how to control females after tending to the affairs of five sisters. Then again, five sisters were nothing compared to one duchess.

"As my father always said, the mark of a true gentleman is his ability to keep his word," Isabelle continued. "Will you keep yours, then?"

It was like a kick to the groin. He was a man of his word. He rarely made promises.

Indeed, when someone required a promise, the weight of the world placed on his shoulders was typically the result.

He had made two other promises in his life—one to his father and one to Isabelle's father, the Duke of March. And he was beginning to feel as if he was balancing the entire planetary system at this point.

But the promise he had made to March three years ago was the one he would not ever fail to keep. And as God as his witness, he'd see it through. No matter what it cost him.

And it was clearly going to cost him. A pound of flesh.

His own.

"You can count on my word, Isabelle. That I promise you. You can count on it."

Chapter 8

On the south side of Hyde Park, the Route de Roi, or more commonly known as "Rotten Row" in its corrupted form, was the place to give one's horse a good run early in the morning. The only drawback was that it was often crowded with young bucks jostling for position in the midst of older but not wiser bucks. Few of the female persuasion dared to set foot, or rather, hoof there. Then again, most ladies were still abed at seven o'clock in the morning.

Isabelle and Mary were not like most ladies. And so they warmed up their mounts and their bodies with a brisk trot on the sandy track shaded by a broad arch of ash trees. Isabelle finally allowed the gray mare her head and broke into a canter, breaking away from Mary on the bay gelding. The wind felt good on her face as she urged her mount toward Serpentine Road in the distance.

The weather showed the first hints of fall—crisp, clean, and ready for change. And so was Isabelle. She'd offered James her hand and he had not accepted it. She'd given herself in his embrace, and he had regretted it. And now there was not an hour of the day when she could not remember it.

At least her days were filled with the mountain of tasks and responsibilities to ensure the March duchy continued to not only prosper, but also to grow. She would not allow any hint of a question on her ability to govern the properties entailed to her and the welfare of people who depended on her.

But her nights? When all her tasks were accomplished and societal obligations fulfilled, she had naught but her memories of that night in the garden. With a man whose words were muddy and gray, but whose embrace was every color imaginable.

This entire summer had been disastrous. He had showed hints of something beyond his words to her. She'd hoped his kiss was something more than just a momentary distraction. It had to be.

She was sure.

She was as sure as the ancient lords were of overtaking the young riders barreling helter-skelter all about her. She was so far in the dark concerning James that she could have been wearing blinders.

Twice, Isabelle and Mary rode down the allée—

each lost in their thoughts, each happy to have the other for company.

"Had enough?" Mary laughed as she caught up with her toward the end of the second run.

"Never," Isabelle replied with a smile. But she veered far left of the wide track to cool her horse at a more sedate pace.

"Agreed." Mary's eyes sparkled with good humor and vitality. Two gentlemen slowed their horses and craned their necks to get a better look at the beauty, who appeared to sparkle as the sun began its march from east to west. Vanity had to be reined in when one was with Lady Mary Haverty.

"So are you ever going to tell me what happened last evening?" Mary looked at her expectantly. "Or am I to pretend I am something I am not—a proper friend who allows you the privacy of your own thoughts?"

"The latter," she replied.

"Not very likely," Mary said under her breath.

"I heard that."

"Yes, I know," Mary replied, her face glowing. "But I fear it's impossible. You know, perhaps I might offer a different perspective. I've known James forever. I spent part of every summer at his family's seat in Derbyshire after his elder sisters and I became great friends during our disastrous first season in Town."

Isabelle diplomatically ignored the reference to

Mary's family's straitened circumstances. "James has a very high regard for you. He has always considered you a model of everything good and proper."

Mary's smile was blinding. "Well, two can play at this game. He told me just last month at Kress's that he knew of no other lady in England who could manage a duchy by herself."

"Oh, I manage it all right," Isabelle said a bit grimly. "By the skin of my teeth since I dismissed my father's advisors the day I came of age earlier this year." Only the sounds of the horses—their hooves hitting the dirt and their breathing—could be heard for several long moments.

"Isabelle?"

"Yes?"

"I know we've not been the closest of confidantes, but I hope that can change. I hope you never believed any of those ridiculous falsehoods circulating about on occasion." Mary's constant cheer was suddenly replaced with seriousness.

"Of course I didn't," Isabelle said, rushing to fill the gap. "I know you and James have nothing more than a deep friendship based on years of acquaintance. And I've always admired your candor."

"That's a nice way to say audaciousness." Mary's radiant smile reappeared.

Isabelle bit back a grin. "Indeed I cannot forget

when I first saw you after years of hearing about you from James. You were purposefully stepping on the feet of some poor fellow whilst waltzing. James's sisters told me it was to punish him for never ever dancing with them."

"I didn't have many requests to dance the rest of the summer. But it was worth it." Mary's laugh floated in the warm summer breeze.

A silence intruded, and only Isabelle's mare nickering and pawing the ground broke it.

"I was surprised you wrote to me," Mary began. "Surprised but so very pleased. I hope you will not take this wrong, but will you not tell me the real reason you asked me to visit?"

Isabelle exhaled. "Because . . . well, because of your good sense. And your knowledge of the ways of the ton and courtship. And of possible suitors. I must marry, as you know. And I hoped you might help guide me."

"And what of James?" Mary finally dared to ask softly.

She kept her gaze straight ahead.

"But you love him." Mary said what no one else would dare.

"I'm afraid so." What was the use in lying? Mary and all of James's sisters knew of her unrequited sentiments. And now even James knew. "But my sentiments are not returned. Never have been and never will be. He made it perfectly clear that he has no interest in marrying me."

"You actually brought up the topic of marriage with him, then?"

She studied her horse's ears straight ahead. "Oh, yes. To my perfect mortification. He would not consider for a moment an arranged marriage with me despite the prince's commands."

They walked in silence, each of them occupying their hands with their mount's reins as they moved over a small rise.

She finally continued. "I refuse to go on like this, mooning over him. Even if it were not for the royal command that all of us marry, I would find a husband. I have a list of candidates and . . . well, I hoped you would help me."

"Oh, Isabelle, of course I will," Mary breathed, "You cannot imagine how fond I am of you. But I always thought you had little regard for me."

"No," she replied, "that's not true. I am just like every other lady with eyes in her head—impossibly envious. In fact I am wondering if you would consider wearing padding around your middle and hideous, matronly turbans if we have to stand next to each other at entertainments."

Mary shouted quite inelegantly with laughter. She mopped her eyes. "I like you. Very much. And yes, because I am so delighted we are to be friends, I shall let you choose whatever you would like me to wear!"

Isabelle finally smiled. "Mary, I can never thank you enough," she said with great earnestness.

"Well, I think you've hit upon an excellent idea. I adore lists. And they work remarkably well. Verity and I employed a list of questions for suitors not two months ago—and you see, she is blissfully happy with the Duke of Abshire now."

James's middle sister, Verity, was indeed, married to Abshire, James's former archenemy in Derbyshire.

They had come to a halt beside a stand of trees. Isabelle could not stop the question she had never dared to ask anyone familiar with the past. "Was James violently in love with Catharine Talmadge?"

Mary's green eyes studied her. "I don't believe he has ever been 'violently' in love with anyone. It's not in his nature. But, yes, when he was engaged over a decade ago it was considered a love match. Although . . . while I do not like to speak ill of the dead, I must tell you that Catharine had no female friends apart from her younger sister. There was falseness to her character that was evident to ladies but not to gentlemen, who were all blinded by her appeal."

"But James's sisters hinted he had changed when she died, no? Is that why he is so reserved?"

Mary tilted her head and gazed into the distance, thinking. "They were both fairly young when they were betrothed. He was more lighthearted then. He was always a devoted son and brother. Loved nothing more than rambling and exploring nature with his likeminded mother and sisters. But as the years passed, he gained a seriousness and remoteness to him. I can't tell you the why and how of it. But yes, certainly there was a part of him affected that summer. And when his mother died, too. She was the light of Boxwood." Sunlight filtered through the leaves on the branches above them and cast lovely shadows on Mary's face. "But, I've always wondered . . ."

"Yes?" Isabelle encouraged.

"I've wondered if he has silent burdens like so many of us." A faraway look clouded her deep green eyes.

Isabelle regarded Mary. "Well, I shall find out. I don't like unanswered questions."

"Are you certain that is the best course, Isabelle? Privacy is everything to James." Mary glanced at her sideways.

"Of course. James gave my father so much—such peace in the end. I owe him even if he has pricked away at my pride," Isabelle said.

Mary regarded her slyly. "You are a better woman than I."

"Why do you say that?" Isabelle leaned forward and patted her mare's shoulder.

"Because when Lord—" Mary paused, her voice

caught for a moment. "—Hadrien threw me over last year I had not an inch of compassion."

While Mary was endowed with great beauty, she had not been lucky in love. The great love of her life, Lord Hadrien, had without a word shockingly disappeared, to cast his lot with an aging countess who possessed ten thousand a year.

"Rightly so," Isabelle said quietly. "But that was a bit different. Would you like me to shoot him for you?"

"What a lovely idea." Mary forced a laugh and patted her horse's shoulder with her gloved hand. "James always said you were an excellent shot. But I like to think Hadrien is suffering more—living under someone's thumb with nothing more exciting than fetching shawls, playing bridge, and wishing he was in Town. He loathed the country. Oh, I sound like a wretch."

"Well, my lovely Queen Anne pistol is at the ready. Doesn't require much powder, very little recoil, and best of all . . . lethal."

Mary's expression softened a little, just as Isabelle had hoped. She pressed forward.

"Then again I could use a Brown Bess. Excellent for hunting accidents. I can prime, load, and fire almost as fast as James."

"Thank you, Isabelle." Mary's expression eased and she truly laughed. "And truly I am beginning to think you will need very little guidance from me in the mating rituals. Your instincts and your heart are in the right place."

Isabelle knew she had to say the rest, even if it was difficult. For if they were to be friends, they must be open. "I cannot tell you how sorry I was to hear about the MacGregor. I don't know how you managed on the heels of the other." Mary's hastily arranged betrothal to a Scottish laird after Hadrien disappeared had also ended disastrously when the MacGregor died of a lung fever before Mary even had the chance to meet him in person.

Mary would not meet her eyes. "I understand he was the best of men. I grieve for his family." She finally looked at her. "Indeed, Isabelle, I fear you are at grave risk befriending me. My bad luck is legendary. Let us hope it is not infectious."

"Luck is an illusion," Isabelle said. "I'm very glad you are spending the Little Season with me."

Mary sighed. "Then we are of like mind. And I, like you, cannot dally any longer. I'm giving the marriage mart one last chance. If I have not secured the affections of a worthy gentleman this year, I'm retiring to live with James's sisters, as they're determined to leave the Derbyshire and retire to a lesser estate."

"How ridiculous." Isabelle would not say more.

"No, it's not ridiculous at all. It is what one does when one has no fortune, and one's prospects are limited," Mary said quietly.

"Oh, pish," Isabelle replied. "The day your prospects are limited . . . If you do not have ten gentlemen vying for your favors at all hours of the day, it will be the end of time."

"Is this when we have to waste time complimenting each other, and not planning what must be done? Do you have the list on you? The one with—"

"Lady Mary Haverty! And Isabelle," the Duke of Sussex exclaimed, riding his magnificent beast of a stallion to a halt in front of them. A smile was ever fixed on his handsome face as he jumped from the saddle and pressed a quick kiss to each lady's hand. "Delighted to see you both. And so convenient. But why aren't you both still abed? Don't you know it's not at all the thing for ladies to be up at this hour?"

"And what would you have us do?" Isabelle adored Edward. He was always so open and kind, and charming. And never afraid of being made a fool.

"Languish in bed with lace caps while having someone peel grapes for you," he said, his green eyes twinkling.

"I might be willing to do that if it could be apples instead of grapes," Isabelle said, wrinkling her nose.

All amusement fled Edward's face. "There are no apples in this scenario."

"But I like apples," Isabelle insisted. "Peeled grapes are slimy. Sort of like overripe bananas. Apples are the perfect fruit—sometimes tart, sometimes sweet, and they last forever."

"There are no apples in this scenario," Edward ground out again. "Peeled grapes or perhaps bacon. Yes, bacon."

Mary chuckled, unwilling to participate. "So why is our meeting here so convenient to you when Isabelle and I should still be abed and consuming something other than chocolate, which everyone knows is the only thing palatable in the morning?"

Edward smiled at her. "I have taken a decision this morning."

"Sounds ominous," Isabelle inserted.

"Actually, it's the opposite," he replied. "I find I cannot spend another night under Candover's roof. Impossible, I tell you. Impossible. The man has no idea how to treat guests."

"Really?" Mary arched a brow.

"I'm for Richmond," he continued, put out.

"Your estate just beyond London?" Mary continued, "I've heard it's one of the loveliest places."

"You must both come, too. That is why it's so convenient, you see. I'm decided on a house party. You must come."

"How delightful," Mary said, looking toward Isabelle. "What say you?"

He did not wait for her answer. "Isabelle, I insist you bring Calliope Little."

For a moment she thought she spied something in Edward's regard that was a little too serious. "You are very kind to think of my little cousin. Indeed, I didn't think you even knew of her existence."

"She is not meant for Town," he continued. "She needs air and nature."

Why on earth was Edward focused on Calliope's needs?

"And I suppose her abigail must come too," he said casually.

"Miss Primrose?" Mary queried.

His face became a mask of disdain.

"I haven't even given you my answer, Edward," Isabelle said, holding her excitement in check. She longed to leave Town. But she could not.

"No matter," he insisted. "I will not take no for an answer, so you should save your breath."

"Well . . .." She was acquiescing far too quickly. She had her plans in place for the Little Season and they did not include dallying in nature. "But . . ."

"But what?" He fidgeted in the saddle.

"I fear I cannot unless . . . Oh, this is far too embarrassing."

"Anything, Isabelle. As long as you all come. A week from today. What is it you require?"

"You know the Prince Regent's demands. I fear I cannot go unless . . . well, unless certain eligible gentlemen are there as well. I have a list."

"Ah," he said, a smile breaking through. "A lady without pretense. Very good. I shall promise you a house full of gentlemen since you are providing a house full of ladies."

"Is James to be one of the party?" Mary asked slyly.

"No," Edward immediately replied. "I refuse to include a man who provides houseguests with fare only interesting to horses."

"This explains your aversion to apples," Isabelle said with a smile.

Mary chuckled and then looked at Edward with her most alluring expression. "Well, I for one will not go unless James is there as well."

Edward's eyes widened. "Will wonders ever cease? Do you have a *tendre* for him, Mary? Lucky, lucky fellow."

She glanced at Isabelle and laughed. "Actually, I have my own list."

Sussex looked at Isabelle and scratched the back of his head. "I see. Anything more I should know?"

"James has a list, too," Isabelle said as casually as she could.

A grin overspread his face. "Ah, this I would not miss for the world. I suppose I could invite him. But there is one condition."

They looked at him expectantly.

"I have an aversion. It is so deep that I get hives if I am within ten feet of it."

Mary giggled. "Yes, we know. Apples."

"No. *Lists*," he said innocently. "Don't like 'em. Don't need 'em."

Isabelle cocked her head. "Maybe not for the moment. But have you forgotten that sooner or later His Royal Highness will look in your direction? Wouldn't you rather pick your poison instead of having it thrust down your throat?"

"Perfect analogy, my dear. Not that I don't adore and admire all ladies. But any female attempting to marry me against my will . . . well, arsenic would be preferable."

Isabelle seized the moment. "Why do you look at Amelia Primrose with scorn?"

He started, but recovered nicely. "It's not scorn, Isabelle. That is something altogether different. Amelia Primrose might look like an angel, but I assure you that no one should trust her. She is the Devil's handmaiden."

Angelus Abbey, the prime seat of the Duke of Sussex, dominated a picturesque, sleepy village in Richmond, just a few hours west of London. A massive gatehouse fronted the mile-long entrance to the circular drive bordered by low-lying black-painted chain links and posts. Few flowers or shrubberies decorated the wooded landscape. But that merely drew attention to the stark beauty of the structure built soon after William the Bastard conquered England. One corner of the towering edifice showed signs of ruin, proving man's handi-work could not withstand the havoc wrought by seven hundred years.

James studied the structure through the rain-splattered window of his carriage as his equipage made its way down the long drive.

It was the last place he wanted to be.

And yet, he'd had little choice.

A loud snore interrupted his thoughts. He looked at the elderly gentleman slumped across from him. His Grace, the Archbishop of Canterbury.

It was the last person he wanted to see.

And yet, again, he had little choice.

Whoever said that with power and prestige came responsibility had been putting it mildly. Indeed, no-blesse oblige was a millstone one wore while maintain-ing a benevolent air one rarely felt.

The archbishop let loose a highly inappropri-ate sound for a religious man. James had a flash of memory from the night of the outrageous party. In his majestic robes, the archbishop had nearly drowned in the Serpentine while trying to swim with the swans. James shook his head. He had the vague nightmar-ish notion that he might have been the one who had revived him by blowing air into his mouth. Yes, the Primate of All England facing him had downed more of that wretched brew provided by Kress than any of the rest of them. His Grace might sleep as soundly as the dogs now slumbering at their feet, but it was astounding the man did not wake himself, with such a devil-like symphony emanating from him.

James felt he should not be here for more than one reason. First, no Duke of Candover was ever supposed to set foot on these sacred grounds *for good reason*. Second, Isabelle would be here, as well as a host of gentlemen from her damned list she did not need. Third, there might be ladies from that double damned list she had provided.

He was here for only one reason: to put to rights something of which he knew next to nothing, other than the letter he held in his hands. The one he had nearly memorized.

My Lord Duke,

Only the most serious circumstances force me to ask this favor. Would His Grace be kind enough to arrange for His Grace, the Archbishop of Canterbury, to attend the Duke of Sussex's house party?

Your servant,
AP

Why had Amelia Primrose made such an outrageous request? And since she had never asked him for one thing in all of the years she had been with the family, James was loath to refuse her. Clearly something was grave beyond reason. And since she had not told him what was afoot, he would have to find it out himself.

Not a quarter hour before James's carriage drew in front of Angelus Abbey, the archbishop awoke, yawned hugely, and finally smiled, his little mouth forming a vee. "This carriage is very well sprung. Delightful outing. Say, Candover, would you happen to know if Sussex's wine cellar is as well stocked as—"

"No idea," James interrupted. "Now that you're awake, I must ask you again—how long ago did you form an acquaintance with my sister's abigail?"

"Is this the Penelope creature you spoke of?"

"Amelia Primrose," James repeated for the fifth time in three hours. "Originally from Scotland."

"A rather heathenish lot, those Scots, don't you think?"

"How do you know her?"

"Penelope?"

"No," he ground out. "Amelia. Primrose. As in a rose that is prim."

The archbishop blinked. "Never heard of a flower being prudish. Are you certain you haven't been nipping a bit of brandy?"

"There are no spirits in this carriage. But if you

answer my question, I will arrange for a bottle of the best brandy in the region for you tomorrow."

"Actually, I prefer Armagnac. The Dowager Duchess of Helston introduced me to the delights of—"

"I shall deliver a case of it to your chambers tonight. Just please, for the love of God, tell me how you came to know Amelia Primrose."

"Everything I do is for the love of God."

James rolled his eyes.

"No need for a tantrum, Candover." He winked. "Amelia is a far lovelier name than Penelope, don't you agree?"

He refused to reply. As soon as the Little Season was done, he was for Derbyshire. Living with four sisters would be a relief after this.

"Hmmm . . . She's your abigail, you say? A bit long in the tooth for an abigail, no?"

James sighed heavily. "I told you she was my sister's abigail. You apparently know her."

"Your sister Prudence?"

"I do not have a sister named Prudence."

"A fine brother you are. Forgetting your own sister's name."

He stared at the archbishop.

"You have half a dozen sisters if I recall. Your parents were models of propriety. Let's see, let me help you remember. Prudence, Temperance, Levity, Morality, Chivalry, and, oh yes . . . Amelia."

"I have five sisters. Faith, Hope, Verity, Charity, and Chastity. Amelia was Verity's abigail. She is now employed by the Duchess of March."

He furrowed his brow. "By my dearest Isabelle? But she does not need an abigail. She's fully mature at thirty-two years old. What she needs is a husband."

"She is eighteen."

"The Duchess of March, you say? Eighteen?" He scratched his balding head. "Are you sure?"

James could not open his mouth.

"My, you are awfully short-tempered, Candover."

James clenched his molars and prayed for deliverance from the Valley of Death by Archbishop. "Do you know Miss Amelia Primrose or not?"

The archbishop appeared greatly affronted. "Why, I do not *know* ladies in the biblical sense—other than my wife, of course. May I remind you, dear boy, that I'm the spiritual leader of our great country? You cannot imagine the pressure."

James looked toward the abbey, still half a mile in the distance. If it were not so important, he would stop the carriage and walk the rest of the way. He attempted a different tactic. "Do you remember anything from that infamous night with Prinny and the rest of us?"

The elderly gentleman instantly retorted. "Of course I do. I have an excellent memory."

James could not resist needling the man. "So you remember swimming with royal fowl?"

"I would never—"

"And drinking Kress's god-awful absinthe and—"

"My dear," the archbishop interrupted. "One should never condemn any part of God's cache of earthly delights. Is it *still* raining?"

"No. You see, it's very easy to answer a question. Will you do me the very great favor of answering mine?" He was considering torture.

"Of course, I will grant you a favor, Candover. As long as it's in my best interest, of course."

"Forget it," James muttered. It was a testament to his state of mind. He never muttered.

"I never forget anything, dear boy." And with that the archbishop tilted back his head and closed his eyes.

The carriage rounded the second to last wide turn toward the abbey. James had no choice but to insist that Amelia explain all directly. He was loath to do so. Both he and Verity's former abigail had taken great pains to maintain a very formal rapport after she bore witness to his father's great secret. It had been the only way, given the embarrassment.

He stared at the abbey ahead. He knew they were most likely the last ones to arrive. He had planned it that way. Less time with the hordes of guests.

And less time with Isabelle.

He would have to make a point of never finding himself alone with her. He stilled his hand, which was tapping the carriage bench.

He had missed her the last week. And now she was haunting his dreams. That face of hers . . .

She had the most expressive eyes. Highly unusual and not unlike a lioness. And her mass of shiny, lovely brown hair. Not as dark as his own, but a beautiful lighter shade, more like maple that shone in the— Lord, since when had he attempted poetry? And at this moment? Across from a demented tonsured religious? The madhouse was in his future.

God, how she had felt in his arms. So vibrant, and feminine, and bold. He closed his eyes for a moment and remembered her face—open, trusting, passion-filled. He feared what might have happened had they been alone, far from anyone else. He, who had prided himself on his control. Well, he learned from his mistakes. He only had to do one thing. Remember the Duke of March.

She had always been very much like her father in temperament. Stubborn, proud, smart as a whip, a natural leader. Indeed, she was the best thing that had ever happened to the Tremont duchy.

He wondered how much of her mother Isabelle had truly inherited—if anything at all. The former Duchess of March had been such a mysterious, grave lady. Far younger than March, very quiet, seemingly devoted until the day she left, the winter Isabelle had been ten years old. In his distress, the Duke of March had shared with James the note his wife left behind when she departed England with a lover. Oh, they had done excellently in covering up the sordid event, telling all that Her Grace had gone to Brussels to care for a consumptive relative and become ill herself and died there. The last had been true, at least. James's own mother had been quite different from the beautiful young former Duchess of March. And while both had been holding up the pretense of a loving marriage, his mother lived a joy-filled life raising her children and filling up her days with her passion for nature. She'd had the rare qualities of goodness, loyalty, and grace under all circumstances.

They were the very qualities Isabelle possessed in abundance, but did not know it.

A loud snore erupted from the archbishop once more. He hoped he himself did not snore. And suddenly he felt more alone than he had ever felt in his life.

There was no one who would ever tell him if he snored. Certainly not his servants. And his sisters would not dare to set foot in his bedchambers. And of the ladies he'd bedded, all rich widows with nothing to lose, he had never stayed to slumber in their presence.

What had possessed him of late? James closed his eyes and leaned his heavy head against the edge of the carriage back. Why was he so damned tired all the time?

And why was he dreaming every damned night of

Isabelle Tremont? He could not stop reliving every hot moment—the way her form had molded to his so damn perfectly it made his mouth water. He had wanted to touch her, peel down that scrap of a silk bodice of hers and taste her.

And in his dreams he had.

Her face, creamy white under a waxing moon, had suddenly been bathed in the candlelight of his chambers in Derbyshire. And he had kissed and caressed her supple flesh as she moaned. His mouth had trailed his hands until he reached the juncture of her thighs. He had urged her slim legs apart intent on driving them both mad with desire. In the dreamy haze of thick passion, he had parted and stroked and finally tasted her as her sweet sounds of excitement changed to wild abandon.

Until he hadn't been able to bear the strain of pent-up desire. He had crawled up her body with a deep guttural growl and positioned himself, nudging her thighs ever wider. The heaviness of his arousal had rested against the soft invitation of her body, and he'd gritted against the wave of intense desire to take her. And in his dreams he did. And each time, the wild rush of pleasure crashed the moment he took her innocence and he caught the shattering depth of hurt he had seen in her eyes that night in the garden.

He looked down at his hands in his lap. They were shaking like leaves of summer, against the rush of autumn's first gusts. He would not let go. He would not give in to temptation. He would be damned more than he already was if he broke his word. He closed his eyes against the pain of it.

God, he wanted her.

And yet, he didn't want her at all.

Bloody millstones.

Chapter 9

Letter from HRH the Prince Regent

My dear Duchess,

More lists. Unless you can unleash that marvelous creativity I've seen in your young mind. Don't ask how I've managed it—but the best and brightest flowering young ladies of the Little Season (albeit some are seconds and thirds since the best of the crop are usually already plucked by the start of summer—except you my dear, as we both know you have your pick of the curs) are on their way to Sussex's drafty pile.

And if I were you, I should give up on Old Sobersides, as your delightful Miss Calliope Little refers to James Fitzroy. Candover is not worth your efforts, my dear. Onward and upward I always say.

And as for the rest of the royal entourage, you are to make sure the Duke of Barry finds his way toward marital bliss for he is A Good Man. But don't bother with Sussex—you shall have your hands full with all the characters gathering for the grand marital hunt of the season.

Write to me, my dear. And give my warmest regards to that dear Calliope Little creature. I adore aging crones masquerading as girls of four and ten. From a distance.

À Bientôt
G.

Nota Bene

The list of Hopefuls and Has-beens:

Lady Pamela Hopkins—*likes to wager. A lot.*
Lady Katherine Leigh—*whinnies. A lot.*
Lady Judith Leigh—*the giggler of the lot. Her flaming hair makes up for it. Almost.*
Lady Susan Moore—*always with the headache. (Or causes my own.)*

Until I receive Candover's list of (certain to be) rubbish, I shall send the only gentlemen I can coax from their hunting boxes:

The Marquis of Haverston
The Earl of Bronway
Mr. Parker *(widower with two squalling brats to entertain Miss Calliope Little and occupy Miss Amelia Primrose.)*
Mr. Adams *(a handsome gentleman but with an unfortunate tendency to discuss shop instead of assuming a proper tonnish facade of world-weariness.)*

Keep this list. You will need it. They all look so much alike—the simpering ladies in white dresses and the wasp-waisted gentlemen peacocking about with quizzing glass ribbons lacing their fingers.

James had never enjoyed déjà vu. One should not have to repeat nightmares. And this house party of Sussex's was like an awful re-creation of the visit to the Duke of Kress's ancestral estate in Cornwall. Then, James had been ordered south to oversee the marrying off of the most notorious members of the royal entourage. But this time? He had no one but himself, and

Amelia Primrose, to blame. Not that he would ever blame her for anything. It was just the opposite. He owed her too much.

These were his thoughts as he surveyed the lounging guests in Sussex's ancient cavernous great room, of which one side featured a fireplace that could roast a half-dozen pigs at once. Clearly designed to fulfill the master's porcine addiction.

The medieval chamber featured more than a few seating areas, perfect for private conversations. And every corner of it was filled with the same ladies who had been in Cornwall. Only now they were joined by a covey of gentlemen all preening and vying for the attention of . . . Isabelle and Mary, at first glance.

He clenched his teeth. No. He would not go to Isabelle. He scanned the chamber once more for Amelia Primrose, without luck.

His eyes were drawn back to Isabelle. Candlelight played across her features, illuminating her lively expression. His gaze traveled to the delicate hollows of her collarbones, and to the elegance of her shoulders and hands.

She conversed with . . . he squinted . . . *Devil take it.* What was the Duke of Barry doing here? Prinny had ordered him to make himself scarce after Cornwall. Why, if the populous in London learned Barry had woken up across from a dead man in Carleton House the morning after the night of sin, it would renew rebellion against the aristocracy. The newspapers had learned and trumpeted all of the excesses of the bachelor night except that one, hideous fact that Prinny managed to keep secret. Not one month ago the country was in anarchy and on the brink of revolution. If the news leaked about the lifeless man across from Barry, well . . .

James walked toward the pair as his peers pretended not to watch his every movement. When he met one gentleman's eyes, the peer lowered his gaze as a mark of deference. It never failed to make him feel like a different species of animal.

"Barry?"

The younger duke glanced up from his chair across from Isabelle. "Ah, Candover."

"What brings you here?"

"Delighted to see you again, too." The other man chuckled.

"Isabelle?" James said with a short bow. "I hope you are well."

"Very well, thank you. Barry and I were just having a most lively discussion on gaining wisdom in advanced years."

"And the conclusion?"

"It's an illusion," she said with an artful smile. "One is either born wise or not. The rest is mere education. He agrees with me."

"Of course I do," Barry said. "How could I not after we each confirmed the other was born wise?"

"But you are forgetting experience," James said. "And one can only gain that with age."

"Pfft," Isabelle retorted.

Barry was studying Isabelle's profile while James studied him. "I'm all amazement, Barry. Didn't Prinny suggest he would skin you alive if you dared show your face again this year?"

"He did."

James respected Barry. He was the only one of the entourage who had earned it. Barry might have done something unpardonably grave the night in question, but at a very young age he had earned great valor during the war against Bonaparte. A former Lord Lieutenant of the 95th Rifles, Vere Sturbridge, the new Duke of Barry, had retired from the battlefield last year at the age of twenty-four when he unexpectedly ascended to a distant cousin's duchy with a single crumbling castle, crippling debts, and no fortune.

"So?" James inquired.

Barry glanced at Isabelle across from him. "Isabelle and I were just discussing our dilemma. It seems I'm not the only one to have received a royal command two weeks ago to," he lowered his voice, "marry."

James looked between the handsome young man and Isabelle. A coldness invaded his spine. "I see."

Barry did not notice the drop in temperature. "But as I decided to take a wife when I inherited, now is as good a time as any. The prince has only hastened what I intended. Family is everything in life, don't you agree, Isabelle?"

She glanced at James before returning her gaze to Barry. "I do."

Barry looked at him expectantly, but he said not a word.

"How have you managed to avoid the prince's eye, Candover?" Barry finally asked.

James glanced at Isabelle's bowed head. She was fiddling with the fingertip of one glove. It was what she did when she was ill at ease.

"I have not," he replied quietly. "What's that?" He nodded toward the paper in Barry's hands.

"Ah," Barry said, scratching the back of his head. "Something very convenient, actually. Isabelle was kind enough to make up a list for me."

"A list," he said arctically.

"Yes," Barry replied, good-humored but with the seriousness of a man who has seen too much death on a battlefield at too early an age. "I'm unfamiliar with some of the ladies here. And Isabelle made a few suggestions."

Isabelle finally spoke, with coolness. "Barry *likes* lists."

"Would you care to join us, Candover?" Barry gestured toward an empty chair.

"Thank you but no," James replied. He turned to Isabelle. "I'm looking for Miss Primrose. Is she here?"

"Of course," Isabelle replied. "She and Calliope are out gazing at the stars. I believe the archbishop is with them."

"Thank you," he replied, but did not move. For some reason he did not want to leave Isabelle and Barry to their own devices.

She smiled. "Perhaps your desire to see Miss Primrose is in conflict with your desire to *not* see Calliope."

"That's untrue. It's rather that Calliope would not like to see me."

"Why don't Miss Little and Candover get on?" A hint of amusement colored Barry's face.

"I think it has to do with the fact that they are both unused to hearing 'no,' " Isabelle replied. "They do not take kindly to anyone questioning their authority."

"I disagree," James replied. "It is because neither of us likes to wait. And neither of us suffers fools with good humor."

"I can't imagine what you're thinking. I actually wait *and* suffer fools very patiently," piped up a young, familiar voice behind him. Calliope, in the flesh. "What I don't care for are people who lock away other people and forget all about them."

"Lock away?" James raised his eyebrows.

"Without a drop of tea or stale biscuit to gnaw on."

"I know precisely of what you speak, Miss Little," said the Duke of Sussex as he strolled toward them. Mary Haverty was beside him. "I, too, have endured such treatment. And worse. Such a distinct lack of manners. What shall we do in retaliation now that he is under *my* roof?"

"You are incorrigible," Mary said to Sussex.

"Agreed," James said dryly.

"*Both* of you are incorrigible," Mary said, turning to Barry with a sly smile. "I've often wondered if all dukes are born as such."

"I don't believe so," the Duke of Barry said. "I never had the slightest impropriety attached to my name until *after* I unexpectedly became duke."

Mary suddenly laughed. "I've an idea. A brilliant idea. Let's test my theory and see if dukes are more incorrigible than the rest of us mere mortals." She looked toward Sussex. "But it will require your help."

"Anything, my dear," Sussex replied benevolently.

"Would it be possible to arrange for all of us to play a round or two of golf at the Royal Blackheath Silver Club tomorrow?"

"I do not play games," James ground out.

"Don't we know it," muttered Isabelle.

He raised his brows. "I would not disappoint you, Mary," James informed her. "But the course is reserved for gentlemen." *Thank God.*

Sussex grinned. "I do believe the combined forces of three dukes, one duchess, and an archbishop might sway the rule keepers. Who would be of the party?"

"I say anyone who enjoys competition," Mary replied. "Isabelle, have you ever played this game?"

"Once or twice with my father. I would love to spend the day out of doors," she said with a smile. She looked toward Barry.

"Never tried," he replied, "but I'm always ready to try new things and up for a challenge."

Isabelle's smile shone a little too brightly in James's opinion.

"Such an admirable point of view," she said.

"May I play on his team?" Calliope piped up, looking with devotion at Barry.

"Of course, Miss Little. I'd be honored."

James would have given his eye teeth to know what sort of miracle Barry had performed to have her eating out of his hand. "Perhaps we should ask Miss Primrose too," he said as offhandedly as he could manage.

Sussex's expression darkened. "Excellent idea. Would not go without her. Where is she?"

"Still naming all the constellations with the archbishop," Calliope said, rolling her eyes.

"I think we should invite everyone to go," Isabelle said, pointedly looking in James's direction. "The more the better. There are so many, many other ladies and gentlemen with whom to socialize."

"I agree wholeheartedly," Mary inserted.

"If we are to play," James said, "I would request the honor of having you as my partner, Mary."

"Of course," she said, chuckling. "I'd be delighted."

Calliope shook her head.

"Thank you, my dear," he responded, his calm restored.

"She's Scottish, remember?" Calliope loudly whispered in Isabelle's direction.

"Indeed. Half." Mary smiled. "My mother's side."

Calliope's impish grin reappeared. "Didn't the Scots invent golf?"

"They did," James replied with great hauteur. "We dukes might be incorrigible but we know how to win."

Calliope could not contain herself. Her whoops of laughter caused the other guests to turn around.

There was one other person listening nearby, hidden on the other side of the door. She, too, was Scottish.

And she was ready to play to win, too.

It had not gone according to the prior evening's plan. Then again, nothing had gone according to anyone's plans since the day (or rather, night) the royal entourage had embarrassed themselves, the entire ton, and worst of all caused a populous uprising against the Prince Regent.

The view in front of her, Isabelle thought as she watched fifteen of Sussex's guests limbering up for the outing on the five-hole course, did not promise to improve the situation.

For some inexplicable reason, Sussex had insisted she be his partner, and so she'd had to turn down Barry, a man of unquestionable character, open to the idea of marriage, quite handsome, and so very kind. A prime candidate if ever there was one. He had blasted his way to the top of her list.

But at the last moment, when so many guests jumped at the chance to play, it was decided they would all form foursomes. Calliope had pleaded with Mary to be in her group. James had relented, but only on the condition that Amelia become his partner.

Isabelle shook her head, which was spinning from all the changes. Her foursome now included Sussex, Amelia, and James. The foursome to follow them was Mary, Barry, Calliope, and the archbishop.

Isabelle knew most of the ladies but not the gentlemen in the other groups. She had met Lady Pamela Hopkins at Kress's house party. Lady Pamela appeared to like billiards more than anything else. Or cards. Or anything that involved wagering. Then there was Lady Katherine Leigh, a great horsewoman, and her red-haired sister, Lady Judith Leigh, who spoke few words but laughed quite a bit, especially when she was nervous. Lady Susan Moore was also in attendance, which was unusual. She almost seemed too fragile to endure athletic pursuits. But perhaps that was an illusion due to her affected manner of speech; her lisp was of the Georgian era.

Two of the other four peers on Isabelle's list were playing: the Marquis of Haverston and the Earl of Bronway. The last two, a Mr. Parker and Mr. Adams knew better than to play this demented sport.

"So," Sussex said as he chose a club from the bag a caddy held. "You know how to play, do you, Isabelle?" Before walking up to the first tee, he took a practice swing and sent ten inches of sod soaring. Amelia and James had not joined them yet.

She cleared her throat. "Yes. About as well as you."

He took another swing. His club was so far above the ground that the grass did not move. He chuckled. "The thing to remember about golf is that honor, integrity, and knowing and following the rules are all vitally important."

"You sound like my father," Isabelle retorted. "Don't worry, I reread all the rules last night." What else could she do since she had not been able to sleep? James was presumably sleeping in chambers not three doors down from her own in the southern wing. It reminded her of the times he would come to visit her father, during the spring and fall equinoxes each year. She had sometimes dared to sit outside his door at night. It seemed shocking and very intimate when she had been four and ten. It was the same year she'd fallen in love with him.

Amelia, James, and another caddy joined them as Sussex took a few steps to the raised mound of grass, planted a tee and ball, then stepped back with great pomp.

"Yes, the game is often won or lost on knowing and employing the three hundred eighty-four rules," Amelia stated.

Isabelle started. "But there were no more than a dozen rules listed in the guide in Sussex's library."

"That must have been a first edition," Amelia said quietly. "This is the latest edition." She pulled a thick book from the straw bag she carried.

"I choose my partners carefully," James said, taking a few strides to stand beside her.

Isabelle raised her chin. "I wouldn't expect any less of you." It had hurt that he hadn't asked her to be his partner. And it irritated her that she felt that way. She should be playing with two eligible gentlemen, not just one.

"Well, I know the rules well enough to know one thing," Sussex said, a bit irritated. They all turned to look at him on the mound. "One is supposed to be very quiet and stay motionless while another is about to hit the ball."

"He's right," Amelia muttered.

"Of course I'm right," he replied coolly. "I am always right."

"Of course, Your Grace," Amelia said without a trace of a smile. Funny how Miss Primrose was capable of agreeing with someone, but with her posture saying just the opposite. Isabelle simply adored her.

Sussex harrumphed as he awkwardly bent his

knees, arched his back, and wiggled his backside in the manner of a . . . duck shaking water from his tail feathers. Isabelle caught herself before she laughed. Sussex stilled and then repeated the motions.

And a third time.

James leaned down and whispered in her ear, "Is he about to lay an egg, do you think?"

She was so surprised by his unexpected humor that a quick ball of mirth erupted from her. God, she hated when James did that to her. Just when she decided he was a dry old stick, as Calliope suggested, he killed her with humor.

Sussex straightened and stared at her with ill-humor. "You are my teammate, Isabelle," he said sourly. "A little respect, please."

"Sorry," Isabelle said.

James cleared his throat. "Do you think we could speed things up a bit so we finish before tomorrow?"

Edward narrowed his eyes.

No one dared say another word as he again went through his exaggerated motions. Sussex finally raised his silver-headed club behind his left shoulder and swung it through the air, missing the ball by a good three inches.

"One," Amelia announced.

Sussex looked at her incredulously. "What are you talking about? That was a practice swing. It doesn't count."

"I'm sorry, Your Grace," she said, her sweetness taking on a tiny edge. "It didn't look like you were still practicing."

"Anyone could see I was still practicing," he insisted.

"Did it look like that to Your Graces?" Amelia asked, looking at her and James.

"He was definitely practicing," Isabelle replied.

"He was definitely laying an egg," James said.

It was impossible not to laugh. Isabelle tried desperately to make up for it by adding, "And you are only proving Mary's suggestion that all dukes are incorrigible."

"What's good for the goose . . ." James replied, amusement in his eyes.

When he looked at her like that, with laughter in his expression, and his famous reserve in retreat, Isabelle had to look away. She would not love him any longer. She had a mind, and she could control her sensibilities. He didn't truly want her and she would marry another, per the Prince Regent's suggestion. "Do let's get on with it. Others are waiting behind us."

"I'm not going to hit my ball," Sussex insisted peevishly, nodding toward Amelia, "until she or someone official"—he glared at the caddies who were polishing the faces of clubs nearby and pretending not to listen—"acknowledges that my *practice* swing does not count."

James nodded toward the caddies. "You may leave

us," he said dryly. "We shall carry our own bags." The caddies disappeared quietly, apparently quite used to the eccentricities that emerged when usually well-bred aristocrats trod these lawns.

Isabelle looked at Amelia and nodded toward Sussex in the universal feminine signal to let a gentleman who was being infantile and stubborn have his way.

"Don't do it, Miss Primrose," James said softly.

"Don't you start," Isabelle ground out to James.

"You're only suggesting we give in to him because he's your partner," James retorted.

"Don't be ridiculous," Isabelle insisted. "Golf is a game you play truly by and for yourself. He might be my partner on paper, but I'm playing against myself."

"Exactly," Sussex said, delighted to watch Candover be put in his place.

"That's true," Amelia said, raising her chin. "And so those who cheat—only cheat themselves. Do you want to cheat yourself, Your Grace?" She looked at Sussex.

"A fine one to talk of fair play," Sussex replied hotly.

Isabelle did not know what was going on between Edward Godwin, the Duke of Sussex, and Amelia, but it was obvious it had nothing to do with a silly little leather ball stitched up with feathers inside. "Oh, go on, already. I will take the point," Isabelle said to end the stalemate.

Sussex shook his head and approached the tee again. Without any further preening, he finally hit the ball, which surprisingly landed unseen, but fairly near the green.

Candover took his place when Amelia and she refused his invitation to precede him. He displayed far more elegance of form than Sussex and considerably more strength. His ball landed in the bunker on the far side of the green. Sussex coughed in amusement. Isabelle could see a muscle tic in James's cheek. It was amusing to see him take this all so seriously. It was supposed to be a lovely little outing on well-manicured lawn, not a battleground of male pride.

Amelia insisted Isabelle go next. And so she gathered her skirts in one hand, a club in the other, and ascended the first tee. She shaded her eyes and surveyed the lay of the hole and the entire field of play. Foursomes littered the course in every direction. Behind her, Barry, Mary, Calliope, and the archbishop were walking toward them from the gathering house.

Isabelle turned, knelt to place the ball on a tuft of grass, straightened, eyed the green, and trained her eyes on the ball as she swung. The little white-painted ball made a satisfying arc and landed a respectable distance.

"Excellent shot," Amelia said as she walked up to her.

Isabelle felt nothing but relief at not having made a fool of herself. She rejoined the two dukes to watch Miss Primrose.

Amelia went stock-still after sizing up the fairway and addressing the ball. In an extraordinary movement, she hit the ball, which landed not three feet from the hole.

Without a word, Amelia descended to collect her bag and marched toward the green, leaving the others speechless behind her.

"Do close your mouth, Sussex," James finally said, "although it will be hard to do with that foot of yours in so deep."

Sussex coughed on an oath to disguise it and marched toward the green.

Isabelle bit her lip to keep from laughing.

James turned to her, his brown eyes expressive. "Your form is lovely."

She could not reply for a moment. "Thank you."

He nodded and they walked behind the other two.

"What is going on between them?" Isabelle asked.

"No clue," James replied. "But I assure you I won't allow it to continue much longer."

"I've never seen Sussex like this. Normally he is utterly charming, especially among all ladies. What are you going to do?"

"Amelia Primrose knows how to correct bad form in others. And I know she would prefer to handle this her-

THE ONCE AND FUTURE DUCHESS

self. She is everything good and kind and proper," James said. "Very much like you in character, except . . ."

"Except what?"

"She does not have your stubbornness"—he gave her a look when she opened her mouth to defend herself—"or your sense of humor, your noble bearing, or your beauty."

And now Isabelle felt just like Sussex as she stopped, her mouth ajar, as Candover's stride lengthened and he left her side to find his ball in the sandy bunker. She quickly recovered and reminded herself that while he might say such things to her, he had also refused her. Compliments did not a husband make. He was most likely feeling guilty toward her for pricking her pride.

The four of them played on with few words except the occasional muffled oath, mostly by Sussex when he sliced and slaughtered the ball.

Near the next green, Sussex took out his masher, studied the difficult lie with exaggerated movements, and somehow managed to land the impossible putt. He squealed with delight.

"You are a disgrace to our sex," James announced.

Sussex's retort was sustained laughter as he looked toward Amelia. "Scots might have invented the game, but I daresay the English could teach a thing or three to the Highlanders."

"But not a Lowlander," Amelia muttered as she passed Isabelle toward the final tee.

Isabelle shook her head in disbelief. What was it about this game that seemed to bring out the worst in everyone? She would go for a gallop over golf any day of the week.

James sidled up behind her. "I refuse to play another hole with him."

"Why?"

"He's a damned cheat."

"Really."

"Yes," he insisted.

"How do you know?" Isabelle could not believe how juvenile men could be.

"He played my ball."

"Maybe it wasn't your ball."

"Of course it was my ball."

"How do you know for certain?"

He smiled in a particularly sly fashion Isabelle had never imagined he possessed. While he was being ridiculous, it somehow made him more human. More lovable, oddly enough.

"Because I played his ball," he said with a peculiar light in his eye.

"And look how that turned out." She shook her head in exasperation. She did not wait for his response. Instead, she made her way toward Sussex, who was pretending not to watch Amelia mounting the fifth tee.

James caught up and the three of them silently

watched Amelia hit the ball so brilliantly that it landed within inches of the last pin.

"You play very well, Miss Primrose," James said as Amelia descended the mound to join them. "If I did not know your whereabouts the last decade, I would assume you spent many hours on the links."

"I suppose," Amelia replied, "I should have told Your Grace that I have my father's clubs, and sometimes your sisters and I would amuse ourselves by hitting a shuttlecock at Boxwood when you were in Town."

"Well, I've never thought much of the sport," Sussex muttered.

"Why is that?" Isabelle inquired.

"It reminds me of croquet," he replied, his jaw set. "Only it takes twice as long, and *some* people play by a mysterious, ever-changing set of rules. Where's the fun in that, I ask you? Foxhunting is far more enjoyable than whacking balls."

"I like whacking balls," Amelia announced.

Isabelle tried to intervene, but Sussex would not be denied.

"It's quite obvious you like to *whack balls*," Sussex seethed. "A lot."

Amelia paled, and James immediately stepped in front of Sussex. Nose-to-nose, he said softly, with an edge, "You go too far. Apologize."

Sussex regarded him with unrestrained anger.

"It's rather the other way around. She might look like a saint, but I assure you she is a bloody thief in the night who robs gentlemen of their dignity and far worse."

In a blur of motion, James grabbed the knot of Sussex's neck cloth and twisted his fist.

"No, Your Grace . . . he is correct," Amelia said, and stepped forward.

James did not let go. "I would sell my soul before I'd believe that," he said hotly.

Isabelle couldn't breathe for the tension. She'd never seen him so angry. "James," she whispered.

He ground his teeth and released Edward in one swift motion. "I will have a full accounting," he said, pinning Sussex with a furious gaze.

She had to stop this disaster from unfolding further. She grasped Sussex's arm and tugged on it. It felt rather like trying to pry an old oak tree from the ground. "Come along, Edward." She looked pointedly at the other man. "James . . . not here. People are in front and behind. Obviously there's some sort of misunderstanding. We'll settle this later when—"

"There is no sodding misunderstanding," Sussex insisted, glaring at Amelia. "The conniving mushroom dared to steal my name that night we were all of us half dead with drink. She plays the martyr very well by the by. But I assure you there is not a single reason she could concoct to defend her abominable actions—even if she suggests she was foxed to the gills."

"Whatever are you talking about—" Isabelle began faintly.

"Go on, tell them"—Sussex's eyes narrowed to slits—*"wife."*

Isabelle had never seen eyes as tortured as Amelia Primrose's. And James's face was stark and drawn tight as he gazed down at the exquisitely beautiful woman with her blond hair drawn back at the nape of her swan-like neck. He did not turn to face the man he addressed.

"If you were not who you are, Edward Godwin," James whispered, his hands clenched at his sides, "with God as my witness, I would—"

"No. Please listen," Amelia interrupted, finally breaking under James's steadfast gaze. "I've said he's correct. But it will be annulled. I guarantee it."

James's tortured gaze was still fastened on her sorrowful face. And then he leaned down toward her, and for one terrible instant Isabelle thought he was going to kiss her. Instead he whispered something in her ear.

Isabelle thought she heard James say something about always protecting her, taking care of her.

Sussex cleared his throat and appeared ready to do murder.

Isabelle could not breathe. There was something so strong, so powerful, so . . . *wildly raw and protective* in

James's hard features as he stared at Amelia, that she felt like the wind had been sucked out of her lungs.

Without a word, James finally turned and stalked toward the gathering house ahead.

Isabelle inhaled raggedly. God. Was that it? Was James in love with Amelia Primrose? And why had he not acted upon that love? Surely not because she was an abigail from the Lowlands. But still . . . his reaction was beyond chivalry, beyond everything. It was . . . primal.

Amelia turned to her, her face paler than the sands of time. "Go after him. Please. I beg you."

God. Oh God. Oh God. And Amelia loved James.

She tore her eyes from Amelia when Sussex finally said tightly, "Oh, go ahead. Don't worry. I won't kill her," adjusting his neck cloth. *"Yet."*

They were all mad, Isabelle thought as the world she thought she knew spun out of control. Amelia and Sussex married? James loved Amelia? She had less than no desire to go after James. But she had to get away and so she pretended to do as they bid. Her legs felt like rubber and would barely do as she wanted. She kept moving forward until she stumbled behind a copse of trees, light-headed and disoriented.

Once behind the low-lying branches, she fell to her knees on a carpet of moss and leaves. She was ill. More ill than she'd ever known. A cold film of sweat broke out on her forehead. She would not retch. She would not.

Instead, she drooped down on her side and curled up in a ball, her arms wrapped around her knees. Her hands gripped her arms and finally, blessedly, she gulped in air to ease her aching lungs. She concentrated on breathing. She would not cry.

Duchesses did not *ever* cry.

Chapter 10

It could not be true. James was certain. Amelia Primrose would not marry a man who was three sheets to the wind and not in possession of his faculties.

Especially not the Duke of Sussex.

Unless she had had no choice. And he would wager his last farthing that at the heart of her actions, she had married Sussex to somehow protect his own family's secrets or the Duke of Sussex. God, he was sick of secrets. Sick of burdens. Tired of the game. And Isabelle . . . dearest, loveliest Isabelle. At so many points during the round she had made him remember what he had felt during his youth—the joy of shared laughter and lighthearted fun. And when she worried the edge of her bottom lip with her teeth as she addressed her ball in the rough, he had wanted to pull her behind a tree and kiss her senseless.

But it was not to be. He should know better than to indulge in that dangerous game.

He only wished he had pulled her along with him when he left the hellish scene. There had been a look in her eyes that he wanted to ease. But he had a more powerful urge to protect her from the secrets and the ugliness that he had to untangle on his own.

And so he churned on, toward the gathering house, and forced his mind toward a plan. At least now he understood why Amelia had asked him to bring the archbishop to Sussex's estate.

Abruptly, he changed direction, cutting through a small wood toward the archbishop among the last foursome behind him on the course. He would pin down His Grace, Mr. Divine High and Mighty Divert All Questions right now.

Too late, he spotted Calliope Little in his direct path. Bent over, obviously searching for her ball in a stand of trees, she looked up and then straightened.

"What's going on?" she asked with her usual disregard for his station. "It looked like you were about to knock down Sussex."

"Not your affair," he ground out.

"Nothing ever is," she retorted. "Since when has that mattered?"

"For once, we are in complete agreement." He kept walking, and she glued herself to his side, trotting to keep up like one of his greyhounds. "Miss Little, for the love of God . . ."

"How ridiculous you always are with me. Look, I know you like me. You don't have to *pretend the opposite* all the time."

He stopped dead in his tracks. Sometimes, if one was very lucky, and one truly paid attention despite the chaos all around, one was given the chance to learn a truth.

He looked into Calliope's wide brown eyes, brimming with intelligence. "What did you say?"

She snorted. "They say hearing is the first thing to go with age." She chewed on a thumbnail as she examined him.

"Stop that," he said stiffly. "It's inelegant."

She did as he bade. "I said sometimes you are extremely pigheaded."

He refused to comment.

"I said, 'I know you like me.'"

"No. The other part."

She gave him a look that suggested he was an idiot. "I said you don't always have to pretend the opposite. Everyone knows that if someone is irrational and irritated with someone else all the time they either love the person or truly loathe them. Although, some married couples seem to bicker endlessly. In those cases . . . they love and hate each other at the same time." She stopped and blinked.

As she was speaking, it had all fallen into place. Sussex *loved* Amelia. Even if Amelia had married Edward against his will and full knowledge that awful night, the man James knew as well as he knew himself . . . *that man* was a gentleman and would not behave like an ass unless there was passion beneath all that hurt pride. Of course, he would still have to knock Sussex senseless in private. What he had said was unpardonable, and he hoped Amelia would make him pay for it the rest of his days.

Calliope Little was speaking again and he regained focus. " . . . but no one could ever possibly loathe *me*. My father always insisted to anyone who suggested otherwise that I'm extremely lovable."

"Miss Little?"

"Yes?"

"Your father was a highly intelligent man."

For once she did not utter a sound.

He placed a hand on her shoulder. "I wish I had known him."

She gulped. "I do, too," she said in a small voice that broke his heart. She would not meet his eye. "Your Grace?"

It was the first time she'd condescended to him. "Yes, Miss Little?"

"Calliope."

"Calliope." He waited.

"Please don't let her down."

He frowned. "Why would you ever think I would let down Miss Primrose?"

"I'm referring to Isabelle. You know, she might be the strongest, best person I know, but everyone needs someone they can count on," Calliope said quietly, not answering his question. "In fact . . . Oh, hello Isabelle."

James followed Calliope's gaze to find her walking toward them, her head down. "Isabelle," he echoed quietly.

She nodded without stopping, and continued walking along the line of trees on the edge of the expanse of lawn—toward the threesome. The archbishop was taking practice swings on the mound.

He turned back to Calliope. "I require your aid."

"Anything," she breathed.

"Look, I don't have time to explain, but will you chaperone Miss Primrose and His Grace straight away?"

Calliope broke into a wide grin. "I'd *love* to."

He nodded and abruptly strode onto the center of the fairway toward the threesome.

"Hey," Calliope called out, laughing, "take care." She pointed toward the archbishop, addressing his ball on the tee.

James plowed forward and muttered, "Old canker doesn't have a prayer of a chance of hitting me in the middle of the—"

"Fore!" Calliope screeched.

He had just enough time to bend forward and grab the back of his head before the ball hit his back. Pain radiated near his spine. He held back a string of oaths by the skin of his teeth and waited for Calliope's certain laughter.

He looked up to see her shrug helplessly. "You all right?"

"Perfect," he said dryly.

She darted off in the opposite direction, one of them older and wiser—the other just as wise as she had always been.

James lengthened his stride to reach the archbishop, who stood on the mound, his gnarled hands still gripping the club. Even at this distance he could see vast amusement coloring the old man's face.

Isabelle had not stopped walking. She was petite, but she had always been able to walk faster than any other lady of his acquaintance as well as three-quarters of the gentlemen he knew. "Isabelle," he called out to her.

She was almost to the threesome and continued her pace. Obviously, she had not heard him.

Mary, the archbishop, and Barry were listening to Isabelle when he finally caught up. " . . . and so, if Your Grace would be kind enough to consider my—"

"Pardon me, Isabelle," James interrupted. "This is my affair and I require a private word with the archbishop."

The archbishop ignored him and kept his attention on Isabelle. "I'm sorry, my dear. You were saying?"

Out of the corner of his eye he saw Mary's warning glance. He bit back the primal desire to protect Isabelle from the certain to be sordid mess to be corrected.

"I would request the honor and privilege of a private interview at the soonest opportunity that did not inconvenience Your Grace."

The little old man actually smiled.

James was not sure he had ever seen the man's teeth until now.

"My dear," the archbishop said very kindly. "It's obvious to me that something very grave is on your mind. Does this concern Miss Amelia Primrose?"

He started. Where was the archbishop who had ridden in his carriage for two solid hours, who thought Amelia was Penelope, who was not one of his sisters named Morality, Temperance, and—

"Yes, Your Grace," Isabelle said simply.

Mary's face filled with concern. "Isabelle, what is wrong? You are not well. Please take my—"

Barry grasped Isabelle's arm before James could turn to examine her face.

She gently rebuffed Barry's support, but there was not a hint of color in her face. And her eyes were devoid of emotion—like the blank orbs of the busts of great philosophers who stared into space at his great hall in Derbyshire.

"My dear," the archbishop continued, concern on his serious face. "Let us return to Angelus Abbey at once, where we can converse in private. I sent a note to Miss Primrose last evening, responding to her request for an interview this afternoon. I shall leave it up to your good judgment if you would like to include Miss Primrose. Or not."

"There is no question that *I* will attend," James insisted.

Barry chuckled. "How's the back? Or was it the neck?"

James examined the former Lord Lieutenant. "Remarkable humor for someone who should be worried about his own neck."

"Lady Mary," Barry said, his expression darkening, "I do believe we have somehow managed to lose Miss Little. Would you care to join me while I go in search of her?" He bowed stiffly and offered his arm to Mary, a lady nearly five years his senior but appeared five years his junior given his war years.

As the handsome couple walked down the fairway, James, not for the first time, wondered if Mary Haverty did not like Barry very much. He did not have time for these stupid thoughts. He returned his attention to the archbishop and Isabelle.

Her features had still not returned to their usual vivacity. Above all else, he wished he could have a private word. But he could not. He must attend to familial duty first. He exhaled and addressed the archbishop. "I fear we must postpone the pleasure of the last hole. We can all of us return to the abbey in my open carriage if you like." He extended an arm to Isabelle, who did not move.

The archbishop studied first Isabelle and then him, as if James were a fly on a jam pot. "I never discuss anything of importance while facing a horse's bum," he announced, reverting back to his nonsensical self. The man was an out and out actor of the highest order. "I shall return silently on the back of the horse who carried me here. But I shall be in the orangery at four o'clock." With that parting remark the old man turned on his heel.

He motioned for Isabelle to proceed with him. She would not meet his eye, but after a long moment she walked forward. He matched his stride to hers. "Isabelle," he began. "I'm more sorry than I can say that you were forced to witness all that."

"I'm not," she said woodenly.

"It was not fit for a lady's ears."

"I'm a damned duchess, and was brought up to understand all parts of life—the good, and the ugly."

They had reached the edge of the shaded wooded area and she suddenly stopped short. He did the same and faced her.

He hooded his eyes. "Perhaps. But that doesn't mean

you should have to go out of your way to involve your-self in something ugly that does not concern you."

"I assume you're speaking of Miss Primrose?"

"Of course."

"She's in my employ now. Not yours," she retorted.

"Perhaps," he replied calmly. "But this is my con-cern."

"That is quite obvious," she replied.

"I beg your pardon? What are you implying?"

"That I finally understand the way of it now."

"Go on, then."

"You don't need my damned list. You are in love with Amelia Primrose."

He exhaled but did not blink. Here was finally a way to kill any possible remaining expectation. "I think you mean Amelia *Godwin*," he replied.

"And you have no one to blame for that travesty but yourself," she said hotly.

"I agree," he said quietly, his throat closing. He was very good at killing love everywhere he went.

"At least I can be glad you had the grace not to agree to marry me." She paused, finally fully meet-ing his eye. "I am glad I have finally seen your true *character*."

He stiffened. "And what is your opinion?" He was surprised by how much he cared about her answer.

"You are not the man I thought you were. You reject

anyone and everyone. Reject any possibility of love. You prefer to live your life all alone."

His heart stuttered and his mind for perhaps the first time in his life failed to think logically. Indeed, why was she talking about love? "Go on, then," he said, his voice uneven.

Isabelle exhaled roughly. "For as long as I remember, I looked up to you on all levels. I wanted your approval even more so than my father's. Do you know why?"

He remained silent, unable to form words.

"Because you had confidence in me. You were certain I would succeed at everything I had to learn to be the future Duchess of March." She swallowed. "And you gave me your attention—your time. You came twice a year for as long as I can remember and you were the one who taught me how to sail, how to shoot, how to sit a difficult horse, how to judge a person in my employ, and bookkeeping. You taught me about cultivation, and how to ensure the comfort of tenants, and even about the beauty of wildflowers, and every last bird and insect. And you—" Her voice broke off abruptly and she looked away.

He edged closer. "Yes?" The tension was unbearable.

"You spent hours with my father, especially when he was dying, reassuring him, telling him I would not fail. And I will never be able to repay you for all you did for me, for him, for everyone who depends on me. But," she looked at him with sadness, "I now see that you did not do any of this due to a sense of love. You did it out a sense of duty."

"There are many who would argue that duty is a form of love," he murmured.

"It isn't when it's something you use to keep yourself apart from everyone and everything. And I know why. You don't want anyone to see who you truly are. To be vulnerable. But that's no way to live life, damn it, James," she said, her hands clenching at her sides. "It might protect you a bit more from pain, but it also dulls all joy in life. I . . . I'm not like you and I never will be. I don't know who you are. And I don't think you want anyone to truly know you," she said with finality.

Her eyes were so remote there could have been two continents between them. She finally glanced away, took her leave, and left him there rooted to the spot like a two-hundred-year old oak.

And that was when he feared he might have taught her the last lesson she would ever learn from him. *Disappointment*. Isabelle Tremont, the eighteen-year-old Duchess of March, in possession of the soul of someone three times her age, was now finally, thankfully, beyond his touch.

It was a relief really.

Except it was not.

He stared at her petite form marching regally away from him. And he cursed the same foul word three times. He then cursed his father, her father, and every other person to whom he had given his word in the last thirty odd years. He then cursed Sussex, the archbishop, and even God . . . for making a female he could not have. A female he had carefully kept at a distance because it was decided she was far too young for him, and her father—his godfather—had very clearly specified on his deathbed that he wanted him to guide her toward a marriage with someone her own age. The old duke's May-December marriage had proved disastrous in the extreme, and he was adamant in his last wish that James was to make certain that his daughter not make the same mistake.

His godfather's words were burned in his memory: *No wife should have to feed her husband porridge. And I won't have the same for Isabelle. She will marry a man no more than three or four years older than she— not one of your contemporaries, James. You are all too jaded and old for Isabelle.*

But now she had become a woman. A beautiful, passionate, wholehearted woman. A lady mature far beyond her years. And ready for any and all of the difficulties she would surely encounter in her life. And only hoped she would not become like him and face the world alone.

The caw of a crow flying low in the sky jarred him from his thoughts. He closed his eyes and breathed deeply to bring calm to his mind. He felt twenty years older.

He took one last deep breath, opened his heavy eyes and finally forced his legs forward. There was no more time for reflection and pain. He had to hurry. He had to meet the damned archbishop in the orangery to find out if Amelia's marriage to Sussex was official, recorded, or whatever it might be. But first he ought to privately meet Amelia and find out precisely what had happened that night. He was certain that she had done something to save the man's ass. Or worse, maybe his own.

And then . . . and then?

He had to fix the greatest problem of his life.

He had to go to the woman whose opinion mattered to him more than any other, for some damned reason, and he had to make things right and good. He might not be able to have this lady whose face would not leave his mind at night, and whose lithe elegant body pressed against his own that night in the garden still haunted him—but he would be damned if he could leave it quite so badly.

He had to figure out a way to leave it better than this. He would be haunted forever by the distress in her eyes.

He wanted to shield her from pain. It was a near primal emotion that rose up within him.

He had no idea what to do or say to her. For the love of God, he was losing his mind. His methodical thinking stuttered into a lower gear. A more base cog.

Bugger life and the carriage it arrived in. Bugger abstinence, golf, promises, duty, and responsibility.

And most of all . . . bugger love.

Hell. He needed a damned drink.

And he would have it.

Chapter 11

Isabelle made her way to the orangery at the appointed hour despite the blazing headache that was now her ugly companion.

The archbishop was a difficult, albeit kind man. A man of the cloth, and devoted supporter of the Prince Regent. But his intelligence often parried with nonsense. And while she knew he admired her, she sometimes had the vague feeling that he liked watching her as well as everyone else commit gargantuan sins if only so he could resurrect them from their misery.

For that reason she always listened to him with a grain of salt the size of a cantaloupe.

The orangery door was ajar and so she quickly entered and closed the door behind her. She searched for the archbishop in the first chamber filled with palms of every shape, most likely used during balls. A ball was never a ball without palms. They were very convenient, really. They were good for hiding, kissing in secret, and disposing of terrifyingly bad canapés.

Ah, he was hiding beside the tallest palm. He was reading a book that did not appear to be the Bible. It looked more like a novel. He quickly closed it and hid it in the foliage.

He cleared his throat. "My dear Isabelle, so we meet to discuss the fate of Miss Amelia Primrose—perhaps Amelia Godwin, if I understood from the lady's note. Is that it?"

"Yes, Your Grace."

"My dear Isabelle, you must not worry so. Miss Amelia Primrose is not married to Sussex. I assure you I would remember something that important." He scratched the bald crown of his head. "I think. Well, in any case, even if some bastardized form of a ceremony might have—but not probably—taken place, there would be carefully documented records."

She willed him to continue silently. It was vital he did not get off track when he was in this sort of mood. She had learned from experience.

"I would remember writing them. It requires great care and excellent penmanship—at least by one of my scribes—and I'm quite certain there were no scribes or anyone capable of writing anything coherent, I'm sad to admit, in attendance that night. At least I am almost certain."

"Even if the document had been drawn up," Isabelle said carefully, "and no one has admitted to seeing it or watching anyone draw it up, correct? Well, it would have to be found, and then filed officially, no?"

"Precisely, my dear. And I would remember that, too. Officially recording and filing it. Right." He said the last with a hint of uncertainty.

Flattery always helped him remember. "Your Grace is famed for always performing the rituals of your office with great care. I stand in awe of your great service to the Crown."

He narrowed his eyes. "So why are you so interested in this affair?"

"I'm certain I don't understand what Your Grace is implying."

"Men of the cloth always know when someone is lying through their teeth."

She felt like an ant. He was very good at making a person feel like an insect.

"And where is Miss Primrose?"

She shook her head. "I could not find her. Perhaps she is still on the course."

He shook his head sadly. "So you are here to solve the problems of a Scottish abigail you've only recently employed?"

"Yes, Your Grace."

His eyes suddenly gleamed. "I suppose you do this because of a sense of duty?"

She stiffened. That was James's overriding attribute, not hers.

"No answer?"

"No. I'm not here because of duty, really. I'm here out of kindness. She needs my help."

"Well, I shall pay you a kindness, my dear. Let people solve their own problems. You will be doing them a favor. Unless a life is at stake, of course. And don't bore people with advice. Let them sort it out. It will make them stronger or kill them." He smiled benevolently, as if he had just carved one of Moses' own tablets.

"Isn't Your Grace not following your own direction by giving me advice?"

His smile abruptly disappeared.

"I shall make it clear, then, my dear, as you've suddenly become your true age."

She'd made a huge tactical error and now she must pay the penance. "Thank you, Your Grace." She bowed her head.

"Have you not wondered why the man who has the most to lose has not sought me out? Has not said one word to me about this entire affair—probably all imagined by Miss Primrose. The Scots are not of the Church of England, after all, and they like to stir the pot, if history is any indication."

Her vision blurred.

"Yes," he continued, "if the Duke of Sussex wanted

an annulment to this imaginary farce of a marriage, where is he? Why are you here and not he?"

There was a reason this small man was the Archbishop of Canterbury. He was capable of reducing duchesses and dukes to fools. He was very, very, very good at it.

"And if Candover truly wanted to correct this situation, where is he? And Miss Primrose knew of this rendezvous, too."

She could not speak.

"Even children know actions speak louder than words. And it was very clear to me by the way you and Candover were behaving that there was something more involved than the fate of Amelia Primrose and Sussex." He harrumphed.

Wordlessly, Isabelle curtsied deeply, signaling her pardon and her intention to beg her leave.

His words stopped her. "You know, my dear, everyone makes mistakes. Even me." He shuddered. "Almost never, of course, in my case. But . . ." He paused for breath. " . . . the mark of a truly good soul is to learn from mistakes . . . and more importantly to acknowledge it all by apologizing."

She nodded.

"Paying homage to me also helps," he said with a self-satisfied smile. He extended his hand.

She leaned forward to lower her lips to within an inch of his hand as a sign of deference.

She regained her feet and looked at the wise man.

His smile was as satisfied as a matron who had just married off the last of five daughters.

James paced the floor of a small chamber in Angelus Abbey. It was cold in this north-facing room, but he'd been led here by Sussex's butler, who had doubted any of the other guests would have reason to come here. Except the one person whose presence James had requested.

A draft of wind rattled the sole window and he moved away. He came to a stop before a delicate escritoire. The lengthening shadows of the afternoon light filtered through the window. Glancing down at the writing desk, James saw a number of miniatures in gilt frames. He closed his eyes and forced his head to one side to crack the tension in his neck and then to the other side.

Where was Miss Amelia Primrose?

He dropped his head forward and reopened his eyes, only to focus more fully on the little paintings. He stilled.

The first was obviously a likeness of Sussex's mother. Edward had her same alluring, even, happy combination of features, except for one or two.

This was the woman his father had loved. And lost. And had privately longed for the rest of his life whilst he married another to set up his nursery for that was his duty.

It was not hard to understand why his father and the former Duke of Sussex had fallen in love with the great, wild beauty in the picture before him.

James forced himself to move his gaze to the next miniature. Sussex as an adolescent smiled in the picture. Edward had been and ever was of easy temperament and wit; he had obviously inherited his charm and nature from his beautiful mother. James's gaze wandered and stopped on a tiny watercolor, half hidden among the others. Slightly faded, it depicted an eye, green and familiar. As he reached to examine it, someone knocked on the door.

"Yes?" He withdrew his hand in haste.

Miss Primrose's face peeked around the heavy door.

"Do come in," he requested.

"I'm sorry I kept Your Grace waiting," she said, closing the door behind her.

He acknowledged her and walked from the escritoire to the window. "Will you join me? The view is quite lovely from here."

Without a word she crossed to him but bowed her head, unwilling to take in the colors of a late-summer afternoon.

"Why did you do it?" He kept his tone even and low.

"I won't pretend to misunderstand," she said, almost

all trace of the lilt of her homeland gone. "I am more sorry than I can ever say, Your Grace. I fear—"

"James," he said quietly.

Her eyes darted to his and then toward the view beyond the window.

He could palpably feel her discomfort. "James . . ."

"I'm sorry for interrupting you," he stated. "Please go on."

"I've always been too reticent," she began. "Especially with Your Gr—with you. I know why, of course. It's because of the gratitude and esteem I hold for you. I thank the Lord every night for your intervention, you see. You employed me without references, without—"

He raised two fingers to stop her, and forced a smile. "No, my dear. Your gratitude is misplaced. You forget that it was very simple. There were no other candidates who applied to me for the position. Verity was infamously ungovernable." He stopped and looked at her.

She rushed into the awkward silence with an explanation. "I should have come to you straight away at Carleton House that night . . ." Her voice faded. "But I did not. In the end I decided I would not. It was the least I could do to repay you for taking me in. I would have starved under a hedgerow if not for your kindness so many years ago."

"Don't be absur—"

"No. Please listen to me. It was not Barry who shot

that man in Carleton House the night before your wedding," she said harshly. "I shot him, and I nicked the Duke of Barry, who passed out cold in the process. I *killed* a man."

Silence settled between them like a dense northern fog.

A hundred questions crowded his mind, competing to be spoken aloud. But she plunged onward.

"And because I was such a coward, I had the archbishop marry me to Sussex, both of whom were blind with drink." Wretchedness turned her lovely face into something so remorseful that it was hard to witness. "I married him," she continued softly, "to protect myself from the gallows. Everyone knows it would be next to impossible to hang an English duchess but very easy to dispose of an abigail from Scotland."

"This has my sister's signature lunatic reasoning written all over it," he surmised darkly.

"No," Amelia insisted. "I knew what I was doing."

"I don't believe that for a moment," he retorted. "But why did you shoot this man? Who was he?"

"I shot him—" She swallowed. "I shot him because he was threatening me in the gaming room."

He was not surprised. There were too many stories of gentlemen taking advantage of females such as Amelia Primrose. "Go on, then."

"We argued and he would not see reason. Without thinking I grabbed one of the dueling pistols from the display case and cocked it, shouting a warning, which he did not heed. The Duke of Barry must have heard us and stumbled through the door behind the man. And Verity trailed Barry's footsteps. I don't remember firing . . . just the smoke, and the shock on your sister's face." Her voice proceeded haltingly as she looked away in shame. "When I think I could have accidentally killed Verity. Your own flesh and blood. The person who means more to me than just about anyone—"

"And I am guessing it was my dear sister," he repeated, "who instead of going in search of me, chose to take matters into her own hands and insist you marry Edward Godwin, and set up Barry to take the blame. But why she had to involve two dukes instead of just one—"

"I should have never agreed to her idea. Although I've always thought Mary Haverty and Barry would marry, and . . . and—" She stopped herself and evaded his glance. "And your sister was not the one who killed this man. I take full responsibility."

"I can see it all—Verity propping up the body at a card table and dragging a drunken Barry, to sit on the other side."

She shook her head almost imperceptibly. "I'm certain I helped her."

"I'm certain you didn't," he said dryly. "It's a miracle this didn't end up in my sister's infamous *Duke Diaries*, stolen and printed in the newspaper."

She didn't form a reply for a beat. "As you can see, you were very right to chastise me recently, about the absinthe."

He shook his head sadly. "You were not the only one who made a mistake that night. You forget."

Faint grooves of anxiety appeared on her forehead. "James . . ." she began softly.

"Yes?"

"I should not have agreed to marry Edward. I know I should not have. I knew you would be horrified . . ."

"Amelia, tell me. Who was this man you shot? "

She glanced away. "It was Edward's heir . . . Percy Godwin."

James started.

"He was in such a state of blind, evil excitement, insisting he was in possession finally of some document." The pale sheen of embarrassment crested her cheeks. "He was mad in his triumph and I was just in the wrong place at the wrong time . . . He was about to take advantage of me—"

"You don't need to say it." He clenched his hands into balls of fury but held back a choice oath unfit for anyone's ears.

"He was looking for Sussex and the Prince Regent that night, and Percy just happened to find me instead."

A ball of fury formed in his gut.

"I grabbed the book of documents after." She studied

her fingers. "And I threw it in the fire while Verity determined Barry was merely passed out from drink, and Percy dead."

A rush of impotent fury and relief burst in his gut.

"Verity does not know who it was. And I did not tell her."

He instinctively grasped her hand and bowed, wordless.

"I won't have your gratitude," she insisted. "And if you must know, I did not throw the book in the fire because of what you think. I did it for Edward. While I should never have played God, I am almost glad Percy threatened to abuse me for at least I do not have to feel very guilty of depriving the world of this particular Godwin," she finished in a whisper.

"I only wish I could have killed him myself," James replied, and exhaled harshly. "Well, as I see it you've two choices before you," he continued, sensing she wanted the comfort of formality. "I can either arrange for you to disappear and live in complete ease—a safe haven. Or I will ensure that you retain the protection that Edward's name will provide. If the worst came to light, the word of a duchess, without proof or motive otherwise, would stand in the House of Lords. It would be a risk—a risk of embarrassment, but there is also a risk to go into hiding and without the protection of a duke's name. What would you prefer to—"

At that moment the unwilling bridegroom of the

hour, Sussex himself, opened the door to the small chamber without a single warning knock. "Get your bloody, sodding hands off my wife," he roared, plowing toward him like a bull at a red flag.

James pushed her away a half second before Sussex's body collided with his. James hit the edge of the escritoire before he landed on his back with Sussex on top of him.

"Get off of me," James rasped, and pushed Sussex away from him. "I was thanking her, not abusing her, you idiot."

Sussex coughed once and then regained his feet while appearing as embarrassed as a schoolboy caught fighting behind a schoolhouse.

"Only a child takes out his anger on someone who is not responsible for it to begin with, Edward," Amelia said, raising her chin.

Sussex changed direction and prowled inches in front of her.

James nearly gave in to the urge to pummel him. Sussex knew not what he owed her.

"I told you I am not leaving this alone until you give me an answer, Amelia Primrose Godwin," Sussex growled. "Why did you hoodwink me? You could have at least asked if I would marry you."

She sniffed and would not meet his glance. "I've acknowledged my full guilt in this ridiculous affair. And I've promised to make sure it is rectified, annulled, and the evidence buried so deep that no one will ever know that a Scotswoman got the best of the new, oh so powerful Duke of Sussex. And I can promise you will never have to see me again. But, *Your Grace*," she said a bit stronger, "there is something I think you have completely forgotten."

"Really," he said, put out. "And what is that, *Your* Grace?"

"I thought you said I would never call myself 'your duchess.'"

He ignored her bait. "Damn you woman, w*hy did you do it*? I will not be diverted."

James had never seen even half the anger in Sussex's face before. It was more shocking than snow in July. "Back down, old man," he warned quietly.

"Stay the sodding hell out of this, Candover," Sussex continued, returning his glare to Amelia. "Why?"

Chapter 12

From the gilded side table of HRH the Prince Regent

Isabelle shook her head in disbelief, and reread the handwritten top of the express a footman had just delivered to her in her chambers. She had no time for the regent's absurd witticisms. But like trying to look away from a lady's atrocious hat or a silly dandy, she could not ignore the lure of the prince's notes.

My dearest Isabelle,

It has been an age. I'm beginning to worry my affections and concern for your well being are not returned in sufficient amounts.

No news? No darling little stories to take away the sting of little progress? No more talk of the importance of plans? No more delightful lists to consider and revise?

May I remind you that we are on the brink, the very rim of the brink, of complete anarchy and chaos—or perhaps you will try harder if I insist the entire future of England depends on you. Hmmm. It's so difficult to motivate people today—especially members of the ton. They want for nothing. And I've never had a flare for threats. They always take an air of unoriginality or—

She crumpled the gilded edges of the future king's note without reading the rest.

There was no more time for lists or for exchanging witticisms with His Royal Highness. And all her plans and attempts to hurry her fate had gotten her nowhere.

She had very possibly made an error in judgment. Or not. None of it felt right—and that was not usual. James had always taught her to trust her instincts. Well, nothing made sense. A little nagging voice in her head kept asking why James had not simply denied what she had suggested concerning Amelia.

And then an awful idea came into her head. Perhaps he knew her true sentiments toward him and was desperate to dash her sensibilities to his person.

She felt ill. No, he would not be so dishonest. He

could not. His first advice had been about honesty and that lies ate away at a person's character and breached trust. And he said that one should never wager more than one can afford to lose and a lie was always a wager that never died.

She felt ill. She had lied to him. She had lied when she proposed marriage. And he very likely knew the truth. He knew she had always loved him. His sisters knew and all the rest of their clutch of friends knew. And she had wagered on a lie and lost.

But it was not settled between them. Every fiber of her being demanded truth.

She knew what she had to do.

It was simply the last thing she wanted to do.

And that was always a sign. It meant it was the right thing to do.

She had to have the courage to do what she had told James he must do. Open herself up for a very great chance of more disappointment.

But the truth was all that mattered.

And so she departed her chambers after a last glance in the looking glass, which revealed an anxious face, yet resolve in her eyes.

She flew down the cool stone corridors of Sussex's abbey and asked the footman stationed in the main hall where James might be. Not a soul seemed to have any knowledge of his whereabouts. She darted glances behind each door, and beyond each window.

But she could not find him. Nor could she find Amelia or Sussex.

James Fitzroy had disappeared as swiftly as her righteous disgust toward him. She had to give him the benefit of the doubt. Perhaps he did indeed love Amelia. And perhaps there was a reason nothing had come of it. Perhaps Miss Primrose had refused *him*.

Or perhaps the archbishop was right and there was nothing between them. Sussex was very likely in love with Amelia, as the archbishop had suggested, or he would have corrected his secret union immediately.

Amelia and Sussex were not her affair. They never had been unless Amelia requested her aid. And she had not.

Was there any question why every man in Creation appeared to love Amelia Primrose? She was a woman of substance. Everyone loved Amelia—man, woman, or child—especially Calliope, and Calliope had proven to be uncanny in her character assessments.

Oh, where was James? She searched the entire estate for the next two hours in vain until she gave up and retired to prepare for the evening meal.

When Sussex, James, and Amelia did not appear at the lavish supper that night, Isabelle had further proof that she was a fool for having put her nose into something that was not her affair. No one wanted her involvement.

And she appeared to be the only person in the drawing room prior to dinner who noticed their absences in the magnificent wood-paneled drawing room. Sussex's butler had informed the two dozen houseguests that the Duke of Sussex was sorry to inform them that an urgent matter required his attention.

Calliope gently tugged on the skirt of her pale blue silk gown. "Isabelle?"

"Calliope, dearest, you must stop doing that. You must announce your presence in some other fashion than pulling a person's attire."

Her young eyes were wide with worry. "All right. But where is Old Sobersides? And what of Sussex? And Miss Primrose?"

"It's not our affair," Isabelle replied.

Calliope frowned. "Of course it's our affair. They're our friends."

"Since when have you considered His Grace your friend?" Isabelle's tone was cool, but her cousin didn't seem put off.

"Since today. I've decided I like Sobersides. He's still a bit stiff about the edges, but he can't help it."

"And why is that?"

"He might try to hide it, but he worries about everything and everyone," Calliope said, shaking her little head. "He's worse than a mother hen with a clutch of chicks."

"And how do you know this?"

"Can't you see it? The more he likes or worries about someone the more he acts the opposite."

"And why does he do that?" she asked faintly.

Calliope shrugged. "Why do I have to figure out everything? I am just a child."

"I thought you said that at fourteen you should be treated as an adult."

"And you said that fourteen was the height of being contrary. I am just living up to your opinion of me."

Isabelle laughed and hugged her beloved cousin to her breast.

Calliope hugged her back. "I'm truly worried," she whispered.

"I am too, dearest," Isabelle admitted.

"You're not supposed to say that," Calliope murmured dejectedly. "You're supposed to lie to me and say that you will fix everything and it will be all right."

"We've already discussed the cost of lies."

"Yes," Calliope said, disengaging from Isabelle. "But that would not be a real lie. That is a lie adults tell children to foster security. It's only when you are officially deemed old enough that those same adults yank the carpet of security out from under you."

Isabelle shook her head as she stroked Calliope's head and glanced down at her bespectacled large eyes. "Dare I ask why they would ever do such a thing?"

"To toughen you up," she said sadly.

"And how do you know that?"

"Because that's what old Sobersides told me the last time I saw him."

Isabelle felt a stab of sadness. It only grew in intensity when the guests queued up two by two, ranked by seniority to enter the echoing dining hall, where the ghosts of ancient monks seemed to lurk in every flickering light bouncing off the stone walls. An endless round of dishes was served to an endless array of guests. Isabelle played her part with little animation and much effort.

No one else appeared concerned about the state of affairs. Mary was seated opposite Isabelle and chatting with great animation with Barry. Isabelle shook her head. Mary always insisted she was far too old for Barry, as she was more than a few years his senior, but Isabelle had always witnessed such genuine warmth between them and maybe even sensed something more intimate.

It was with only the most stalwart effort that she managed to hold her own during the conversation with the two gentlemen on either side of her at the table. It was ridiculous, really. For all her talk of lists and nailing down a husband while here, she had done a remarkably poor job of sizing up two of the gentlemen that the Prince Regent had insisted she consider: the Marquis of Haverston and the Earl of Bronway.

It did not take her long to make out their characters, in the end. While the Earl of Bronway was a kind gentleman, he had a very distinct lisp, an extraordinary girth, and far more interest in the fare being served than anything else. The Marquis of Haverston was a great wit with a dashing air. But sadly, it was obvious to anyone with ears on their head that he was a bit too pleased with himself. During the dinner hour he had told Isabelle his entire life story without once asking her a single question. He then turned to his other dinner companion at the table, a Lady Susan Howard, who giggled in an extremely grating fashion, and proceeded to repeat all his anecdotes to her.

When thankfully the meal was consumed, Isabelle was one of the first to rise. Calliope dogged her steps.

"You'll find him now, won't you?"

"I promised you, Calliope."

"And you'll make an effort to be nice to him?"

"Only if you agree to amuse yourself for the rest of the evening?"

"The archbishop and I have so much to discuss that it will not be difficult." Calliope smiled as sweetly as a cat in cream.

"You like the archbishop, too?"

"Of course. I ask about various sins and he discusses penance. It's vastly amusing. The penance never really matches the crime very well. Although His Grace sometimes becomes creative."

Isabelle was so on edge she could not laugh. She

continued softly, "We will go riding together tomorrow if you like."

Calliope nodded and turned on her heel. "May we invite Sobersides?"

"Perhaps." Isabelle shook her head. "We shall see."

Her cousin had enough sense not to press the issue.

Three-quarters of an hour later Isabelle still had not found James Fitzroy. She had searched everywhere. The butler, the footmen, and the stable master insisted he had not left the estate. She had dared to knock on his chamber door, and even peeked inside. He was not with the other guests in the card room, library, or gardens. And he certainly wasn't in the music room, where two young ladies were murdering a lovely little sonata by Mozart.

Isabelle looked inside every chamber on the main floor, and accounted for every guest. She didn't dare knock on the door of Sussex's study when a man who appeared to be his steward informed her that Sussex was indeed inside conducting a private interview of some importance. Isabelle heard Amelia's voice for a moment before it lowered. She returned her gaze to the steward.

"Is the Duke of Candover with them?"

"Your Grace," the man bowed with deference, "it is not my place to say."

She had the audacity to push her nose two inches from his face. "Is he in there or not?"

He stepped back, unmoved. "No, Your Grace."

She feared she might very well have lost her last shred of dignity as she left the poor man alone and continued her search.

Finally, blessedly, she found him. He had hid himself well.

She hesitated but a moment before she slipped between two statues blocking a path through a dusty corridor strewn with stone and other building materials, leading to a new east wing, still in construction. Everyone knew Sussex was mad for renovating every last inch of the duchy's entailed properties he had just inherited. Indeed, Sussex would be officially inducted into the House of Lords upon the reopening of Parliament—and the Prince Regent was so delighted by one of his favorites' elevation that His Royal Highness had planned a formal celebratory ball that included every last member of the Upper Ten Thousand and even some of their hanger-on relations.

Edward clearly intended for all of the duchy's estates to bear his signature good taste before then.

She pushed down a loose lever on a door at the end of the corridor. It jangled a bit but would not open.

A sound emanated from the other side. It sounded remarkably like a crow. Unintelligible, and harsh.

"Are you in there? Let me in." She rather liked her authoritative voice.

Silence.

"I know you're in there." Her authoritative voice never seemed to work well with this particular bird.

"If you do not let me in then I will—"

"Hurf, 'nd . . . purf, 'nd . . ." His voice faded.

"What did you say?"

"Go 'way."

She could make out that baritone anywhere. "Absolutely not. Let me in, James Fitzroy.

"No' by the 'air of my chinny, chin, chiny, chinny-yyyyy chin chinny." A brusque laugh, the sort she had never heard him ever make before, wafted through the door.

Isabelle glanced around her and found a discarded stone in the rubble. Grasping it, she struck the lever as hard as she could. The door swung open in a small whirl of dust. She coughed as she entered and waved her hands in front of her eyes to shield them.

"Delight-ed." He sat on a crude wooden bench with a bottle and a glass half filled with amber liquid. "Welcome to the 'ouse o' sticks."

She carefully relatched the door and studied the spectacle before her. Indeed, there were pieces of wood in every direction, helter-skelter along the walls and floor. A single candle illuminated the large chamber.

"I thought you gave up drinking."

"Did." He picked up the bottle and held it up to the

candle. He squinted his eyes and examined it. "Did you know that yer eyes are this eg-xact same color?"

She took a deep breath and exhaled.

"But yer don't taste like Armin—Armin . . . Frog water. You taste like—like . . ." He was concentrating so hard that he frowned.

Good God. She walked toward him shaking her head. "All right, big bad wolf, how much did you drink of that bottle?" She could see a little more than half of the bottle was empty.

"No' enough."

Thank the Lord she'd had Calliope teach her how to converse with recalcitrant individuals. "I see. And are we sharing?"

His eyes swung back to her. "No."

"Do I have to ask another little piggy to help me?"

The murkiness in his eyes receded a little and he smiled hugely. "Only if the piggy don' eat rashers o' bacon."

"But swine eat absolutely everything and anything," she retorted.

"Don't I know it," he said, more shrewdly than she thought him capable of, "'specially when they're stayin' at my town house in *Lonnon*."

"Look, I won't even try to understand what you're talking about." She grasped the neck of the bottle he held, and he immediately slapped his other large, hot hand on top of hers.

"James," she said softly, pleading, and kneeled to his level.

He stared at her, his eyes glassy but more direct than she had hoped.

"I need to say something to you, but you need to be clear-headed. I must apologize, I think." Her voice trailed lower with embarrassment. "But first I need you to tell me the absolute truth. Are you in love with Amelia Primrose or not?"

He laughed darkly. "I thought we settled that point."

"No we did not. I assumed but you did not confirm. *Directly.*"

"You have no idea what-er you're talking abou'."

"You're doing it again. And changing the topic." She could not hold their locked gaze. She broke away first. "And you're three sheets to the wind."

He laughed without any amusement in his voice. "I can be sober if *absolully necessess—too many esses.*

"Tell me," she insisted.

"Oh, all right." His glassy eyes became half shuttered. "I'll answer any question you want. But you'll have to play me for it."

She shook her head. She'd never imagined he could be like this. And she was uncertain of his answer, uncertain of his frame of mind. She would have to go along with his mood until he was steadier. "Play you for it? Since when did you begin wagering?"

"I always wager when I'm foxed."

"Well, at least you are sober enough to know how ridiculous you are."

"Truth serum. Spirits always work in that fashion, don't you know?"

"*Now* you tell me." She shook her head.

"You're not going to use it against me, are you?" His brown eyes were huge in his long face and for the first time ever Isabelle spied a hint of boyish innocence in their depths.

"Oh, no," she said, careful to keep her smile to herself. "Not at all."

"I can tell when you're lying," he said with the smallest slur.

"Okay." It was best to agree with him at least half the time when he was this combination of, ahem, blind and all-seeing.

He placed the bottle on the nearby end table and stood up with remarkable fluidity and ease.

"Where are you going?"

He walked to a circular foot-wide object somehow mounted on the wood beams in the half shadows of one corner. He was plucking things off it. "Here."

"Illuminating."

"Darts are always illuminating."

"I refuse to wager on this. I've never played."

"Your choice," he said. "No wager, no answer." He walked back to her.

"But I told you, James. It's a simple, very small . . . easy question." She paused. "And I'm really here to apologize if I've—"

"Done," he replied. "Forgiven."

"But I haven't even fully explained what I've done or why I must ask your forgiveness."

He extended his hand and opened it. Six wooden darts, each wrapped with a bit of lead, lay in his wide palm. He ignored her words and instead nodded toward the darts.

"Are those crow feathers?" She wasn't sure if that might be a good sign or bad, given her experience in London.

"Turkey."

"Lovely," she said, feeling quite the opposite.

"We'll play . . ." He paused. " . . . *going bust*."

"Perfect." *Just perfect.* Exactly as she felt.

"Three darts. Whoever is closest to the center wins. If I win, you answer my questions. If you win, you get to bore me with an apology that isn't *neccessessss*—" He shook his head and the irises of his eyes seemed to slosh about. "Yes, well, and I'll answer your questions." His smile was too large. "Perhaps."

She sighed loudly. "I never knew you were so competitive in spirit."

"There're a lot of things you don't know about me, Isabelle." His eyes burned with intensity.

She grasped three of the proffered darts, touching

the flesh of his hands. She tried hard not to show how his skin always made her remember their kiss.

"It's a little like using a firearm. Remember what I taught you?"

"Of course I remember." She remembered every last bit of it. How his large arms felt three years ago when he'd insisted on teaching her, in case she ever found herself alone and in danger. His chest and arms had been so warm and something much more than just comforting as he'd stood behind her and shown her how to grip, aim, and fire. How that scent of his had drove her to nearly turn and kiss him. How she had not been able to think or speak properly without acting and feeling like an idiot. And she had been so self-conscious she had spit out the absolute stupidest things ever. And she had even giggled. *She never giggled.* Only children would do such a juvenile thing. And all the while she was certain he had known what she was about.

"You, first." He waved his arm in the direction of the target.

She did as he bade. The dart fell far short of the board. "This isn't like shooting at all."

"I know," he said with a grim laugh.

"Have you always been this insanely determined to win?"

"Golf should have been your first clue." He stepped

up to the mark, and threw his first dart within an inch of the center.

Without thought, she asked, "How do you do that?"

"Simple," he replied. "Just envision Sussex's face in the center. In your case, you can envision mine."

She was getting nowhere. She had to win this blasted, silly game. Isabelle's second dart flew wide of the center, but at least it was fairly close to the same horizontal plane. "I get it. But I might need a few more practice shots before we begin."

"Nope," he announced like a common sailor. "Play has begun."

This was ridiculous. "Don't you dare. This is important. And you're not like this normally. You're acting like Sussex at his worst. And you're not like Sussex."

"I know," he said cryptically. "I'm not like him at all." He had moved into position. He pulled back his arm and let loose.

This time it barely caught the edge of the bottom of the board.

"Now look what you made me do," he said.

It was so uncharacteristic of him that she chuckled.

"There's no laughing in darts."

"Is this sort of like how there's no picking up someone else's ball in golf?" He was being ridiculous.

"If you laugh at me, the wager is off," he stated, his

head tilted as if it was too heavy to hold up. "Unless I win, of course."

"Of course," she repeated dryly.

He might have become quite a wit when foxed, but she knew better than to take him seriously. The man simply could not go against his natural character to live up to his word. He would answer her questions if she won.

And so she took aim one last time. Then held her breath, closed one eye as she focused down the line of her raised arm. With a quick motion back, then forward, the dart flew within a half inch home. She did not move, did not react. She knew better than to utter a word to Mr. Drunk as a Sailor on Leave and Proud of It. She still had not won, and he had most likely about three thousand and one more games under his wildly competitive belt to her one round.

And then he did something Isabelle had never, ever, ever seen James Fitzroy do.

He took her place in front of the target without a word.

He took his aim.

And then shockingly, instead of throwing the dart, his arm, seemingly acting of its own accord, slowly returned to his side, the dart still in his hand.

She could not understand. But when her eyes flew to his face, ashen beyond recognition, a blast of cold enveloped her body. He appeared to give up.

"Play the last dart, damn it," she whispered harshly.

His bleak eyes turned dark, his pupils overtaking the irises. "If you insist." He tossed the dart sideways and it disappeared between two adjacent boards. "You win."

And she suddenly didn't like the sound of those words. "I win what?"

For the barest second she spied behind his mask. Unbearable sadness lurked in the depths of his dark eyes, and beyond that . . . the weight of a world of secrets.

Chapter 13

"What do you want to know? If it's about Amelia Primrose, the answer is no."

"No to what?"

"I'm not in love with her. At least not the way you might think, Isabelle. I admire the person she is, but I am not romantically inclined in her direction by any degree. And I never was."

"Then why did you look at her—" She halted. "—touch her . . . say—"

"Because I would protect her from any harm, as I would anyone for whom I hold a deep respect."

He seemed as sober as she had always seen him in the past.

"From whom does she require your protection?"

He appeared to consider her question very carefully. He searched her eyes. "From my *brother*."

Her heart plummeted in confusion and shock. He was obviously more drunk than she had thought. "You don't have a brother," Isabelle said slowly and with great care.

"Edward Godwin, lately the newest Duke of Sussex, at least as soon as the House of Lords declares it, which I've arranged to be the first order of business as soon as Parliament reconvenes." He paused and his voice dropped, "Edward is my half brother."

She could not form words.

"He is the son my father sired before me—the one who should have been his heir if there was any right in the world," he continued quietly. "But there is little right, is there? You see, my grandfather got wind of my father's intention to marry a woman far beneath his station. And my grandfather would have none of it."

She closed the distance between them and took one of his hands between her own. It was as stiff and as cold as a frozen glove lost in a snow bank.

"My father loved her, as I understand it." He could not seem to form the next words, and then he did. "And they anticipated the wedding. The next day my father went to my grandfather and told him his intentions. My grandfather put an end to it quite effectively."

"How?" She could barely breathe.

"Very easily. He immediately shipped his heir to a

naval commander whom he had supported, and then my grandfather tried to pay the young female a stipend. She refused. But soon after, she and her family left the neighborhood. It is not difficult in retrospect to understand why. She was not only ruined, but with child. And so, in humiliation and in secret, she bore the infant." He looked away blindly. "Edward. My half brother."

She prayed he would tell her all before he—or rather, she—broke down. "He doesn't know, then," she said flatly.

"His mother or our father would have told him if they wanted him to know," James said, emotionless. "She thought my father had deceived her, used her even when he did not come after her. She didn't know my grandfather had arranged for his own son and heir to be impressed and dragged out to sea to join the Royal Navy. And when my father returned when his father died and finally learned what had ultimately become of her, it was too late."

"I see," she said faintly. The sadness of it was staggering.

"You see, she apparently had beauty and youth on her side." He swallowed, and she could see his Adam's apple bob awkwardly. "And fortunately, while she lived in a remote nowhereshire corner of Wales, she caught the eye of the reclusive, tonnish neighbor of her aunt with whom she had been sent to live, buried in a suitably obscure cottage."

"The former Sussex," she said as calmly as she could.

"Yes." His eyes were old and sad. "Does that answer all your questions?"

She looked at him, not wanting to stop the flood of information.

"Of course not," James said, and he shook his head slightly. "So then, to clarify . . . Edward is not the new Duke of Sussex, and yet he is."

"Well," Isabelle said, "if his mother was married to the former Duke of Sussex when she gave birth to Edward, he might be your half brother in theory, but in name he is unquestionably Sussex."

"Edward was born a month prior to her marriage. The former duke was infatuated by her—said he could not live without her—despite all. Apparently she gave birth before the former Sussex decided to marry her, saddled himself with an heir that was not his, gave up the lease on the house he had taken in Wales, and then he took her on the Continent for three years to hide the truth from everyone in England."

"And how do you know all this?"

"My father was a man who left no stone unturned when he was determined to find something out . . ." He paused. "And then he got on with his life, and performed the duties of his station, but he never forgot. My father bade me to always watch over Edward when he lay on his deathbed and admitted all to me."

"He asked you, the younger of two gentlemen, to look after the elder?"

He would not answer.

"But what has this to do with Amelia?" she badgered him.

"She is the only other person who knows. My father dared not allow me to be the only living person who knew the truth. Indeed, he trusted no one. I do not blame him, considering his father's actions." He shied away from her hand that reached out to him. "He asked Amelia Primrose to bear witness. She heard my father ask me to watch over his firstborn. The one who resembled him in looks, manners, and speech. His rightful heir. The one who should have been the Duke of Candover when he died."

"He did not say that," she whispered, horrified.

"Yes, he did," he said stiffly. "And he meant it."

"He absolutely did not mean it," Isabelle insisted. "Why would you suggest that? Your sisters once told me their father loved you more than any of them. More than anyone, they said."

He spoke so softly she had to lean in to hear him. "Really? Is that love? Informing me that the love of his life was not my mother? That he had been living and breathing a charade with his wife and family? That he still loved the Duchess of Sussex, a blacksmith's daughter who had borne him a son, the true heir he always regretted not being able to see?"

His face became a mask without a hint of emotion. It was the face she knew all too well.

"Yes," he began sardonically, "well at least Sussex's duchess had a sense of humor. She named her only child after my dear grandfather, the one who had impressed his own heir and offered her money to disappear, all because he would not have a butcher's daughter for his son's duchess. But I digress."

"Go on," she whispered. The only thing she could do now was bite her tongue and listen. It was what he needed.

"I only tell you this to show you the error in your thinking regarding my father," he said stiffly. "We have always been frank, something rare. At least for me."

She nodded, her heart heavy with his pain.

"Do you truly think he held much affection or even esteem in his heart for me—as you suggest—when he beseeched his second son, me, the product of an arranged marriage to a lady of impeccable lineage—to watch over the son of his heart?" He closed his eyes and shook his head when she tried to speak. "And insisted my sister's abigail witness it in its entirety?"

"Oh, James," she said sadly.

He stared at her, his tic beating a tattoo along the edge of his jaw.

"He was," she whispered, "secretly in love with

her his entire life, obviously. And he had not protected her. He had done the worst thing a man can do to a female—left her unprotected. He was obviously mortally ashamed, and deeply wounded by his father. Imagine how he felt. And you—so dutiful, so careful to place your family's needs above your own. Just look at how you are with your sisters. You were the only one he could trust with the bitter truth." How could she help him to see something she was not even certain was true? "Obviously, he had to make certain this part of him was at least protected—and not alone in the world. Sussex knows you're his brother, right?" She had an awful feeling it was the reverse.

"Of course not," James said, annoyed. "For Christsakes, have you not been listening? My father didn't want the son of his heart to be *burdened* with the knowledge of his mistake."

She felt so ill she did not know what to say. She finally uttered blindly, quietly, "Your father should not have involved Amelia. He should have overcome his distrust and told you alone, and in a loving way. It would have been far better had he written it all in a private letter to be opened only if you died without an heir. But—"

"I have an heir," he interrupted. "Everyone seems to forget."

She waved her hand. "I'm sorry to say what no one

else would dare to voice—all in the spirit of frankness, of course. Frontine Fitzroy is a sweet young man, but he shows no early signs of becoming a great duke of the realm. I'd make sure your stewards are the best in the land. Oh, Frontine won't ruin the duchy, but it won't prosper, and he's as dull as a fourteenth-century looking glass." She stopped, appalled by her own lack of gentility. When he did not comment, she continued. "In his fifteen years Frontine has not shown a lick of wit, refuses to exchange his pony for a horse, cannot be counted on to converse on any subject with brilliance, cries at every opportunity, cannot add the figures in ledgers, and cannot be trusted to shoot anything unless it's his own foot, and—" She ran out of steam and halted.

The barest hint of a smile appeared on his face. "And?"

"And he has not a single tooth going in the same direction and his hair is already thinning. No lady in her right mind would have him, no matter how great the fortune," she said flatly.

A darkness filled his eyes, and his glance fell on the bottle still on the nearby table. "Oh, they'll have him," he gritted out. "You have only to remember the Duchess of Sussex to know that. And also the . . ." His voice died as he turned away and strode to the table to grasp the neck of the dark green bottle.

She rushed to stop him and placed her hand over his.

"And? And who were you going to say? My mother?"

His eyes glittered as he stared at her. "I refuse to answer. I would not insult you. And your father was one of the most intellectually superior gentlemen I've ever known. "

She didn't know whether to shout at him or thank him. No one ever mentioned her mother—or what she had done—in front of her. There were times Isabelle wondered if her mother had ever even existed or was some phantom in her imagination. Every trace of her beautiful, wistful, mysterious mother had been removed from her father's estates within twenty-four hours of her running off with another gentleman. Her father had concocted the story to be disseminated outside of the estate and Isabelle held her tongue. Her draconian governess, Miss Hackett, would have been proud her efforts had not gone wasted. But servants used gossip and household secrets as currency with other servants in neighboring estates, and the circle of gossip had welled outward like the ripples caused by a stone thrown onto a pond.

Everyone knew. Yet everyone held their tongue around her. But she could always see it in a person's eyes when they first were introduced to her.

She finally released his hand, holding the bottle. She watched him pour a shot of Armagnac. Instead of drinking it, he offered it to her.

She tossed it back like a seasoned Corinthian. It was like drinking fire. She would not cough or show a hint of discomfort, but her voice dropped by three notes. "Thank you for at least reminding me that she once existed."

"You might look like her, but you are your father's daughter through and through." He poured another shot and downed it.

"Well, I would say the reverse about you after I saw your parents' portraits in Derbyshire. You look like your mother, and according to your sisters, you used to share her interests until your father died and you assumed the title," she said quietly.

He stilled, and his eyes became remote. "Thank God for my mother. She knew her duty. She was the most amazing mother in the world. She ensured a glorious childhood. And all the while she knew my father's heart was not hers. But she never said a word."

"And so you became like her—and like him. All duty. All a facade. Hiding every true feeling. All sadness behind a proper mask. All everything, even true joy, probably. I feel ill for what your father endured. At least she had her passion for her work, and her children to love. Why did you give up your interest, which matched your mother's?"

"Do you want another?" he replied coolly, nodding to the bottle.

She grabbed the bottle and threw it in the corner.

Splinters of glass and liquid burst, but neither reacted. "Listen to me, James," she said, trying to shake him, but it was like trying to shake a tree.

"He didn't trust me," he said. "What is love if not trust?"

"He loved you. Look, I might not have known him, but he loved you," she choked out. "He told your sisters that you would be the best Duke of Candover that England would ever know." She felt ill. She knew how it felt to be the rejected child.

She finally took his stiff body in her arms. "Look, I know how it feels. I was not the boy my father wanted—merely a girl child. Impossible. Useless. Even my mother had no use for me—did not take me with her. But I refuse to give up trust. Or give up on love."

His head finally fell on her shoulder, and slowly, ever so slowly, his arms came around her loosely. After long moments he whispered into her ear, "I'm glad you were born a girl."

She swallowed against the emotion that threatened to engulf her.

"And you are the most courageous lady I know," he continued. "And you never back down from a challenge." His arms tightened and he pulled her deep, as close to his heart as she had once dreamed.

Then he lowered his lips to her forehead, which felt like a benediction to everything good. His lips fell to her cheek, easing the tension there, and crossed to her ticklish nose, her eyelids, and came to rest on her lips, which craved his.

Her uneven breath fanned the hollow of his cheek as she tried to stop the trembling of her body, without success.

His mouth took possession of hers and she gave over to the wild thrill of the moment, which seemed precariously balanced on the precipice of everything fantastic. He coaxed beyond her lips and teased her tongue to engage with his own. And she felt like she was falling, falling. The taste of Armagnac and the poignant remembered scent of shaving soap and his cologne dangerously dabbled with all her other senses, and she grabbed his sleeves with a fierceness born in her breast.

The feeling of his lips trailing down her neck to the sensitive skin below was nearly her undoing. She couldn't breathe.

He raised his head for a moment to gaze at her; his eyes were stark against his bronzed face and filled with palatable need. His eyes would not leave her face as he passed his hand over her breast once and then delved beyond the edges of her pale yellow silk gown. She squeezed her eyes shut so she would not make a sound.

He traced a light circle on the tip, increasing the pressure until he paused and gently squeezed her tip drawn up tightly. The sensations were so shockingly exquisite the back of her throat closed and she gasped.

"No more." He kissed her temple and nuzzled her ear. "No more, Isabelle."

He withdrew his hand, but she covered that large bronzed hand with her own, halting his motion.

"I will not forgive you if you stop," she whispered, determined to see this through. "I swear to God I won't."

"You don't know what—"

"And don't you dare say something so condescending to me. Look at me, damn you."

When he fully engaged his eyes with hers, she tugged his head toward her. "I want you," she whispered fiercely.

Gathering her in his arms in one motion, his glance swept the dusty chamber, searching. In the shadows lurked a discarded billiard table of the last decade, piled high with old fabric. He laid her upon the soft mound.

He kissed her with utter abandon while his hands worked at the hidden bow beyond the lace of her bodice.

And then his lips replaced his hands and unerringly found the tip of her breast. His tongue swept in circles and he teased her flesh by blowing the wetness until she writhed. Using the edge of his teeth, he tormented her while his hand caressed her other breast with great care.

A deep, heavy place within her contracted and long waves of pleasure echoed.

He groaned and the reverberation sent sparks of longing throughout her.

He broke away. "This is insanity, Isabelle." He stared at her, his pupils nearly overtaking his irises. "For the love of God don't ask me to—"

"Go on," she interrupted.

"No," he whispered harshly.

"I am asking. Again. One day I hope it will be the reverse. I am so tired of always grasping, James. It's your turn. *Please*."

He groaned in frustration, and she grasped his head between her fingers, entranced by the sleekness of his hair, which grew coarse as she traced the path below his temples toward the coarseness of his shaven face. She had never known such intense pleasure combined with a wild happiness such as this. She loved him, and would ease the ache she sensed deep in his soul.

Without knowing, she dropped her hands to grip his broad shoulders, which were as hard and unyielding as stone. Her neck gave in to the tension and her head dropped back. She loved the feeling of his skin against her own but wanted to feel more of it. The heat of his body warmed hers. And the softness of her yielded to the strength and hard angles of him. She went still when she became aware of a thickness jutting from him, straining between the layers of stiff fabric that separated them. Heat seared her senses and she wanted to be free of every last article of clothing.

She knew, understood, the promise of paradise when she imagined what it would feel like to eliminate all the barriers between them.

And suddenly one of the two candles in the room guttered and the room was plunged into near total darkness.

"Enough," he rasped, lifting his head from her body. "It's a sign."

She could not stop trembling. "It's a sign, all right. And it's saying not to stop or . . . or I might have to kill you." A dark hint of wit laced the intensity of her words.

And for the first time that night she spied amusement in the darkness of his eyes.

"I think I must take my chances," he said, his eyes suggesting he wanted just the opposite. "It's a gentleman's code, Isabelle."

"I don't want your damned duty. Or your gentleman's rules of gentility, damn you," she whispered roughly. "I want you. I want to see you. Know you."

He began to shake his head until—

Isabelle Tremont, the Duchess of March, did the outrageous. Something no proper and innocent duchess would ever do. She eased her hand between them; dared to trespass the gap in the flap of his breeches and touched the part of him that strained against her.

Oh, it was not at all what she had expected—such an intimidating, unyielding strength that pulsed against her entire hand, which could not fully grasp him. But he seemed stunned and incapable of speech. And this power she finally wielded encouraged her to want to give him the same pleasure he had shown her.

He went as still as an ancient oak as her fingers traveled over his length right down to the root. Her fingers stroked the drawn up pouch below as her other hand continued to explore his iron-like arousal. When she reached the bulbed end, his body surged toward her, telling her what he wanted. And the wild passion she finally saw coloring his dark eyes spoke of a need so long denied, so passionately desired, that she knew . . .

James was hers. And she was his.

James could not have stopped to save his life. Or hers.

She had not stopped until she pushed him to the brink, dislodged his facade and forced him to unload the burden of his soul. And she had done it through trust—the very thing his father had withheld from him at the moment it most counted. It was the element everyone needed to feel genuine and accepted.

And she had not backed away from his ugly revelations. She merely challenged his every thought. And she would not let him down.

Ever.

She would trust him to protect her, to love her, to provide for her every need, even now when he had no right, indeed it was just the opposite.

And there was no falseness between them. She didn't need him. She was perhaps the only woman in Christendom who was his equal on every measure. And she had chosen him—not for his position, not for his wealth. She had chosen him because she *liked him*.

No . . . His mind, the person beyond the strictness he wore like a suit of armor, resisted for a blind moment. She loved him.

He nearly cried out at the knowledge of it.

He had found the only person in the world who had the strength to offer him comfort. A person who would accept the weight of his burdens without complaint, stand up to him and shove aside his mask, truly want to know who he was, allow him to be himself—flaws and all. And above all else offer strength and loyalty against the storm, and love him in truth that could not be feigned.

All these thoughts ravaged his mind when time stilled and she stroked him as he lay paralyzed with desire.

She gazed at him with such raw passion it nearly took his breath away. She showed not an inch of restraint. Until finally one of her arms curled about his shoulders and drew him down to her to meet her lips.

Blindly, he grasped the side of her gown and pulled

the entire skirting above her waist. He could not wait another moment. But she would have none of it. In a quick motion she drew the yellow silk gown above her head and he yanked it off, popping the buttons on the caps of sleeves.

While he frantically worked the complicated stays, and the busk, chemise, and soft undergarments that hid her from him, she pushed at his lapels, tugged on his neck cloth and proved that she cared even less about the buttons that would be forever lost as she yanked his shirt from his torso.

He lay down beside her, turning her face-to-face, the mystery of her eyes beckoning him.

When she reached for his flap again he brushed her hands away. "No, it's my turn," he growled.

He pushed her back as he rocked toward her, and relished the sight before him as he prowled her body with his free hand.

Her skin was luminescent in the low light as he studied every small hill and valley of the perfection of her femininity. She was every inch a woman.

A woman unlike any other. And she wanted him.

He growled like a predator when his hand caressed her thigh before he instinctively sought her mound of soft curls. They were softer than in his dreams.

He heard her breath catch, and he controlled his desire to take her. His arousal felt like a twelve stone length of iron as it pulsed against the tent of his breeches.

His gut clenched with need as he grasped her knee and urged her to open herself to him. Her leg trembled for a moment and then stilled. A harsh sound of shock escaped her lips when he finally slid downward to trace the folds of her essence. She was so soft, so very wet, like hot velvet in the rain.

She violently trembled and tried not to writhe as he glided his fingers along her crest again and again before he inched beyond the merest edges of her. She was so responsive to his slightest touch; her uneven breath and the tension on her brow beyond her eyes closed so tightly.

He imagined what it would feel like to be inside of her. To join his body to hers in a perfect union. He just knew with every inch of his being that it would be perfect. Her depths would be his balm, and his hardness and strength would be something she could grab onto.

She had no one to lean on in her life. The reality hit him as never before.

And here he was taking from her when he needed to give. It was his duty—his reason for being born. To oversee, to protect, to give.

Well, he could at least give her more knowledge—more pleasure for her alone. He massaged the sensitive peak of her folds without ceasing.

He slid his long index finger down her dark valley and paused at the well of her. And then he entered her gently; her muscles clenching against the invasion.

God, she was so soft, so wet, and yet so tight. His mind screamed against the reality of it while his heart refused to be denied.

He worked her untried passage rhythmically and slowly inside of her, until her hips began to move against his hand, straining to meet him.

His other hand stoked the engorged peak of her sex, and she struggled to reach a plateau she did not know existed. But he had to make sure she reached it.

She had to understand, and he could teach her.

Her eyes opened as her breath came in ragged notes.

"Close your eyes, my love," he said softly. "And grab onto me. Don't let go. And I promise you I won't stop."

He lowered his body down her slim form and fully spread her knees open. A rush of near primal wanting pounded through the blood in his veins as he glanced at her beautiful sex. He settled himself between her thighs and wordlessly met her trusting, passion-filled eyes before he allowed himself to taste her, satisfy the most primal need to know every part of her and tend to her every need.

She was everything he had known she would be, genuine and true, unshocked by his actions, trusting him and opening herself to him. He spent long minutes stroking her with his tongue and teasing every fold. He knew how to draw it out slowly, make the tension build to excruciating levels that were a pleasure unto themselves.

He listened to her ragged breaths, and finally nudged her hands to her knees as he urged them farther apart. And farther still.

"Mmmm," he murmured as he returned his attention to the glistening, swollen crest. "Hold your breath, my darling, when you can't stand it anymore," he whispered, "and then let it come to you and hold onto it for as long as you can. Trust me to take care of you."

The only sign she gave that she had heard him was when she lifted her head and stared at him, a haze of desire coloring her face.

In one long, smooth movement he dragged his finger down her crest and entered her to tease the place inside of her that was most sensitive. At the same moment he tugged her peak into his mouth and refused to stop until he had learned what brought her to the pinnacle.

He plunged and retreated, stroked and licked, and then he heard it, that catch in her breath. The rustle of the fabric on the table as she curled her body forward and became still, as every muscle in her slim body focused on what he was doing with his fingers and his mouth.

A cascade of pulses raced across his finger and his tongue as she suddenly gave herself over to the pleasure he had promised.

At least he had been given the joy of sharing this with her. He was nearly spent by the restraint of holding back from ripping off his breeches and taking her.

He dragged himself back up her soft body and

she wrapped one arm about his shoulder. The other dropped between them.

She was still trying to catch her breath, and he was holding onto his desire when he felt her hand undo the falls of his breeches and slip beyond.

"What are you doing?" he growled.

"What you just did to me," she said, surprisingly composed.

His eyes closed when she naively found the exquisite notch of pleasure pain on his arousal.

And just like that, gone was his reserve, his iron grip on any possible chance of checked motion.

"Isabelle," he ground out. "Stop. For the love of God." His body spasmed in an effort to reverse desire.

"No," she whispered, and emboldened by his reaction, began to stroke him with a wickedness he had not guessed she possessed.

He lay between her soft thighs and rested his forehead against the fabric on the felt table, gulping a great lungful of air.

And suddenly a sort of cold calm invaded his body. He kissed her, and raised his head to look down at her. "Is this what you truly want, Isabelle?" He could barely breathe. "You should not trust me. You know that, don't you?"

"I have always trusted you." Her voice did not waver. "And I always will."

And again she touched him with her soft hands, uncertain but bold. He strained into her fingers, urging her to never stop. He had crossed a line, the line that turned a man into pure instinct.

In one practiced motion as ancient as all mankind, he covered her small body with his own larger one, urging her legs once again apart with his own. He grasped behind one knee and pulled it higher until her delicate foot lost its anchor.

Pushing his hips forward, the tip of his length sensed her feminine heat and impossibly inviting depths. The wait was excruciating, and yet he would not move.

And so he wavered on the edge of disaster—damned if he did and damned if he didn't.

Temptation was upon him like an unbearable midsummer's night, the pressure of a storm bearing down. Then, in the blazing tension of the moment when the crickets and night birds fell silent, he knew what would happen. The heavens would tear open and loose their fury.

Just like he would do to the only woman he knew who was a slice of paradise in this private corner of hell on his earth.

All the muscles in him pulsed as he pushed the slightest fraction of an inch more inside of her. He desperately wanted to tell her something important, assure her of something he could not, comfort her, and yet he couldn't unclench his jaw to open his mouth so the words would pour forth.

And so he closed his eyes, gritted his teeth, and gave

in to the great hunger to strain closer.   He could feel the muscles of his back popping with exertion as he entered her, and felt an unbearable ring of pleasure that made every fiber of his being long to surge past.

He could feel beads of sweat forming at the base of his back.

Then he heard the smallest sound, and he opened his eyes to glimpse raw pain on the face of the woman whom he trusted—who trusted him—whom he loved and would always love even if she stopped loving him.

Duty came roaring back into his head with a vengeance at the same moment she disengaged her knee from his grasp, ground her feet and lunged up to take the choice from him.

Exquisite physical pleasure battled temporal horror at his guilt. "I'm so sorry. Oh Christ, Isabelle. Don't move," he rasped.

And when she stilled, he finally undulated forward, working just the edges of her, slowly. He shifted as he dared to pulse ever deeper. He nearly lost his thin grasp of control when he felt her warm fingers tracing the muscles of his arms and then down his spine.

He tried desperately to be gentle with her and feared he was failing miserably in a battle between slaking a burning need to wildly possess her and to go slowly. He was so lost in a sea of sensation that he could not hear anything except a roaring in his head.

And suddenly all thought left him and blinding need

took over. His muscles locked when there was no more depth inside her to plunder.

Just when he thought she could take no more of his length, something loosened inside of her and she cried out so loudly he heard her through the mist of pleasure. The twin points on the base of his back tightened, and he could no longer stop the wild fury of his release. It unleashed him from his past and bound him to a future that was not his to live.

And he had done the unpardonable. He had lost complete control—become an untamed animal, barely leashing his brute power over her. Already the black specter of a far greater guilt was rising up from his soul.

Gathering her in his arms, he rested against her before the full weight of his actions overtook him. She smelled of woman. Of serenity and happiness all packaged in perfect femininity.

She was quietly saying his name and wisps of words he could not make out for the life of him as he was drawn back behind the mask he had never let slip before. He was a blackguard. His father had been right not to trust him. And he had grossly broken his word of honor to his godfather, the one man whose opinion mattered more to him than any other.

He felt her gaze as she studied him, and finally met her eyes. She said not a word and neither did he. There were no words he could form. Oh, he knew what the future held. He supposed he always had. He was not above history repeating itself. Only he had helped it along quite famously tonight.

Her face was painfully open and honest, and he sensed she was waiting for him to say something. But he dared not say a word before he had thought it all through and planned what must happen.

So instead of speaking, he eased his great weight off her and pulled her against him in the cradle of his shoulder. It was all he could do. The shock of what he had done, what he was capable of doing when he had allowed his facade to fall from his form appalled him. She did not move beside him after settling her head on his arm.

He understood so little of what had overcome him. There was only one thing he knew with crystal clarity. He had been an utter fool to think that he was a gentleman. He never deserved to be the Duke of Candover. He belonged in the gutter along with the rest of mankind without character. He had ruined the woman he held above all others. He'd shown no restraint, none of his famed but false good character. And to boot, he had failed to protect Amelia. He had failed the most important people he was put on this earth to guard and defend with his life.

And he knew why.

He had never truly wanted or deserved the title. And so, he thought blindly, he had failed *on pur-*

pose. The thought had lurked in the furthest recess in his mind, mocking him. He had not wanted to be the next Candover. In his darkest moment after the monotony of days where his only joy was ensuring the tranquility of all those who depended on him, he would dream.

A life at sea and on distant lands would have been his preference had he been given the choice. He loved the hidden mystery of the sea's blue depths, and exotic lands. He had felt most at ease with the salt in his hair and on his skin during those long summers when he was a boy and his mother had returned to her parents' estate on the southeastern coast that looked toward the unseen Bay of Biscay far, far away.

He'd wanted to be a naturalist, an adventurer, a charter of maps and unknown species of animals and plants, responsible for no one or anything beyond foreign horizons. Yes, all those many summer days endlessly long ago, when his mother had taken him on miles and miles of nature walks and then taught him how to sail. Both pairs of eyes had rarely strayed from the horizon—ever in search of new seabirds to discover and draw.

And yet now he was so different from this beloved mother. He very much feared he had become just like his father.

It was the last coherent thought he had as his mind blanked at the enormity of his failings. James Fitzroy, the last man who should be the premier duke of

England, a man who never slept at peace, let go of the world finally and fell into a slumber so deep that he did not know that the love of his life got up and left him while he snored loud enough to rattle the walls of this house of sticks.

Chapter 14

Isabelle knew her greatest strength. The ability to remain calm in the face of a crisis. And this was beyond a crisis.

She paced the floor of her chamber, ignoring the pain of her torn and aching flesh. She'd washed all evidence away in private, donned a thin summer night rail and then a winter pale blue robe to stop the chattering of her teeth.

She barred her thought beyond an iron will. She would not think of him. Yet. Oh, what did it matter? She knew what would happen. She'd already seen it in his eyes. He would never fight it and she had been a fool to think he would.

But more than anything, she had seen the truth. He did not love her. And his guilt was the proof.

The desolate guilt she had seen was not the simple

one—the one where he would feel ill at ease for taking her innocence when she had in fact forced it on him. No, it was not that, because love had the power to overcome a guilt like that.

His eyes had reflected a deeper, uglier emotion—something made of despair, horror, and the knowledge that he would regret this to the end of his days.

Because he did not love her.

But he'd eventually let guilt overwhelm him, come to her. He'd be on one knee tomorrow. And he'd do it properly. She had the gravest certainty that he'd act the enamored lover with great élan once the cool mask was drawn back over his features.

Oh, where was Amelia Primrose? She had no patience anymore. If Amelia did not appear within ten more minutes, she would go to her.

Isabelle halted and drew in a shaky breath. God, what had she done? She did not regret it in the least, but oh, if she was with child . . .

The sound of a rap on the door had her hurrying to pull Amelia inside.

"Is Calliope all right?" Amelia's face showed her concern.

"She's perfectly fine. In the adjoining chamber, sleeping. I merely told my maid that as an excuse for you to come to my chambers."

Amelia relaxed.

"Look, I need to apologize for interfering in your

affairs. I just wanted to inform you that you are not officially married. The archbishop told me. And so I wanted to offer you my protection."

"But, I don't—"

"Pardon me, Amelia, but I must tell you all quickly for I—I must arrange for all of my affairs to be packed at this late hour." She put up her hand to stop Amelia's words. "I've taken a decision. Calliope and I must leave at first light. I very much want you to come with me. But only if you want that, too. Candover told me of all the difficulties you witnessed for his family."

Amelia's eyes filled with shocked. "Pardon me?"

"We shan't speak of it, unless you like. I shall always be here if you need to unburden yourself. But I sense you might choose to do the very opposite. You will find peace in my household, Amelia. I just wanted you to know that. I know you're very close to His Grace's sisters and that perhaps you'd be too gracious to be honest with me. I am sorry to give you such short notice but would you like to accompany me to the duchy's seat in the Lake Region? We would leave in four hours."

Amelia shook her head. "You are very kind, but I shall remain here."

Isabelle cocked her head. "But where will you go? To His Grace's sisters? To Scotland? Have you really family there?"

"No," she admitted, wryly. "But I have family here. Or soon will."

It was obvious Amelia did not want to confide, and Isabelle would not pry. "Amelia, I'm arranging for a sum to be in your possession within three days. I refuse for you to be beholden ever again to anyone. With me it is different. You know I don't ever want to see it again, but I won't argue against your pride. I know it too well."

Amelia raised her blond eyebrows. "I won't need it, but thank you."

Isabelle waited.

"I've already plans of my own in place. Please don't worry about me. I promise I will turn to you if I ever become desperate or must protect another." Amelia paused as if choosing her words carefully. "But you have been far too generous."

She grasped Amelia's hands. "But have you chosen a plan? And where are you going?"

Amelia smiled. "Why do you ask?"

Isabelle opened her mouth and then snapped it shut.

"Where is Your Grace going?" Amelia's eyes glittered with feeling.

"I told you. And please, we are friends. You're no longer in my employ. There's no need to stand on ceremony."

"If you will pardon my interference, I must beg from you one favor."

"Anything," Isabelle replied.

"Don't leave," Amelia said softly. "Please. Don't leave him."

It was the second time in less than a day that someone had asked her to help him—first Calliope and now Amelia. But they did not know how it stood between them, and she could not confide in anyone. Tears pricked the back of her eyes when she realized that she had just lost her first and best confidante—James Fitzroy.

Isabelle could not hold back the tears that had been forming since she left James in that dust-laden lair in the easternmost corner of Sussex's abbey.

Amelia enfolded her within her thin arms. "He needs you. He'll never say it. But everyone needs somebody. It's hard to admit, but it's truth. And . . ."

"Mmmm," Isabelle mumbled, a new wave of emotion rocking her.

"He is the man for you. Don't let him push you away. He will try. And . . . Oh, Isabelle, I hold you in highest regard. But, don't go. Wait. Please."

She could not make a promise she would not keep. She gently pulled away from Amelia and stroked her face. "I could give you the same advice."

The other lady nodded. "But my story is not the same as yours. I fear mine is far more outrageous."

"You've never done anything outrageous," Isabelle said with certainty. "I know you well enough to know you are the greatest lady in this abbey."

"I fear you do not know me at all. I am quite capable of the gravest of sins. Indeed I shall roast for it, if not hang—I mean pay for it, dearly."

A tickle of uncertainty itched Isabelle's brain. Amelia was so proper she probably thought she'd go to hell if she'd allowed Sussex to touch her. "Well, you could always marry Sussex in truth," she joked through her tears, "although I am afraid that he'd lead you very far off the path of righteousness. But I daresay it would be worth it."

Amelia refused to laugh. "Will you promise me you'll stay? Give him a chance?"

"I am willing to compromise," Isabelle finally said. "I will stay three more days. But . . ."

"Yes?" Amelia waited.

"You must tell me what is going on. Oh, I can see you are too embarrassed to tell me the how and the why of how you ended up married to Sussex. But really, can't you tell me if you will marry him again, properly or not?"

Amelia studied her face and finally made some sort of decision. "I am not supposed to breathe a word."

"Yes? Go on."

She rolled her eyes in fine abigail form. "That's it."

"You're not supposed to breathe a word of what?"

"Of *anything*," Amelia said with great significance.

Light dawned and Isabelle nodded. "Oh, I see." But she had to be certain. "And does *anything* involve the Archbishop of Canterbury and Sussex or does it involve . . ."

Amelia arched a brow. "It involves prayer."

Isabelle gave up. She only prayed Sussex and Amelia would be married in truth. Amelia was the only lady up to the task of outwitting a charming duke wilier than all the rest of the royal entourage put together.

Isabelle had made her promise to Amelia, and so she would endure the interview and the remaining time with the rest of the house party. It was fruitless, of course. But she also knew, within her heart, that if she did not take her leave properly as a true duchess would, it could haunt both of them.

And James was waiting for her beyond the wide sheets of glass of the orangery.

Again the orangery.

The grinning, knowing face of the archbishop had not faded in her mind. She hated being made the fool, and knowing she had been completely wrong on every level.

It was half past six in the morning. Obviously the ideal time for a guilt-laden proposal of marriage.

As she stepped before him in the farthest corner of the chambers, where every sort of exotic plant thrived, he did not fail her prediction. His face was a veritable mask of reserve.

His most famous expression. The one she had loved with girlish infatuation. But now it meant something more. She realized as she gazed into his chocolate-colored eyes that he didn't want to be anything other than this. And she was the fool who had overpowered him while he had been drunk, left vulnerable by admitting the bitterness of his father's actions, and then had taken advantage of him. And it would never be right between them.

He did not love her. And she wasn't even certain he could trust anyone to love him. His father had not trusted him, and now he did not trust himself—last night only compounded it.

Indeed, he might very well be ruined, beyond happiness's reach. One had to choose to see joy in life. It was far too easy to take the other more trodden path, filled with fast-growing vines of despair.

She thought these things, but they sounded false for the first time in her mind. Would she find true joy after this? Or would she become like James—dulling all her emotions and following a grim course of duty between the occasional—very occasional—house party composed of people chasing after little white leather balls filled with feathers hidden in the grasses of a golf course?

"Isabelle," he murmured. He was impeccable, his clothes expertly tailored to his strong, powerful trunk of a masculine body. Not a single hair on his head was out of place or an inch of him reminiscent of last night.

He was the damned premier duke of a royal empire.

She placed her small hand in his large one—the

one that had done such unspeakably wicked things to her—and he automatically raised it to his lips. She kept her eyes on his boots, watching for one to move back.

"Don't you dare kneel," she finally said.

He did not move. "Isabelle, I do not have the right to beg your forgiveness. The only thing I dare to beg of you is to allow me the privilege of making right some minute part of what I did to you last night."

She shook her head. "No, no, you've not the right of it at all. Let me show you the way of it."

He did not utter a syllable as she kneeled before him, their hands clasped between them.

"You asked me not to kneel," he murmured.

"Since when does a man taken by the passion of the moment deny his natural inclinations? Yes, and then this is how it goes. The way I should have considered the day in your garden." She cleared her throat. " 'My dear, please ease the anxiety that fills me, leaving me awake each night. Please make me the happiest of men,' or rather, shall we say, ladies, in this case." Cool resolve filled her when he did nothing to stop this farce. "Yes, and so on and so forth. I see it is not your style. So let's alter it all midway through the calamity."

He did not interrupt her.

" 'So, my dear Isabelle,' is what you would say. 'Shall we not forgo a wedding in St. George's, then? Far too ordinary. Shall we not have the archbishop sign a special license and take on the leg shackle? Yes, let's rush it. So convenient to do it straight away, appease His Royal Highness, and then go back to our lives. You in Derbyshire, and me in the Lake District. We only really need one heir who could wear two hats.' "

His face remained impassive. He removed his hand from hers, as if it was anyone's hand. "Are you finished?"

She stood up. "No."

He waited, like a stone warrior from the Middle Ages.

A ball of fury rose in her, and before she could stop herself she slapped him. "For the love of God, share yourself. Get angry. Show some emotion. Anything but this reserve. I can't stand it. Don't you care about anything?"

He slowly nodded. "You do not know the half of it."

"Then show it."

"I cannot be angry with you, Isabelle. Not after what I've done to you."

She snorted with annoyance. "How ridiculous. We both know I did it to myself."

He smiled halfheartedly and then slowly lowered himself and took her hand in his. His cheek showed the distinct mark of her hand. She thought it must sting like the devil.

"Isabelle, marry me. I will not insult you with false words as you suggested. You know I never have and

I never will. And I will not insult you by playing the draconian tyrant. I approach you as an equal. If you marry me, I promise to do my utmost to ensure your every happiness. It would be a union of kindness and respect—two very rare ingredients I have yet to see in most marriages." His words gained force. "Marry me if only for one incontrovertible fact—you could very well be with child. And please, Isabelle, marry me because I've ruined you. It's unpardonable what I did. And because I will only ever be honest with you, the fact is that if you are not with child and eventually think of m-m-marrying," he stumbled, "another gentleman, you must consider an ugly fact. Many gentlemen will not be understanding—and worse." He would not voice the ugliness of it. Vertical slants of a palm tree next to him cast shadows down his face and form. "So will you . . . have me?"

She prayed she would not allow the bitterness that was taking root in her soul to thrive for any great length of time. She would have to battle it.

She would not honor him with a reply. Instead she turned away, but then stopped, her face toward the exit. "I give you my vow that I will inform you if I find myself with child. I would not worry in that corner. I cannot stop you from feeling guilt. No one can make anyone feel anything. The only thing I insist is that there must be no more private discussion between us. I promised someone I would remain here for the next several days and I will do so. But I do not want to see you again after I leave. And I hereby cancel my membership to the sodding royal entourage."

He did not stop her. Or say another word. She left him, blindly finding her way through the jungle of the orangery.

Chapter 15

Isabelle fled the scene of her greatest nightmare. Oh, it had been even worse than she thought it would be. And Calliope was wrong. And Amelia was very wrong. He didn't need or want anyone. He wanted duty, and kindness, and respect. Passion was madness and unproductive.

And so she ran. She ran as fast as her skirts would allow. And when she could no longer run, she walked. And walked.

She would not cry. She was too barren of emotion. God, she was becoming just like him, she feared.

Well, she would not allow it. She would live her life. She would find her happiness.

She rushed through a patchwork of fields and enclosures. Miles of hedgerows were behind her, and still she walked northward. Toward home.

She would not go all the way, of course. But it eased

the ache of her heart. It was as if her heart was a compass and knew its way home.

Isabelle walked until she could walk no more. These stupid kid boots from the Frenchified boot maker in London could not withstand the rigors of the countryside.

She would rest at the crest of this last hill and then negotiate the hollows and hills back to Angelus Abbey. And then she would immediately begin packing, collect Calliope, and go.

But at the crest of the hill she looked down, only to find a ruined castle.

And she suddenly realized she had walked all the way to the Duke of Barry's neighboring estate.

To one side of the castle stood a two-story square stone structure. An ancient, abandoned pigeonnier—or dovecot. She began to walk toward it, gathering renewed strength, until she ran inside the safety of its walls. There, she lay down in fresh hay, breathing in the familiar scent. And she studied the honeycombed interior walls where doves had at one time paired off and built their nests in the now barren stone ledges.

God.

She wanted to go home. To the Lakes, where she could see the fruit of her efforts. She was tired. She felt different. Older. Worn.

And did she really need a husband at this very moment? She was a damned duchess when all was said and done. And the prince was merely prodding the rest of the unmarried members of the entourage to get on with it and wed, not because the country was on the verge of anarchy. The fury of the masses had been quelled when Abshire married Verity Fitzroy and turned about the entire hysteria surrounding the Duke Diaries. The prince wanted everyone married because he was a careful old bird despite his extravagant ways and the careless ways of his own personal enjoyments. Oh, His Royal Highness would understand and accept her decision.

Her mind whirled in thought, blindly staring at the castle in front of her. Oh, she would one day take a husband. Produce an heir. But, truly, it did not have to be for another half-dozen years. And she would do it the way ninety-nine percent of the aristocracy did it. By arrangement. Everything written out by solicitors— signed, sealed, and stamped with His Majesty's blessing. Just as . . . James would do it one day. She finally understood the way of it. Marriage was not about love. One could not even count on family being about love.

And finally, for the first time since she was a young girl and her mother left her behind to join a mysterious lord in Brussels whom she apparently *loved* prior to her marriage . . . she wept for the mother who did not love her enough to stay. And for her dictatorial father, who married a lady he had loved, and yet drove her away in his demands and increasing fear as her mother became more and more remote.

And while Isabelle finally wept, she wept despite being a proper duchess. Her father was wrong. Duchesses were allowed to cry—especially for the mother who had left her behind. And dukes should cry, too—for the wives who left them or the fathers who didn't trust them.

The Duke of Sussex sniffed out Amelia in the old nursery. She had known she could not avoid him much longer. She was playing a dangerous game, waiting for Isabelle to help Candover see the error of his years of sadness in adhering to promises that were out of date and just plain wrong.

When Sussex came through the door, Calliope took one look at his face and knew a lit explosive when she saw it.

"I do believe the archbishop wants to practice putting on the south lawn," Calliope said, and did not wait for a reply as she sprinted from the brightly lit chamber.

Dust motes floated in the rays of sunlight from the open window. And the symphony of birds celebrating morning's return filled the air.

"I understand the Duchess of March has ordered her affairs to be packed and she is taking her leave," Sussex said. "I assume you will feel compelled to go with her."

"That's what one does when employed, Your Grace," Amelia said.

He snorted. "We both know that is a farce. Calliope needs a governess like Candover needs a nursemaid. Miss Little could rule the world."

Amelia smiled for the first time in a long time. "Women should rule the world."

He pointed a finger at her. "Don't get any ideas."

And then he ran out of steam and she would not break the silence. Instead, she pleated her hands like any good servant and patiently waited for the inevitable crack of composure.

"So, the thing of it is . . ." He cleared his throat and recollected his thoughts. "Look here, I won't let you go until you tell me what the hell happened that night at Prinny's bloody Carleton House of All Things Bad. I know you had a reason to do what you did. And I know it must have been a good reason."

"And why do you know that?"

"Because you're a bloody saint. Everyone agrees. But you've taken it too far. No one likes a martyr."

"I'm not a martyr. I'm simply someone who knows how to repay a debt."

"What kind of debt?" He jumped at the unintended clue.

"Can't you guess?"

"Well, obviously something grave. You married me because it was something so serious you required the protection of my position."

She gripped her hands. She knew how to deflect questions. She'd invented the art. What had possessed her to say something about debt? "There is nothing you could possibly do that would be so awful that you would need my name." His face drained of color. "Unless . . . Did you kill someone?"

She went still. And then lifted her chin.

"Were you asked to kill someone in payment of some *debt*?"

"No!"

"Someone was blackmailing you. I smell it. Tell me who it is. I shall thrash him and then I will kill him. Who—"

"No one was blackmailing me," she inserted.

"But you killed someone." It was said without judgment.

This was the beginning of the end, she sensed. "Yes."

"Are you going to tell me why or not?"

She swallowed against the lump in her throat. It was not her place to tell Candover's secret. But she could admit her own wrongdoing. "I'm not the saint you think I am. But I *was* protecting myself."

"And?"

"And a man was advancing on me after threatening me, and I grabbed a weapon which I did not think was primed and loaded."

"He was an evil man," Sussex said, disgusted. "No man of good character threatens a female."

The balm of kindness invaded her. "Indeed," she replied.

"Was this the mysterious man found opposite Barry?" he asked softly.

"Yes."

"It is not like you to allow another person to take the blame for your actions. Clearly this was someone else's idea. Bloody, sodding hell. Did Candover do this behind my back? He's always had it out for me. The man is the master of deception, I tell you. Can lie through his teeth."

She started. "No!" Too late did she see the glint of untruth in his eye. He was spouting all sorts of nonsense to push her to reveal all. She gritted her teeth.

He sighed loudly. "You know, you are not the only one who is alone in the world. I am, too. I'm an only child. I know loneliness." He looked vastly ill at ease disclosing this, and now he was genuine. "But sometimes you have to trust in someone. Confide in someone. Let someone help you. Let me be the one."

"All right," she finally murmured. "I will ask one favor of you, since I will tell you my plans."

"Yes?"

"Please be kind enough to inform Candover everything I will tell you. Tell him that I have saved most of my wages over the years, and along with all my references from him, his sisters, and now Her Grace, I will do very well in Scotland. No one is to worry about me. But no one is to know where I am, for I will not place all of you at risk by association if all of this comes out later on." She paused. "I have one last favor."

"I haven't agreed to the first request," he said like a bear of a grouch.

Was this the gentleman who had truly charmed half the ladies in London?

"Oh go ahead. I'll do almost anything you want as long as you agree to my last request," he said, disgruntled.

She changed the course of the conversation. Deep in her heart, she feared she would not deny him. Indeed, she had loved him from afar for so long she could not remember when it started. "When you said you were an only child? That you understood loneliness?"

"What about it?" His face flushed.

"Are you truly lonely?"

He stared at her. His silence confirmed it.

"You said that you have to trust in someone," she said softly. "Also have someone in your life to whom you can confide. Let someone do the same. And I think you were speaking about what you need, not what I need. The person who can provide it is not the person you imagine." She pressed onward. "It's Candover. Please insist he should do that, too. With you, Edward. I'm not asking. I am begging. I've only ever begged someone one other time in my life. Please. Do this— for you and for him. Do not relent."

It was the first time she had used his given name.

"All right," he replied quietly. She bowed her head.

"I'll put him in thumbscrews if necessary," he whispered, lifting her chin. "But, my darling, I need more than one confidante. And ladies are far better at it than gentlemen. Let me be yours, Amelia," he urged her. "For the love of God, let me help you."

She raised her eyes to meet his. "Why?"

"Because, well, there is something about you."

When he did not go on, she pushed him. "Yes?"

"It's maddening. Whenever I saw you with Candover's sisters in the past, I had the strongest desire to either earn your respect or kiss you senseless."

She started. "I know what it is," she said with a faint smile.

"And what is that?"

"I am the only one you cannot charm."

Finally a flicker of humor entered his eyes. "There is that. But lately . . ."

"Lately, what?"

He took a step closer and bent down to whisper in her ear, "Lately, I've had more the desire to strangle you."

She stood stock-still. "Perfectly understandable, given—"

Her thought was cut short when he suddenly took her in his arms and lowered his lips to hers.

A wave of wickedness flooded her passionate Scottish heart. She had never been kissed before, and when it started, she feared she would never be able to stop.

His hands caressed her head and expertly removed the pins that always irritated her from the tight chignon she artlessly did herself each morning.

And as her locks of hair fell to her shoulders, he lowered his lips to nuzzle the crook of her neck. Tiny shivers ran down her body.

"So, my love," he whispered in her ear, "do you prefer the rack or the cage? I fear you're in for one or the other, maybe even both . . . if you do not marry me."

She giggled. And then stopped. She'd never heard such a childish sound come from her throat.

"Do that again," he groaned.

And she did. It tickled her throat and allowed a trickle of light into her soul. "Yes," she said, "I will."

And she proceeded to kiss him as she had imagined she would all those years in the little bed and simple bedroom at Candover's seat in Derbyshire. She rather feared as she gave herself with abandon that she would never, ever see it again. But change, she had learned, was good. Very good, indeed.

He settled her into the crook of his arms and began a very long, slow perusal of her neck and far, far below anything that could be remotely described as proper by a Scottish abigail, but not anything bordering passionate enough for a duchess of the realm. "Edward?"

"Yes? Obviously I'm not doing this as well as I should. You must concentrate, I tell you." His hand delved somewhere very intimate.

"I love you," she said softly, the lilt of her native tongue in evidence.

"Ah," he replied, "that makes it very convenient, for I love you, too."

He kissed her again, and she tasted . . . was it *bacon*? She *loved* bacon.

"But I also," he continued, pressing his lips to different parts of her body between each endearment, "cherish you. Adore you. Revere you. Cannot live a single day without you. Need you. God, I will never, ever get enough of you. Come closer, damn you. And whisper in my ear all the other secrets you're hiding in that head of yours. It's the rack and my tongue if you don't. I know burdens when I see them, and I'll be damned if I'll face down that icicle Candover without the fire and brimstone of facts to melt his arse."

Amelia stared at the goodness in his eyes and wondered how long she would be able to hide the truth. He was not a martyr or a saint. He was practical and loving, and charming to a fault. He would not toss and turn at night wondering if he should not accept the Sussex duchy when there was no other Godwin to accept the title. And he would love to know that Candover was his brother. He would laugh for a month straight at the irony, slap Candover on the back and call him "brother" at every private opportunity. And Candover would pretend to hate it, but secretly want it, and happiness would replace the dullness in his heart. But gazing into Edward's green, green eyes, she just could not bring herself to break a confidence. And she had no doubt Edward Godwin would figure it out in under a fortnight.

"Edward," she whispered.

"Yes, my darling love?"

"Where is this rack?"

"Come closer, my little lamb, and I shall show you." He locked the door behind them and proceeded to show her and tell her all about racks, and tongues, and ratcheting up tension, and biting on wood to not scream and alert the maids or footmen patrolling the halls of his bloody crumbling remnant from the Crusades. No one saw either of them for the rest of the day—or knew where they were.

Except for the bevy of grinning servants who knew everything about everybody, especially their master, and especially when it concerned good news in the offing.

And Miss Primrose was very, very good news, considering the other demanding female guests they served during this House Party that Would Not End.

Chapter 16

Isabelle drifted in a haze of dreams, luxuriating in one of the favorite scents of her childhood. There was nothing like the sweet, pungent tang of freshly dried hay. She pushed against all thoughts of him even in her dreams. She knew how to protect her heart. She'd been doing it so long it was second nature. And so she dozed, allowing exhaustion to overtake her until the unmistakable human crush of human footsteps awakened her with a start.

She opened her eyes to find Vere Sturbridge's shadow falling across her.

"Hello, sleeping beauty," he murmured.

"Hello," she said simply, not moving.

"How lovely to find you here," he continued, "and not the escaped cow."

"I've never been mistaken for a cow," she replied without any humor.

He sat on his knees and picked a piece of hay from her forehead. "Would you prefer I leave you to your thoughts?"

Suddenly, rays of sunlight burst through the myriad small openings above them. The clouds had dissipated.

"No," she said, and sat up

"Would you like me to listen?"

His quiet words were like a balm to her frayed nerves. And she suddenly realized that since the day she met him many months ago at her first ball in London, the Duke of Barry had always been very kind and calm. "I'm certain searching for your cow would be far more entertaining."

He laughed and settled beside her. "You don't know this particular cow. She thinks she's a bull. She would have been a good weapon against the French."

She felt a smile tug at her lips. "Tell me about the years you spent in uniform. What it was like to be a Rifleman."

And he did. He told her all about the excitement of joining a regiment, the boredom of training, the terror the night before the first battle, which only grows with the next battle.

"It was as if one knew that each time you survived you were that much closer to having your luck run out," he said gently. "But these are not things fit for your years."

"How old are you, Barry?"

"Three and twenty. A very old man."

She laughed. "Very." But she could see the lines about his eyes. He wore the telltale signs of the toll of war.

He turned wistful. "But I feel twice that age. That, and very, very lucky."

"Some days I feel twice my age, too, and I do not have war to blame it on," she admitted.

"Why were you crying?" he asked gently. "Do you want to tell me?"

There was something about him, such obvious compassion and empathy, that it invited a desire to confide and lay down one's burdens. "I miss my father. And my mother," she murmured.

"Ah, understandable. I know that feeling well."

He pressed a stray lock of her hair away from her face. "I thought it was something different."

"What did you think?"

"It had something to do with Candover. I hope I am not intruding," he added gently.

"No," she said, "I know what everyone thinks. That there is something between us. That we will one day marry. But that is not the case. We will not suit."

"I see."

She knew he was giving her the chance to unburden her soul if she wanted to—or not.

"I suggested we marry earlier this summer," she said, "but he did not think it a suitable match. And later, when he felt it his duty to offer for me, I finally understood that he was right. We will not suit. I turned him down."

Barry's kind eyes, too old for his years, studied her.

And then a breath hitched in her side. James's words would forever haunt her if she did not ask another gentleman's opinion. But she could never—

"Isabelle?"

She met his steady gaze.

"It's all right. Whatever happened to put that look on your face could not be so terrible. I will confide that I've witnessed humanity at its worst. You did not harm anyone, did you?"

His words struck her. She had only harmed herself. "No."

He waited.

"I've done something irreversible. Something that would disgust any gentleman who knew."

He took her hand and squeezed it gently. "Men who would stand in judgment of something, I am embarrassed to say, they might have done as well—are not really gentlemen, are they, Isabelle? And I daresay your intuition will guide you well. I assure you that you are every bit as wonderful as ever, in my eyes at least."

She did not trust herself to speak and so she nodded instead. She retrieved her hand from his, unable to keep the intimacy after such embarrassment.

"But are you certain, Isabelle, that you really, truly do not want to marry him?"

"If you are being diplomatic and asking me if I am letting pride get in the way, the answer is no. While a marriage of convenience is what I will someday seek, a marriage to Candover is impossible and would not bring happiness to either of us. Of that I am certain," she rushed on before he could comment. "Now you must reveal a confidence to me."

"Of course," he said. "It is only fair after you've been so candid and brave in your honesty. And it must be equally important. Let me see . . . All right. Since you're a member of the entourage, I can place absolute faith in your loyalty."

"Of course," she murmured. "And thank you, Barry, for allowing me to confide in you."

"I'm honored you placed your trust in me, Isabelle," he replied. "Now do you remember how I woke up across from a dead stranger—that night at Carleton House?"

"Yes," she said.

"There was an ancient jewel-encrusted pistol I've never seen before in my hands—while my own snub-nosed weapon was still tucked in my vest. And . . . well . . ." His voice faded.

"Go on," she urged.

"This is not a fit subject for a lady's ears."

"Pretend I'm a man. I had all femininity drummed

out of me by my father by the time I was ten, I assure you."

He looked at her, really looked at her, and smiled. "Not true. You are one of the most lovely and admirable ladies of my acquaintance."

"That's what I get for fishing for compliments."

"I will be more specific." His finger returned to the lock he had pushed behind her ear. "Your hair is like silk, your eyes are the color of finest Scottish whiskey, your complexion like parchment, and your ears are like seashells . . ."

A gurgle of laughter escaped from her throat. "Really?"

"Hell . . . I'm no good at this. I do better describing weapons, I'm afraid."

She liked the Duke of Barry very much. She had always thought him overly quiet, but it was not that. He obviously did not talk very much while in company with many other people. But one on one? She smiled. "We've strayed off the subject. You were about to say something not fit for my . . . seashells."

When he smiled, the corners of his eyes crinkled, and eased the battlefield weariness from his face.

"I was bleeding when I awoke in Carleton House. Nothing serious. A ball had nicked me." He tapped his side, a few inches above his waist. "And yet . . . there was no other pistol in sight."

"Does the Prince Regent know these details?"

"Of course. I saw him privately that same awful morning after he sent everyone away. It was hideous—I could remember nothing of the night. And the prince was his usual self, blustering on and on when in fact he could remember nothing as well."

She raised her brows. "Yes, he does that very well. And?"

"And we both concluded someone else pulled the trigger. And in fact, the ball lodged in the stranger probably nicked me first since there was no ball lodged in the wall behind me. The guilty party staged the scene and crept away."

A glimmer of an idea passed through her so quickly she could not grasp it. "But what of the man who died? I know Prinny has hushed it up, but—"

He brought his finger to his lips, the signal that he would tell her a secret. "I should not tell you this, Isabelle. I swore an oath to the Prince Regent. And I'm a military man. But I trust you. You have more honor and dignity and good character than most likely all of the royal entourage combined."

She bowed her head.

"Good. Negating a compliment does neither party justice. So, the thing of it is this. The man was not dead after all. Although . . . well, it's a tricky thing, you see. He's dead now."

She shook her head. "So he was not dead, but he is dead?"

"Precisely. You are very quick."

"Thank you," she said, amused. "So, he died of the wound?"

"Yes," Barry said, "and no."

She waited for him to explain.

"He died that same day, trying to escape from a Carleton House bedchamber window. As the Prince Regent explained it to me, the man was placed in a chamber to recover while he was still insensible. The ball had entered below the collarbone, near the shoulder, and he'd obviously lost a fair amount of blood. He must have woken, decided he didn't want to be questioned, and attempted to leave via knotted bed linen. But he must have lost his grip because . . . are you certain you want to hear?"

She rolled her eyes. "This is worse than a gothic mystery. Go on."

"He fell and broke his neck."

"But who was he?"

"The all-important question. Given the mood of the people in London, Prinny has hushed up the affair. But obviously I cannot rest easy until the entire sordid mess is sorted out. I've arranged for every newspaper in England to eventually be delivered to me. I've been scanning every single one, looking for reports of missing people, without any luck." He paused. "So now you know everything."

A quarter of an hour later Isabelle took her leave of Barry, her heart lighter than it had been in months. She only hoped that one day she would return the favor. He was the kindest, most understanding gentleman of honor. He was solid, and of excellent character.

She esteemed him greatly.

James Fitzroy galloped his gray horse over a stile separating two fields. Where in bloody hell was she? He had privately searched Sussex's freezing abbey for an hour before finally stooping to ask Calliope Little to help him. Three hours later and still she was missing. And now Calliope was worried.

And hell hath no fury like Miss Little in a worry.

He'd had to use promises of future outings to prod her back into the confines of the abbey's library, where not one guest would ever dare to tread for fear of falling into a coma for all the books on sermons found on its vast shelves. Five hundred years of religion tended to leave their mark.

Calliope was delighted. Her favorite topic was redemption these days, now that she had covered all matters of sin and penance.

He had left her to her future and mounted his horse.

God, what had he said to Isabelle? Oh, he knew what he had said, and what he'd done. He didn't know what he could do or say to erase the cool, remoteness that was filling her, so like his own, but he knew one thing.

He had to find her.

And he would not stop until he did. He would do whatever she wanted. He was done trying to control destiny. He would not rest until he saw her happy—the reserve gone from her beautiful golden eyes.

He pulled back on his horse's reins and sat back in the saddle to bring his mount to a halt at the crest of the grassy knoll. Barry's estate was yonder, a patchwork of fields separated by thick hedgerows of yellow gorse and prickled native species of plants that provided cover to rabbits, birds, and all manner of small animals.

It had been so long since he had allowed himself the pleasure of getting lost in the green avenues of nature. What he would give to turn back time and take a long walk with Isabelle, as they had so many times on her father's estate. But then her father's eyes, his hands, so thin due to the ravages of his long illness, gripped his, while he begged James to do his bidding concerning his only daughter, haunted his mind.

A movement caught his eye. And he had found her. Walking across a field, sunshine radiated from her face as she turned her head toward the sun. She was oblivious to his presence. God, she was so beautiful, so vibrant and full of life.

A moment later she looked in his direction and stopped in her tracks. And then plowed forward, obviously determined to ignore him, and quite possibly give him the cut direct as she passed him.

He stayed rooted to the spot.

She crossed his path but halted a dozen strides later. "You are wrong, you know."

"Good afternoon, Isabelle."

She turned again to face him. "I will be just fine. You can stop worrying about me. You can take off that hair shirt of guilt concerning what happened."

"I'll do whatever you ask of me, Isabelle."

"Perfect," she replied. "By the way, Barry asked me to tell you, if I saw you before he, that the Prince Regent sent him a letter asking about you. His Royal Highness would like you to write to him immediately about the progress of the house party—and more importantly, your progress on the list of potential brides I gave you."

"Damn all lists to hell," he ground out. "Enough with these idiotic lists, Isabelle."

"He asked, not I." She smiled, but it did not reach her eyes.

"I am glad you went to Barry," he said softly. "He is one of the most honorable young gentlemen of my acquaintance."

"We are in complete agreement," she replied.

"For once I could never offer you what he can."

She walked back toward him until she was within arm's length of him. "You're absolutely right. But don't hide from the truth of it. You choose to live on an island in the sea of humanity. I tossed you a life raft and you refused it."

He dismounted, his body so tense he found it difficult to get off his horse with any grace. "For Christ-sakes, Isabelle. Was it not earlier today that I insisted we marry? I still do. I told you I won't allow another man to raise a possible child of mine."

"There won't be a child, I'm certain," she insisted.

"How do you know?"

Her face colored. "I know. I should know without any doubt very shortly." She paused. "If history is any indication, tonight."

"Your stomach pains you?" He looked at her with concern.

"I am not going to talk about this," she ground out.

"Have you forgotten I have five sisters? I daresay I know all about it. There's no cause for embarrassment. Soon your mind will be at ease."

"No, James," she said evenly. "Don't put words in my mouth. It is you who will be relieved. I want a child. Many children, in fact. Children who will fill up the empty halls of my childhood home, which is barren now except for me, surrounded by far too many servants quietly waiting to serve far more than one young woman. God willing, I want to be sur-rounded by family. And that will start with a hus-band who truly wants me, children and all the myriad complications and heartbreak, and infinite joy in a shared future. With a husband who will want me just as I am."

He stared down into her passionate expression, so

certain, so determined, so courageously fearless . . .

So like her father.

He teetered on the cliff of duty, nearly fell into the thin air of recklessness—foregoing duty for truth. For letting down the walls so someone could see who he was and love him wholeheartedly, accepting all the complexities of his unique humanity.

In his mind's eye a thousand of the scenes of the life she wanted flew by—her next to him, their children all around them. And he was kissing her, damn the impropriety of it all. The children were whooping and hollering. And yet, his hands did not reach for her. They were tethered by invisible past promises to the father of his heart—her father.

He closed his eyes against the promise of it.

And when he reopened them she was gone.

Chapter 17

He had not appeared at supper the night before. But Isabelle would be damned if she would not hold up her head and attend every last gathering of this infernal house party the next day.

She was leaving tomorrow.

But tonight she was still on display, still gritting her teeth and having a *delightfully good* time.

After a full day—archery with Calliope, a walk to the small village with the other house guests—she again found herself seated to the right of Sussex at the long polished dining table with all the rest of the nattering guests, who were finally showing the inevitable signs of boredom from having spent too much time in each other's presence.

Barry had seated himself on her other side and had been everything kind and attentive to her in his gentle, reserved way. She was now certain that men who had gone to battle and stared death in the face were far more compassionate than others.

She attempted to ignore James, who'd had the good sense to completely ignore protocol for perhaps the first time in his life and seated himself as far away from her as possible. Each time she glanced in his direction, he was conversing with Mary Haverty, who was across from him. His forehead showed no signs of tension, and Mary was all easy charm. Isabelle envisioned—as only a female mind can in the space of an instant— Mary as his wife. They were the same age, they had grown up together, Mary would be the perfect duchess, and she was in desperate need of a husband, given her dwindling funds.

"Penny?" Barry intruded on her thoughts.

"Who knew there were so many ways to serve bacon?" she replied with a smile.

Sussex interrupted them. "She likes bacon." He nodded toward Amelia, who was on his other side.

It was the first time Isabelle had seen them together as a couple in public. Their passion and love for each other was almost painful to witness. Oh, Amelia had not a hair out of place, and the arch of her back was as strict as always, but there was a certain knowing look in her eyes, a slight blush on the crest of her cheeks that gave away the truth: here was a woman who loved and was loved in return in full measure.

Oh, they had not announced a single thing. And no one else in the house party would guess, but Isabelle just knew. And she felt a welling of happiness for the two of them.

"Will you honor me with a stroll in the garden after dinner?"

"Of course," she replied. She was glad to escape the rigors of polite conversation with ladies who insisted of speaking of naught but the weather, the newest style of hats, and the eligibility of every gentleman within a three-day drive.

Out of doors, as she gazed at the stars above them competing against the small lanterns half hidden in the branches of the tall trees interspersed between the landscaped terraces, it felt eerily familiar. Like the evening of the Allens' ball in London.

She glanced sideways at Barry beside her. He was nothing like the seaweed-scented rear admiral. Vere Sturbridge, the Duke of Barry, was tall and handsome. He had a wide, thin mouth, a broad Roman nose, and longish sandy hair. His noble profile spoke of generations of aristocracy. He was a bit lean of frame, no doubt due to his war years, but he had that impossible quality difficult to define.

He had good character.

"I'm glad to have this private moment with you," he murmured, his voice deep. "I've been given leave to pass along a confidence."

She tilted her head to see him better in the encroaching darkness.

"It will also bring you ease, I think. It certainly did to me." He halted and faced her. "It was as I suspected but would not say without proof. Amelia Primrose was the one who shot the man."

"I beg your pardon?"

"It was an act of self-defense. He was advancing on her, had threatened to, uh, possess her."

She looked into the night sky as a flock of mysterious birds flew to some unknown roost. "I knew it had to be bad. That was why she married Sussex—for protection."

"She admitted all in a note, which I burned. She did not say it, but we all know that Candover's sister Verity Fitzroy was there that night, and I am certain she was the one who concocted the entire idea."

Isabelle bit back her agreement. She adored Verity. But really, this was outrageous.

"Miss Primrose begged my pardon most ardently."

"I don't need to ask if you will forgive her."

"Of course I did. I took her aside just before dinner. If only she had come to me sooner. I could have relieved her guilt by explaining that she had not killed him, merely wounded him."

"I wish she had trusted me enough to confide in me," Isabelle said wistfully.

"*I* am confiding in you," he said quietly. "And I hope you will always give me leave to do so." In a natural motion, he grasped one of her hands with his own. "My dear Isabelle, I've been thinking quite a bit about our conversation of the other day."

"You were so very kind to me."

"I would say the reverse is true, my dear."

"I will never be able to express how much I appreciate the kindness and comfort you provided that hour, Barry."

"Vere . . . please." His voice was deep and low, and felt like a comforting blanket on her well-hidden frayed nerves.

She looked at him.

"No one ever uses my given name. I should like you to use it."

She swallowed. "Of course. I should be delighted . . . It's such a lovely name . . . Vere."

He squeezed her gloved fingers lightly. "As I said, I've been thinking quite a bit. And I've come to several conclusions." He glanced over her shoulder and then urged her a few steps closer to the lanterns under an ash tree.

She paused, uncertain. "This sounds serious."

He scrutinized her face and smiled. "It is."

She swallowed awkwardly and hoped he had not noticed. "Go on."

"Are you truly inviting me to tell you these serious thoughts, Isabelle?"

"I hope you feel you can tell me anything, Vere. Especially after the other day."

He seemed to make up his mind. "I've decided that it is, indeed, very likely that love can blossom when rooted in trust, and friendship," he murmured.

His eyes were so expressive it was difficult to stare long at them. She glanced at their joined hands. "And you said you were no good at poetry," she replied.

He chuckled. "Do you want me to go on?"

A small prick of hesitation itched her mind. She ignored it. "Yes."

"We are both of us at a crossroads in life. And it would be very easy to each go our own way." He squeezed her fingers again comfortingly. "We will always share a deep friendship, of that I have no doubt. But perhaps we should not go our separate ways." He stopped.

She went still, uncertainty flooding her.

"Indeed. And perhaps, after careful considerations of all the reasons that need not be said for they are not romantic, we should form an alliance—" He halted mid-speech and shook his head with a harsh laugh. "It is very clear to me and probably to you even more so that I haven't the faintest clue how to make a proper proposal of marriage, Isabelle. It's just that I like you very much."

"You're doing very well actually." She couldn't help but smile.

He exhaled. "I'm a lucky fellow, then."

"I would say I feel precisely the same way. Very lucky to know you. I esteem you greatly," she confided.

He cocked his head to one side. "That is all well

and good, but you have not been kind enough to offer an answer."

She paused, trying to feel her way in the morass of uncertainty. "If I were to agree," she said quietly, "there would have to be absolute truth between us."

"I would not expect otherwise," he murmured.

"It must be understood very clearly . . ." She paused before rushing the difficult words that must be said. " . . . that ours would be above all a marriage of convenience. Between very good friends, as you said."

"But do you believe as I do that love might blossom from deep affection?"

"I do not know. No one can predict the future." She nodded slightly. "But neither of us must expect more, really, because that might only lead to great disappointment." The soft skittering of a little night creature over leaves passed nearby. "I think I've come to finally understand what generations before us have always advised and practiced."

"And what is that?" he urged, a small smile lurking at the corners of his handsome mouth.

"That marriage is a contract to combine property and produce heirs." She felt awkward telling this man, quite possibly her future husband, these things.

"And?"

"And love is *not* a contract. It's a feeling that cannot be controlled by a piece of paper."

"Ah . . ." He looked at her gravely. "But love is an action. And perhaps with enough practice, and given our mutual respect for each other . . ."

"Love is an action. I agree wholeheartedly. In fact, as far as I have witnessed, we see eye-to-eye on everything. And respect and kindness would rule us—which can only promote happiness."

He smiled, and Isabelle realized she had not often seen him do that.

He turned at the sound of distant voices and laughter. A handful of Sussex's houseguests had apparently decided to take advantage of the lovely late-summer night as well and were stepping onto the stone landing, leading to the terraces.

He returned his attention to her and she shyly did the same.

"Yes," she said quietly. "I accept your offer, Vere. I shall be honored to be your duchess, and I shall endeavor to make you happy."

An expression of good cheer and satisfaction formed on his even features. "That will not be difficult, Isabelle. You already do."

Isabelle was still in disbelief. She would spend many if not most of the rest of her days in this gentleman's company. With any luck, she would bear the future Duke of Barry *and* March. Her father, were he still alive, would weep for happiness. Yes, one day soon, if the stars aligned, there would finally be a male child to carry the March duchy.

And the same moment she broke her gaze from his, he bent down and pressed a warm kiss on her cheek. "Will you grant me leave to announce it, my dear?"

A small pit of fear formed in the back of her throat.

"Too late," he said with a chuckle as a night shadow zigzagged toward them.

She looked up and tried to make out the guests coming toward them against the glare of the lantern overhead.

She remembered to smile as the people approached.

But she could not hold it in place a moment later.

"**J**ames," Mary said, her cat green eyes sparking in the sconce's candlelight, "it's so very warm. Shall we suggest a turn in the garden to the others? I should like to take the night air."

He immediately deferred to her wishes. There was something about Lady Mary Haverty that made it next to impossible to deny her anything. Thank God she did not ask for much more than the mundane.

And so they collected a party of eight to join them for a tour. Of course Calliope, the archbishop, who still refused to speak to him (which might just be a blessing), Sussex, Amelia, and two other ladies and gentlemen whose names and titles James could not be bothered to remember, stepped outside into the moonlight. He was glad Isabelle was not of the party. It was just too difficult at present.

He saw them in the distance before anyone else. Without thought he attempted to divert the attention of his party, pointing out the stars in the clear night sky.

He felt a tugging on his coattails.

"Something is going on over there," Calliope whispered far too loudly.

All conversation came to a screeching halt.

"Lovely," Mary muttered, then attempted to drag the attention of all the others back to the constellations, without success.

A small hand slipping into his own dragged him back to reality.

"Come with me," Calliope insisted. "We need to talk."

Words designed to strike fear into the hearts of all males.

He went along with her like a cow to slaughter.

She led him to the other side of the terrace.

"Go and get her before it's too late," Calliope whispered.

"I can't imagine what you—"

"You know exactly what I mean," Calliope said, rolling her eyes. "If you don't, then I will. I'm still her companion. It's in my list of duties."

He looked at her.

"Keep all wolves at bay."

"There are no wolves in England."

She snorted. "Perhaps, but there are handsome Riflemen. Oh, pleeease go and get her."

He gave one nod, turned suddenly and took the stairs two at a time.

If only he had been more coherent he would have noticed that everyone on the terrace took that as permission to follow him.

And as he reached the outer rim of light cast by the lantern they stood under, he heard the words he had always known he would hear. The ones that would be like a knife to the heart.

"Will you grant me leave to announce it, my dear?"

And a moment later . . .

"Too late," Barry said, followed by a deep chuckle, filled with the warm knowledge that he had won the great lottery of the marriage mart.

James could not breathe. Could not make his jaw unclench. He finally became aware of Mary's words near his ear.

"James, look at me. Please."

He couldn't move a muscle to save his life.

He felt a tugging sensation and finally allowed Mary Haverty to drag him a few long yards away from the others.

Some of the gentlemen were already slapping Barry on the back. And the ladies were embracing Isabelle.

A part of him died.

They were just so damned beautiful together. And so perfectly right together. He was only three years her senior, and would protect her, and cherish her in every way. He would ensure her happiness until the day he died. Yes, Barry was the gentleman who his godfather would have chosen for his only child.

He was certain.

James felt beads of cold sweat forming on his spine and on his brow. It was suddenly hotter than blazes.

And they would join portfolios of properties and improve Barry's with Isabelle's fortune until such time as they began prospering on their own.

James could see it all.

The air he had finally sucked into his heated lungs was near to bursting. But he stayed. He stayed and watched all the well wishers offer their congratulations and wander back to the terrace, chattering with excitement.

He unrooted first one foot and then the other to walk toward the official new couple.

Barry made it easy for him by taking over. "I shall ever be grateful to you, Candover, for presenting me to Isabelle at that ball in London."

James bowed without a word.

Mary rushed in. "Oh, Isabelle, James and I are overcome with happiness in your joy. Do let me offer my congratulations, Barry."

He felt Barry's hand on his arm. "I promise to keep

her happy. I am sorry I did not ask you for her hand—as I know her father tasked you with overseeing her happiness."

His head felt disengaged from his body as he swiveled to look at her. He had guessed this might happen. But now he realized he had not truly thought it would.

He almost jumped forward and ripped off Barry's head when the young former Rifleman leaned down and pressed a kiss to Isabelle's face, pale in the moonlight.

It was only later, in the private hell that was his chambers, did he thank God that Mary had been beside him to drag his sorry carcass away.

Her small voice still rang in his ears. "I know, James. I know."

He had not seen Mary's own pain through the haze of his wild agony.

Chapter 18

The Duke of Sussex had stared hard at Barry and Isabelle under the lantern light. Something was off. They had appeared far too comfortable with each other.

It was too ill mannered to suggest it. One just did not say that sort of thing after someone announced their intention to voluntarily take on a leg shackle. Even if it was to Isabelle, one of the dearest, most decent ladies in the world.

He turned his gaze toward the love of his life— Amelia Primrose. Amelia Godwin, almost Duchess of Sussex, whom he would officially wed as soon as he could figure out some bloody secret she would not tell him herself.

Lord, if this was a Scottish way of doing things, he was in for a lifetime of frustrations that would try the patience of a saint.

Why must this figuring out business be a condition prior to marriage? He wanted to strangle her.

He'd never wanted to strangle an angel before.

And yet . . . if he looked deep within himself—the part he rarely examined—he knew it was just the opposite.

Yes, Edward Godwin had been feeling out of sorts the entire day. Not surprising given the fact that he'd been feeling similarly the entire blasted summer. Ever since that infamous night at Carleton House.

But he was feeling particularly peckish today. And he was never peckish. By the time supper was served and not one of Cook's endless series of dishes failed to interest, he knew it was serious.

The time was ripe for a moment of truth. And Edward would be damned if an Englishman couldn't take on a Scot and win. Edward linked arms with Amelia and began to stalk away in the direction of the vegetable garden, ignoring the rest of the onlookers who all drifted away after Barry's announcement.

"Come on, then," he insisted. "Hurry." Amelia stumbled and he reached down and scooped her up to carry her in his haste.

"Edward," she scolded. "Put me down."

"No," he said, stubborn as Calliope.

He reached the tomato vines and unceremoniously put her down.

"I figured something out," he stated.

He looked down and studied her delicate gloved fingers

resting on the dark blue superfine fabric of his evening wear. His shirt was startlingly white in the moonlight.

"Yes?"

"I'm very intuitive you know." He was stalling and they both knew it. "I am also excellent at mathematics."

She brushed at an invisible spot on his lapels. "I will concede that you are most likely good at any subject you set your mind on," she said.

"My cousin has been the bane of my life."

She started.

"You probably don't know him."

She refused to open her mouth.

And that is when he knew. He kept going, like a bird dog on a grouse's scent. "Percy Godwin's greatest aim in life was to somehow manage to become the Duke of Sussex. He had only one thing standing in his way. Me, of course."

Her eyes were huge.

"My steward wrote to me while I was in Cornwall, attending Kress's house party, which was just as exciting as this one." He shook his head. It seemed such a long time ago. "In any case, my steward informed me that Percy had called on me just after I left for Carleton House, but obviously missed me. And my butler informed him I was at Carleton House with the rest of the royal entourage."

Still she said not a word.

"Percy told him, insisted really, that he had something to inform me. Was quite nasty about it. The butler informed him that I was away to Carleton House to attend Candover's nuptials. Of course, all of this was lost on me at the time." He shook his head at her and placed a finger on the tip of her nose. "Yes, I was completely preoccupied at the time due to some-one, yes someone—Verity Fitzroy—who arrived to whisper in my ear that I was secretly married. To you, my lovely."

She nodded. "And aren't you glad how that turned out?" she whispered.

"But my cousin Percy has never bothered to visit or write to me since then. It's not like him. I usually am forced to suffer his person at least three or four times a quarter. I have not heard from him in two months."

She looked ready to keel over.

"He was the one you shot, wasn't he? He went to Carleton House to find me and you shot him. I'm guessing in self-defense. He was a lecherous old fool, always bothering the house maids. But why were you too afraid to tell me? You didn't think I would censure you because he was my cousin, did you?"

She looked away, misery flooding her lovely even features; even in the darkness he could see.

"No, Edward. It was not that."

"Well, I know you don't have his death on your con-science, since Barry told you he did not die by your hand in the end."

She wrapped her arms about herself and looked at him mutely.

"Come here, my love," he insisted. He wrapped his arms around her small frame and tried to stop the vision of his awful cousin's hands reaching for her. He buried his nose in her hair and breathed deep her lovely rose scent. "Why did you tell me to go to Candover, to insist he should be the person I confide in when needed? And then you begged me to insist he confide in me. You said—"

She interrupted by finishing his thought. "That he needed you and you needed him."

He pressed on. "And you mentioned that you owed a debt and that is why you shot Percy."

It was the most frustrating feeling, Edward thought, when pieces of a puzzle could not be made to fit—even when there were only two pieces left, and two gaps remaining on the puzzle.

"Damn it all, woman. Tell me. Tell—" He stopped. "What has Candover got to do with Percy sodding Godwin? What would Candover confide to me?"

Her eyes were huge in her face as she pushed for more space between them.

"And why does bloody Candover always look at me in that stupid cow-eyed way when he doesn't think I am looking at him? He just did it now when we all saw Barry with Isabelle."

"It's not cow-eyed, in any way. That's completely

undignified. The way he looks at you is with his whole heart exposed or—" She stopped and bit her lower lip.

He loved wheedling things from her. And clearly spouting wildly inappropriate lies was the way to goad her. "And there you have it," he pressed. "It's just as I thought, Candover's in love with me."

Her face crumpled.

His arms went numb at the sight of her expression. "I was making a joke, my love."

She buried her face in his neck cloth and he tightened his arms about her. "May God have mercy on me, Edward, of course he loves you. You are his . . ."

When she wouldn't continue, he supplied an answer. "Sinful, secret passion? Well, with God as my witness, I swear it's unrequited."

"Guess again," she said in a very small voice.

He sighed in annoyance. "I am his relation twenty-five times removed?"

"Much closer," she said in a whisper he had to lean down to hear.

"His cousin in some way? I am not Candover's cousin. I do not have any cousins. Percy was the only one. And I am not his uncle either. So that leaves . . . Well, I would know if he was my brother, so surely—" He stopped.

She said not a word.

He shook her a bit. What in hell kind of madness was she suggesting? A growing ball of uncertainty filled his gut.

Still she made not a sound.

He muttered a curse so blue that his Scottish-soon-to-be-wife didn't understand it. "James Fitzroy is *not* related to me."

"All right," she whispered.

"Oh, for God's sake woman. Is he or isn't he?" He paused, stricken. "Lord, help me. I'm a bloody love child, aren't I? Just tell me please that my mother is my real mother. There is no possible way she is not."

"Of course she is," she whispered.

A wash of images and events in his life flew threw his mind as he desperately tried to make sense of all of this. "Well, I must admit that explains a lot. My father—"

She interrupted, her eyes full of concern. "Candover said he was a kind man."

"He was a devoted father," Sussex assured her. "I loved him. But he hated something I loved." He tapped his finger to her nose again at her concerned expression. "Bacon, for one thing. All meat, really. When I think of all the meals consisting of only vegetables and fruits . . . it's a wonder I don't raze this entire garden."

She relaxed in his arms. "You're taking the news very well. Are you certain you don't feel the need to lie down, have a bit of a crisis to ponder your place in the world?"

He smiled hugely and waggled his brows. "Not at all, my sweet. I've just been elevated leaps and bounds above all of humanity, don't you know? I'm a duke twice over, the Secret Love Child Premier Duke of

Candover and Sussex. Why I'm nearly as exalted as a prince of the realm and—"

Amelia interrupted, "A tad full of oneself. Please tell me when your canonization is complete. I have some stockings I need to mend."

"You may kiss my hand," he said, smiling. He enfolded her even deeper into his arms and took over the job of raining kisses down on her—clearly the only living saint who would ever walk the halls of the abbey.

"I have one favor to ask," she murmured finally between kisses.

He could not get enough of the scent of her, and nosed the nape of her neck. "Yes?"

"Please don't tell him I told you."

"My darling, I refuse to play childish games like that. Gentlemen don't do that—and dukes have an even more strict protocol. I will tell him I know I'm a duke twice over at the most appropriate moment."

"And when is that?" she asked with dry skepticism.

"When he needs to be shocked out of his cool-headed, arrogant senses. Extra points if it's in public."

"Oh, Edward . . . don't you dare."

Chapter 19

"Keep your voice down. You're scaring the horses," Calliope whispered more loudly than an offstage prompter at Drury Lane Theatre.

The audacity of this draconian matron in the form of a fourteen-year-old girl was astounding, James thought as he stood in the older of two tack rooms in Sussex's stables. The dusty chamber, which had quite obviously fallen into disuse, was filled with two hundred years of leather, metal, stuffing, and stitching, and smelled like a thousand years of horse sweat and manure.

"I have not said three words," James replied.

"Yes, you have. You just said six more."

"You are again avoiding the question," he ground out.

"And you are using that tone that Miss Primrose tells me is very unhelpful and does not encourage someone to do what you would like," Calliope stated.

James bit back a retort. He was the premier duke of England, damnation. He could *demand* respect.

She glanced around the edge of the door and then wrinkled her nose as she readjusted her spectacles. "The driver has just snapped the ribbons and the carriage is on the way to the servants' entrance to take up our affairs. Isabelle will be here in a trice. But you won't have much time."

"Calliope Little, what in hell are you suggesting?"

Her eyes widened in false horror. "You are not supposed to curse in front of children. It fosters fear and uncertainty."

"Exactly what I intended," he returned, shuttering his eyes. "I'm leaving."

She gripped his arm with the tenacity of a female who would not be denied. "You promised," she wheedled.

"I agreed to take the air with you before you took your leave for London," he reminded her. "And you said you had something of great importance to confide, something which you still have not endeavored to impart. A fantastic secret, in short." The last he said with all the grace and hauteur for which he was famous. "Now, out with it, minx."

Something caused Calliope to dart a glance back around the door. Grinning, she gashed a great tide of words: "She's coming. Here is your chance. Don't you dare let me down, Sober—I mean, um— Oh, there's no time. The secret is . . . that I've decided these plans regarding the Duke of Barry are just entirely unacceptable. Oh, he's a nice enough man. Very nice, actually. You could learn a few . . ." She looked away, only moderately chastened. "But he won't do. Only you will do."

He snorted with annoyance. "These 'plans,' as you call them, are a bit more than that. They are promises they have made—and a *promise* is a bond never to be broken. And they will suit very well. I am happy for them," he said.

"Liar," she announced. "Why must you be so pig-headed? You love her and she loves you. Don't look at me like you've got an icicle stuck up your . . ."

He gave her a look.

"Ummm . . . Well, you understand, I'm sure. Look, please don't let this happen . . . do something. Surely there must be some royal right to trump Barry since you're the premier duke, not just some everyday, run of the mill duke?" She blinked her enlarged eyes behind her spectacles. "Honestly, sometimes gentlemen are so thick-headed. Why must I do all the thinking?"

He wished he could say he had been completely innocent of Calliope's motive behind her demand to take a tour of the park before she left for Town with Isabelle. He could not say it. "It's discomforting to know that four years from now I will have to play the innocent bystander to the complete havoc you will wreak on that Season's crop of ill-prepared bachelors."

"Oh, don't worry, you won't see any of it. By then you'll be ancient and toothless and Isabelle will be feeding you porridge."

The image was the very same one the old Duke of March had voiced all those years ago as he looked into a half-eaten bowl of mush. Coldness invaded his extremities and he shook his head to rid himself of the memories.

Calliope tugged him from the doorway and they entered the hard-packed dirt aisle of the large stable just as Isabelle left the sunshine beyond the entrance in front of them. She was carrying a hatbox and a book, and as she approached, Candover's gut felt hollow and bottomless as he drank in the beauty of her. She was so full of life and promise. So confident and ready for all that fate would throw at her. He desperately wanted to protect her from the future.

Isabelle stopped short a dozen steps from them. "Calliope?"

"Oh, Isabelle. I've been waiting, just as you asked," she chirped, and tugged him to walk forward to meet Isabelle. "His Grace insisted on accompanying me to have a word. Oh dear," the deceiver of gigantesque proportions continued, "I do believe I've forgotten my—uh—my book. The one the archbishop suggested would be good for—"

"Miss Little?" he interrupted quietly.

"Yes, Your Grace?"

"First, I prefer that if you are going to refer to me as Old Sobersides to everyone else, you will have the courage to say it to my face."

She gulped.

"And second," he continued, "quit while you're ahead. Be back here in a quarter hour."

She nodded with the first sign of deference James had ever seen her exhibit, and then she darted away.

The silence that ensued was so great that the everyday sounds of the stable magnified tenfold. The whine of a mosquito, an unseen horse munching his feed while another stomped a hoof.

He finally breached the distance between them by grasping the strings of the hatbox. "May I?"

"Yes, of course," she said quietly and released her grip.

He placed the white round box on a nearby shelf and offered his arm. After a small hesitation she accepted it and they walked in silence toward the sunshine.

"Isabelle," he finally murmured, "I apologize for—"

"Why are you here?" she interrupted, halting.

He faced her. "I won't insult either of us by suggesting this was Calliope's doing. I am glad for the chance to have a word. I promised your father I would always watch over you, and I'm here in that service."

"More service? Service is a pretty word for duty, is it not? I released you from that office long ago. You are not my keeper, James Fitzroy. I don't need your protection. I never did, and I certainly do not now, and my future husband will consider it a grave insult if it is ever assumed in the future."

"You are correct, Isabelle, of course. Will you accept my apology?"

She hesitated.

"Please," he murmured.

"Why are you really here?"

"Because I wanted to privately offer my very good wishes for your new life. Barry is an immensely fine young gentleman of great character. He will make you a very good husband."

"Of that there is little doubt," she said, lifting her determined chin. "It will be a marriage of kindness and respect. A life of respectability, fulfilling our duties to our forefathers and those who depend on us, and preparing the next generation. That is all we can expect in life, no? It is a very good life, and I shall embrace it wholeheartedly."

"Don't, Isabelle," he said gently.

"Don't what?"

"Don't erect a wall between us, please. I cannot bear it."

She snorted with disdain. "A wall? Me? I am the person erecting a wall? You've built an unscalable *mountain* between yourself and everyone."

"Perhaps," he said. "In the never-ending absurdities

of my long life, the only person who refuses to see the impossibility of the challenge is a fourteen-year-old child with reformation on her mind."

She ignored his jaded humor, intent now that she had been roused. "Oh, I know why it's there. You are certain it will keep out all pain. But it won't, you know."

"So we are sharing views after all?"

"No!" she ground out, and then paused. "Oh, all right, go ahead. There won't be any peace until you get on your pedestal. Do you admit that's what you're doing?"

"I'll admit whatever you like if you'll listen with an open mind."

She impatiently waved her hand in a small circle, indicating he should proceed.

"Loss and change is the great toll in life. And it is inevitable. You must prepare for it. So many are crushed by it. Isabelle?"

"Yes," she said with sadness, but compassion in her eyes.

"Well, I don't want you to feel it. You lose almost everyone in the end. What you see in me is not a mountain as you suggest. It is armor, yes. Ugly battle scars of experience, certainly. But there is also a determined perseverance to carry on no matter what the cost."

"And what is the worst of it?"

"You trust, you give your heart, and then it breaks."

"You're talking about your first fiancée, aren't you?"

"Catharine was merely the first. The loss of friendship with Abshire, someone I trusted with my whole heart, second. Then my mother and father, and along with it the destruction of everything I held true about my parents. My father's life was a living, breathing lie, and through no fault of his own. And again, it was all due to loss."

A scudding cloud in the sky cast a shadow on her delicately beautiful face. "But he was happy living this lie, despite his loss."

"Of course not. But he ensured everyone else's happiness."

"Except yours in the end," she nearly shouted. "Yours. He destroyed you. And do you know why? He could not live out his entire life behind a facade. A mountain. Because everyone has an innate need for at least one person on this earth to know them. He needed someone to know the real him—not the one he showed the rest of the world, James. His denial of who he was made him selfish, and in the end he took it out on the one person who most revered this false self he presented to the world. You."

His shoulder became limp, and he nearly toppled over.

"Don't be like him, James. I know enough of you to know that you have nothing to hide. You must find someone who you feel at ease with to let them love all of you. The best of you and the slightly impossible parts." She smiled the smallest bit. "Like this stubborn streak of yours. Your refusal to accept that you can't always be right. And that you cannot control everything as you would like."

She was correct. He knew it. He was very willing to tell her. "Of course, you are correct, my Isabelle." He studied her beautiful face. But she had forgotten the one part of him that was his identity. *He would not break his word. Ever.* Everyone might need to be known by at least one other person trodding along the godforsaken corridors of life, but one had to also have at least one core value. One facet of character that could not be shattered. He would not break his promise to the two gentlemen who had raised him—one with lies and unkindness, and the other with respect, and *love.* "Isabelle, my dear. I shall promise to do your bidding."

Her brow furrowed and she looked away.

He grasped her arm to get her attention. "No, let me explain. I admit I am stubborn. But I can see reason. As soon as you are wed to Barry, and Sussex to Amelia, I shall begin to consider—only consider, mind you—a marriage to produce an heir. If you can be so selfless, then so must I, if only to ease my sisters' fears for the future. And I will attempt to do as you say—form a deep true bond without hiding behind a facade of ill will. I will even get respectfully but sincerely angry from time to time since I know you and Calliope think it impossible. I shall do it all because you've asked me to do it. I know you've asked me because you truly wish for my happiness despite everything."

And in the next moment, he spied in her face what he had been certain had died the night he was solely responsible for ruining her innocence. He glimpsed love in her eyes.

"Isabelle," he murmured, "there is no one I wish more happy than you." He rushed the words he should not say for they bordered on violating a confidence. "You father would be so happy, too. This was his last wish, that I see you happy with someone like Barry. He said he would never consent to a marriage with *someone like me*. Did you hear me, Isabelle? He expressly forbade me to marry you. He bade me to promise to see you married to a young gentleman full of vigor and of excellent character and standing."

Her eyes clouded with anger. "He also told me on his deathbed that I was to defer to my future husband's every decision after I marry. And do you think that will happen?"

"Did you agree to it?"

"Of course I didn't!"

"Too bad for Barry," he whispered.

"Stop it! Tell me once and for all. Do you love me or not?"

And as a ball of fury rose up within Candover to attack and conquer all that stood between them, Vere

SOPHIA NASH

Sturbridge, the bloody, sodding Duke of Barry rode up on his white warhorse. The only thing missing was a rose clenched in his jaws.

"There is my ravishing bride," Barry said with his usual good cheer. "You're not trying to steal her from me, are you, Candover?"

Thank God Barry was occupied dismounting and tugging the ribbons over his beast's head and did not take notice of Isabelle's face.

"Where is the carriage?" Barry asked as he pulled up his stirrups. "And Miss Little? We should take our leave within the next quarter hour if we expect to make London by nightfall. Mary Haverty is joining us too, no?"

"Of—Of course," Isabelle stuttered. Her eyes begged him to say something. Something to stop this.

James was afraid that he would be forever haunted by the expression of dashed dreams on her face just before the imitation of happiness. He forced his legs, which felt like they were stuck in a bog, to walk over to Barry. "I shall see to the carriage."

"Kind of you, Candover," Barry replied, taking up Isabelle's hand and pressing a lingering kiss there. He focused his gaze on Isabelle's down-turned face. "Come, shall we not take a last turn in the garden, my dear? And you must give me a few hints on how I am to coax a smile to the face of your cousin. I've brought sweets for her, but I fear it's going to be a long journey in that carriage for the four of us if she frowns and insists on reading aloud that tract on how we can live hell on earth in our minds if we are not careful." He grinned ruefully. "Why doesn't she like me? I swear she stuck out her tongue at me yesterday when she thought I wasn't looking. Funny, I've never had a problem with children in the past."

"She's not a child," James said softly.

Already Isabelle's eyes had grown remote. This would be how they'd always be in the future.

Barry grinned and shook his hand as they took their leave of him. James heard Barry's next words directed toward Isabelle and something got stuck in the back of his throat—and it wasn't an icicle.

"You did say she will stay with us for a few more months, didn't you, my love?"

Chapter 20

From the gilded throne of your favorite future monarch

Isabelle shook her head. She would miss these little notes from the Prince Regent.

My dearest, loveliest Isabelle,

So you've fixed on Barry, have you? Yes, I always advise to choose beauty before age—unless, of course, you can have your cake and eat it, too. Oh, extra points for me . . . two misused clichés in one! Now then . . . are you certain, my child? You are my favorite of the entourage and I will not have you unhappy.

Again . . . are you certain? I ask for I am your humble servant, or perhaps your benevolent dictator is a tad more honest, and I am very willing (and somewhat determined as long as it will not interfere with my dinner) to have it out with Sobersides and command that he . . . Well, you understand the idea. Unless, of course, you decide to take Matters into Your Own Hands. Duchesses do that from time to time, you know. It's a very annoying thing for a gentleman, but secretly we know that if you are not happy, no one will be happy.

And so, to repeat. . .

It's. Not. Too. Late.

See you at the church—or not.

Hmmmm . . . how many clichés is that? Might be a record.

Your devoted, demanding, manipulative, controlling (but all in a good way) sovereign,

G.

Isabelle took one long last look at the royal missive that had been delivered to her a month ago upon her arrival in London. She tapped it between her fingers, walked to the marble mantel in her chambers in March House and dropped the letter into the glowing embers of the fire that had been set to chase away the chill of autumn.

She had dismissed her maid and had but a few more minutes before she would give herself over to the events of the day. She smoothed the delicate pale blue silk and tulle of her new gown, careful to push aside the small train before she moved to the looking glass to make certain she was ready. Tiny white rosebuds threaded her light brown locks piled high into a soft arrangement. The posies she would carry as she walked into St. George's lay on a nearby table. She leaned into her reflection and pinched her cheeks to bring color to her face.

She had made her choice. She and Barry would do very well together. She had done the outrageous and taken matters into her own hands at the start of the Little Season, as the Prince Regent suggested, and all had not gone according to plan. But she was determined to accept and embrace all the goodness she might share with Barry, beginning today. This very morning.

A soft knock on her chamber door roused her from her thoughts and she called out her invitation to enter.

Calliope's little head peeked around the door, and her expression filled with wonder. She entered, followed by Mary Haverty and Amelia Primrose, now officially Her Grace, the Duchess of Sussex.

"Oh, Isabelle," Calliope said, "how beautiful you are."

"This is entirely unfair." Amelia chuckled. "It will

take at least an hour to admire you, and your carriage is waiting. Oh, you look like an angel. Like a fairy come to life. A—"

"Princess," Mary interrupted quietly. "Isabelle, you are perfection. Then again, you always have been—inside and out."

"Oh yes, I'm perfect, all right—a perfect mass of pudding inside," she said as she crossed her arms and brushed the flesh above her long gloves. "I'm chilled. I should ask the footman to add a bit of coal to—"

"We haven't time," Amelia insisted with a small smile. "I daresay my husband will be pounding on this door in less than a minute. If I had known he could be such a demanding brute, I'm not sure I would have taken him on. Are you ready, Isabelle?"

"I think we still have a little more time," Calliope insisted. "We should call for some tea. And more coal. And my head aches. Please, I need someone to extract half the pins from my head that are"—she glanced at Mary—"stuck into my scalp."

"I'm so sorry, Calliope," Mary replied softly. "I had no idea."

"Mary," Amelia said, shaking her head, "what has come over you? Calliope should be thanking you for arranging her hair. If I have the right of it from the housekeeper—no one could satisfy Miss Calliope Little today. Do I need to return here to bring some sense into you, Calliope?"

"Yes," said Calliope a bit miserably. "Oh, forget it. I know how to leave off of a lost cause. Even I would not leave Sussex if I had him in a leg shackle."

Isabelle had watched the exchange without a word. She missed Amelia terribly. There had been something so right about shouldering the education of Calliope with someone who knew how to do battle with her young cousin, and win her over to correct form without damaging her spirit. Ever since Isabelle had left Sussex's house party with Calliope and Barry, something had been missing.

Someone pounded on the door.

"You can't say I didn't warn you," Amelia said, biting her lip.

"Let's send him down for tea and biscuits," Calliope begged. "There's plenty of time still."

Mary admitted Sussex into the chamber. He looked around the circle of ladies. "You are all of you ravishing. But we are late. Come along, then."

"Is that it?" Calliope inserted. "Where is that silver tongue of yours when it is most called for, Your Grace? Surely someone is going to say something. And you are the gentleman here. You could at least—"

"Calliope," Isabelle said. She tugged at the hem of her gown and moved closer to her cousin. "I'm not certain what is the matter with you, but you will apologize. Now." Calliope was beyond petulant, beyond reason. Even Amelia was aghast.

"No, it's my fault," Mary said, "I should have been more careful with the pins."

An awkward silence hung in the sun-filled chamber, at odds with the mood of the occupants.

"I am sorry," Calliope began quietly, "truly I am, but—"

"It's a quarter past ten," Sussex interrupted, "we really should—"

"But I'm hungry," wailed Calliope. "Really and truly. No one thought to bring me breakfast."

Isabelle examined her shrewdly. What would *he* say? "Did you ring for a tray?"

"No," she replied, "but—"

Edward Godwin, the Duke of Sussex, resplendent in Weston's finest threads made expressly for mornings like these, bent forward and hauled Miss Calliope Little over his shoulder. "Enough, brat. We're leaving."

James Fitzroy was glad he had been given a formal duty this morning. He was simply not at all amused that it involved transporting the Archbishop of Canterbury to St. George's Church in Mayfair. And yet, he was unable to refuse since the Prince Regent had followed up with his own royal command to do the old man's bidding.

It smelled of collusion.

Reeked of it, in fact.

Oh, he was no fool. He knew what was afoot.

Twice during the last month he'd had to entertain His High and Mighty with an appearance at court. Twice the prince had insisted on a private audience. And twice he had endured his sovereign's lectures on the importance of marriage, of heirs, of spares, and most ironically, of love and other nonsense. And then he had been handed a list. The same long list of females Isabelle had forced on him a long time ago.

Every lady on the list was more impossible than the last.

And now he was forced to listen to more of the same in his own landau on the way to St. George's.

"We are given life on this earth to procreate," His Grace, the archbishop, pronounced in his most sonorous voice. "And when we procreate, we honor—"

"And this procreating business," James interrupted, "this is something you've done?"

The archbishop sat up very straight across from him, which was very straight indeed, considering the iron-like gold collar and stiff fabrics of the clergy he wore. "I know my job, Sobersides, do you?"

Good God, would he have to endure this stupid moniker for eternity? Apparently.

The old man switched tactics. "Always liked St. George's Church. Named after St. George, don't you know?"

He would go mad if this continued.

"A martyr, he was. Dead. And now just a martyr and a saint. You know about him, do you?"

It was all James could do not to roll his eyes. Instead he stilled his foot, which had been doing a most irritating thing: tapping.

"This venerated saint slayed a dragon to rescue a king's daughter from a fate worse than death. Do you know what it was?"

"Yes. A dragon eating her alive."

"Not really."

"Then what was it?" He actually wanted to hear the archbishop's sure-to-be-ridiculous reply.

"Unhappiness," he insisted. "He rescued her from a lifetime of unhappiness."

"Of what? Perhaps one minute of pain before death by dragon?"

"You willfully refuse to see reason, Candover."

Enough. James grasped his walking stick and tapped it twice on the ceiling of his carriage. He glared at the archbishop. "I see reason to descend right here, I do."

"But I have not given you leave to—"

"We've arrived, damn it."

A quarter of an hour later, James managed to work his way through the crowd at the west front portico and edge past the six Corinthian columns to make his way near the canopy over the pulpit. Amelia, Mary Haverty, and Calliope waited for him in the first box pew in the church.

James wasn't entirely certain if the roaring in his head was from the crowds of people overfilling the famous church—where anyone who was anyone, and anyone who wished to be someone and could manage it, were married in Mayfair—or if it was imagined.

And why were his feet numb and his hands cold? The three longest minutes of his life ensued as he nodded to a few guests, and then entered his high-walled box, where Calliope, Mary Haverty, and Amelia all waited for him. Handel's organ spewed forth the same mournful music that preceded three-quarters of the weddings in this church.

Before he could think of another thing to dislike, the archbishop appeared from behind a panel and seemed to almost float in his heavy robes to the center of the arched center aisle. Vere Sturbridge, the Duke of Barry, followed him. Moments later Isabelle appeared a few steps away, supported by the Duke of Sussex, whose smile, for the first time James had ever seen, was missing.

She looked like an angel.

Or a king's daughter.

James just wasn't quite sure if he was St. George or the dragon.

Before the last notes faded, the archbishop opened his Bible to a section, looked over the top of his spectacles, and cleared his throat. "Yes, let's see," he said under his breath. "A bit rusty. All right. Let us begin.

The institution of marriage is not to be entered into lightly, or . . ."

James lost track of the words. He had entered into another realm as he stared at Isabelle's profile. So lovely, and intelligent, and dignified. Across from her, Barry wore a look of somber dignity, which was her mirror.

"Who gives this lady's hand in marriage?" the archbishop droned onward.

"I do," Sussex responded evenly.

James could not focus on the answers and more questions. Moments later Sussex bowed, and stepped back to enter James' box. He settled next to James with a loud sigh.

James wrenched his gaze from his worst nightmare and attempted to focus on one of the carved wooden square panels in the box. A little voice, very faint, itched his consciousness and he glanced to his side. "Stop this," Calliope said, her face full of pain and misery.

He closed his eyes briefly and slightly shook his head.

A small cold hand slipped between his tightly clasped hands. "Please," she whispered.

Amelia made an almost inaudible sound of disapproval.

"I know something," Calliope murmured.

He glanced at her without moving a muscle and then returned his attention to the altar.

Miss Calliope Little threw almost all caution to the wind and tugged James down to her level, cupped her hands about his ear and whimpered, "He likes someone else better."

That got his attention. "Who?"

"You know who." She nodded toward Barry. The most wonderful fourteen-year-old girl in the world then gave a speaking glance toward Mary Haverty, whose face was as white as a February day in Derbyshire as she sat ramrod straight, unaware of the conversation.

"Give me your word," he rasped out.

Calliope's eyes grew round and she made an X over her heart while she shook her head.

Bloody hell . . . and heaven on earth.

He swiveled his head toward Edward Godwin, the Duke of Sussex, who murmured for his ears only, "I'd trust her, *brother,* if only because she'll just make everyone miserable for the rest of our lives if you don't."

James did not hear Sussex's appellation. Calliope's words rang in his mind, and all thoughts of duty flew away as instinct flooded the walls of his soul, demanding he protect and profess to the woman he loved. James stood up, unaware of his actions, and unaware of the archbishop's words, or even if it was past the point of no return.

He rapped his ebony walking stick against the marble floor and exited the box to stand before the threesome. Utter stillness gave way to waves of whispers until he cleared his throat loudly.

"Isabelle Delphine Sophie Marie Solange Charlotte Jacqueline Clothilde de Peyster Tremont, Duchess of March? Will you do me the very great honor of condescending to make me the happiest of men in all of Christendom and indeed all corners of this earth, and above? I realize I am asking . . . no, begging, really . . . for you to consider this late request, but you see the thing of it is that . . . well, I love you. And even if you very well do not love me in return, still I must ask."

Isabelle stared at James, darted a measured glance at Barry, followed by the archbishop, whose mouth gaped—most likely for the first time in his life.

"Could you say that again?" Her voice was low.

"Of course, my darling," James said. "Isabelle Delphine Sophie Marie Solange Charlotte—"

"Do you really have quite so many names?" Barry whispered.

"Shhh," Isabelle said. "Yes, I do."

Barry leaned closer to her, and James wanted to reach out and grab her. It was visceral, this need to take that which was always meant to be his love. He didn't want Isabelle anywhere near Barry. He clenched his fists, which were now hot.

"Do you want him?" Barry murmured so quietly James could barely hear him.

"I should say no," she whispered.

"You should," he assured her, and then glanced at Lady Mary Haverty, whose expression was filled with equal parts shock and happiness.

James's chest finally expanded with relief. Calliope gurgled until Amelia elbowed her, unseen.

Isabelle finally smiled. "Please, go on, darling." She nodded to James.

Darling . . . She had said *darling*. The most beautiful word in the English language.

And before half of the ton, James Fitzroy broke his word repeatedly, quite thoroughly, and with great love, for there was one thing above all that he had promised Isabelle's father, the thing that trumped all else . . . He had promised to protect her. Protect her from all harm. And to ensure her happiness. And that this moment allowed him the happiness that might have eluded him—marriage to the only woman whom he would ever love—was merely a miraculous benefit.

"Your Graces," the archbishop insisted, with a baritone that carried to the back of the gathering, "shall we not carry on in private. Follow me. Good day everyone and may—"

James rushed forward to guide Isabelle toward the annex behind the hanging pulpit, forgetting everyone and everything in his wake. He had to have her in his arms. He had to make certain this was real. He pushed and shoved at an enormous tapestry beyond the coved annex until they were shrouded in semidarkness.

There, he grasped her forearms. "I'm so very sorry, Isabelle, my love. Will you forgive me? Will you love me, have me? Despite all?"

"Why now?" she asked, with such tenderness.

"A certain Miss Calliope Little. And Sussex . . . my—hell, he knows. He pointed out something quite correct. I just have to be good, not right."

Without another word, Isabelle went into his arms, and James Fitzroy knew happiness. Tasted happiness with every fiber of his being.

Yes, paradise . . .

And all the while, a rotund gentleman known as His Royal Highness, the Prince Regent, stood in the same annex of the church, unseen. He smiled. He loathed weddings. Abhorred them entirely. His own being his chief complaint. But this morning? Why, he might just reverse his opinion. Ah, yes, love was in the air.

He had accomplished the impossible: five dukes in parson's mousetrap in less than six months.

It must be a record.

And all it had taken was a little hint of revolution. A little soupçon of trickery. A little taste of . . . Oh, how tiring this entire pairing off of dukes could be on one's nerves. Art, architecture, gambling, cuisine, and war were far more intriguing.

The Prince Regent darted a glance about him, and then partook from his glittering gold snuff box.

The entire collection of assorted, bejeweled witnesses of the most outrageous goings-on of the century poured out of St. George's Church, uncertain if they wanted to dash off to report the outrageous or partake in a non-wedding breakfast to celebrate something, of which they were not certain.

A single crow flew overhead, darted through the bell tower, cawed twice, and made its way to an ancient oak tree, where the rest of his murder roosted. His mate cocked her sleek head and tucked her head against his for a moment. Their fellow raven-jacketed friends cackled with joviality.

And much like the starkly handsome duke with his future bride at his side exiting the church below only to be surrounded by a swarm of laughing people, this crow was home.

And now a sneak peek at the first book
in the Royal Entourage series,

BETWEEN THE DUKE
AND THE DEEP BLUE SEA

Available in print and e-book
from Avon Books

A new duke always had hell to pay.

Oh, it had been all well and good when Alexander Barclay, now the newly minted ninth Duke of Kress, had walked into White's Club in Mayfair and been pounded on the back by a blossoming number of friends a fortnight ago.

And it had been *very* good last week when he had met his new solicitors and removed from his cramped and moldy rooms off St. James's *Street* to palatial Kress House, Number Ten, St. James's *Square*.

However, it had gone from the first bloom of bonhomie with the *crème de la crème* of the most privileged societal tier in the world to near pariah status overnight. Alex's avalanche from grace had all started last eve at the Prince Regent's Carleton House, where he provided the spirits to toast His Grace, the Duke of Candover's last evening as a bachelor.

His own induction into the circle that same night, he could not remember.

Alex should have known better. Had not the sages throughout history warned to be careful of what one wished? Barons, viscounts, marquises, and earls would have given up their last monogram-encrusted silver spoon for entrée into the prince's exclusive circle, and all for naught as one had to be a duke of England to be included. For two centuries, the dukes in the peerage of Scotland had pushed for inclusion in the royal entourage to no avail. And one did not speak of the Irish dukes' efforts at all.

Yes, well. Being a duke was anything but entertaining right now. More asleep than not, Alex shivered— only to realize his clothes were wet, and even his toes were paddling circles in his boots. Christ above, he would give over a large portion of his newfound fortune if only someone would lend him a pistol to take a poorly aimed shot at the birds singing outside like it was the last morning the world would ever see.

Sod it . . . What on earth had happened last night? And where in bloody hell was he?

The fast clacking of heels somewhere beyond the door reverberated like a herd of African elephants. A sharp knock brought stars to the insides of Alex's eyelids before the door opened.

"Hmmm . . . finally. Thought we'd lost you," shouted a familiar feminine voice.

Footsteps trampled closer and Alex pried open his eyes to find a blurry pair of oddly golden peepers and coils of brown hair floating above him. Ah, the young Duchess of March, the only female in the prince's entourage. Alex wished he could make his voice box work to beg her to stop making so much noise.

"Although, you," she continued, looking at Alex's valet stretched out on a trundle bed nearby, "are not Norwich. Come along, then. The both of you. Prinny is not in a mood to wait this morning—not that he ever is." Isabelle displayed the annoying habit of tapping her foot as she stared at Alex.

When he did not move, Isabelle had the audacity to start pulling his arm. Dislocation being the worse of two evils, Alex struggled to regain full consciousness and his feet as his man did the same with much greater ease.

Ah, at least he had one question answered. They were still in the prince's Carleton House. *Thank the Lord.* Any debauchery that might have occurred had at least remained within the confines of these gilded walls. There had been far too much gossip lately of the immoderation of their high-flying circle.

"Look, if we're not in His Majesty's chambers within the next two minutes, I cannot answer as to what might happen," the duchess urged. "Honestly, what were you and the rest thinking last night? There must have been quite a bit of devilish spirits to cause . . ."

He held up his hand for her to stop. Just the thought of distilled brews made him wince.

"Must have been the absinthe," his valet, Jack Farquhar, said knowingly. "Englishmen never have the stomach for it."

"You're English," Alex ground out, his head splitting.

"Precisely why I never imbibe. But you . . . you should be *half* immune to that French spirit of the devil incarnate."

Isabelle Tremont, the Duchess of March, had a lovely warm laugh, but right now it sounded like all the bells of St. George's at full peel.

"We *must* go. You too." She nodded to Jack Farquhar, before she continued. "Kress, do you have the faintest idea where Norwich is? Were you not with him during the ridiculous bachelor fete? You two are usually inseparable."

Alex made the mistake of trying to shake his head with disastrous results. "Can't remember . . ." As the duchess pulled them both forward, Alex's toes squished like sponges inside his now not so spanking white tasseled Hessian boots.

The effort to cross the halls to the Prince Regent's bedchamber felt like a long winter march across Europe to St. Petersburg. Alex looked sidelong toward his soon-to-be dismissed valet. "Absinthe, *mon vieux*?"

"'Twas the only thing in your new cellar . . . eighteen bottles. Either the last duke had a partiality for the vile stuff or his servants drank everything but that—in celebration of his death."

To describe the pasty-faced, hollowed-eyed jumble of gentlemen strewn around the royal bedchamber as alive was a gross kindness. Four other dukes—Candover, Sussex, Wright, and Middlesex—as well as the Archbishop of Canterbury formed a disheveled half-circle before Prinny's opulent, curtained bed where the future king of England reclined in full shadow.

"Your Majesty would have me recommence reading, then?" The pert voice of the duchess caused a round of moans. "I'm sorry, but Norwich and Barry cannot be found, and Abshire is, umm, indisposed but will arrive shortly." She blushed and studied the plush carpet. "As His Majesty said, there should be no delay in a response to these outrageous accusations." She waved a newspaper in the air.

Alex swiveled his head and met the glassy-eyed

stare of the bridegroom, the Duke of Candover, who turned away immediately in the fashion of a cut direct.

"Uh . . . shouldn't you be at St. George's?" Alex would have given his eyeteeth for a chair.

"Brilliant observation," Candover said under his breath.

"Late to the party, Kress." The Prince Regent's voice was raspy with contempt. "Haven't you heard? Candover has been stood up by his bride on this wedding morning. Or was it the other way around, my dear?"

"It appears both, Your Majesty," the duchess replied, scanning the newspaper with what almost appeared to be a hint of . . . of *delight*? No, Alex was imagining it.

"Lady Margaret Spencer was tucked in an alcove of the church, but her family whisked her away unseen when Candover did not appear after a ninety-minute delay," Isabelle read from the column.

"Why wasn't I woken?" Candover grasped his wrenched head in obvious pain.

"James Fitzroy," the duchess replied, disapprobation emanating from every inch of her arched back, "you should know. Your sisters and I woke to find every servant here on tiptoe. You, and the rest of you"—her eyes fluttered past the prince in her embarrassment—"commanded upon threat of dismissal or, ahem, dismemberment that you were not to be disturbed."

"I remember that part very well," inserted Jack Farquhar.

In the long pause that followed, Alex imagined half a dozen ways to dismember his valet. He was certain that every duke in the room was considering the same thing.

"Continue reading, Isabelle." The royal hand made a halfhearted movement.

"Let's see," the duchess murmured, her eyes flickering over the words of the article. "Uh, well, the columnist made many unfortunate assumptions and . . ."

"Isabelle Tremont, I order you to read it," ground out the prince.

"Majesty," she breathed. "I—I just can't."

John Spence, the Duke of Wright, who at seven and twenty was the youngest of all the dukes, chose that moment—a most opportune one—to sway ominously and pitch forward onto the future king's bed. Without a word, the Duke of Sussex hauled Wright off the royal bedclothes and laid the poor fellow, who was out stone cold, on the floor.

Alex strode forward and grasped the edges of the paper from the pretty duchess's nervous fingers.

"Ah, yes, much better," the Prince Regent said sourly. "Might as well have the man"—his Majesty's hand pointed to him—"who is to blame for the ruin of us all, read it."

Head pounding, Alex forced his eyes and mouth to work. " 'In a continuation of the regular obscene excesses of the Prince Regent and his *royal entourage*, not one of the party made an appearance at St. George's earlier this morning, with the exception of our Princess Caroline, darling Princess Charlotte, and Her Grace, the young Duchess of March. His Majesty's absence and that of the groom and groomsmen caused all four hundred guests to assume the worst. And, indeed, this columnist has it on the very best authority, partially one's own eyewitness account, that not only the august bridegroom, His Grace, the Duke of Candover, but also seven other dukes, one archbishop and the Prince Regent himself, were seen cavorting about all of London last eve on an outrageous regal rampage. Midnight duels, swimming amok with the swans in the Serpentine, a stream of scantily clad females in tow, lawn bowling in unmentionables, horse races in utter darkness, wild, uproarious boasting, and jesting, and wagering abounded. Indeed, this author took it upon himself to retrieve and return to White's Club their infamous betting book, which one of the royal entourage had had the audacity to remove without even a by your leave. In this fashion we have learned that the Duke of Kress lost the entire fortune he so recently acquired with the title, although the winner's name was illegible . . .'" Alex's voice stumbled to a halt.

"Happens to the best of us," the Duke of Sussex murmured as consolation. That gentleman was as green about the gills as Alex felt.

"And the worst of us," mumbled the Duke of Middlesex, as he finally gave in to the laws of gravity and allowed his body to slide down the wall on which he was leaning. He sunk to the ground with a thud.

"Don't stop now, Kress. You've gotten to the only good part." Candover leaned in wickedly.

Alex had never tried to avoid just punishment. He just wished he could remember, blast it all, what his part had been in the debacle. He cleared his throat and continued, " 'Even the queen's jewels were spotted on one duke as he paraded down Rotten Row. Yes, my fellow countrymen, it appears the English monarchy has learned nothing from our French neighbor's lessons concerning aristocratic overindulgence. As the loyal scribe of the Fashionable Column for two decades, you have it on my honor that all this occurred and worse. I can no longer remain silent on these reoccurring grievous, licentious activities, and so shall be the first plainspeaking, brave soul to utter these treasonous words: I no longer support or condone a monarchy such as this.'"

Alex stood very still as the last of the column's words left his lips.

At precisely the same moment the other dukes cleared their throats, and one valet tried to escape.

"If any of you leave or say one word, I shall cut off your head with a . . ."

"Guillotine, Majesty?" Isabelle chirped.

In the silence, a storm brewed of epic proportions.

Thank the Lord, the chamber's gilded door opened to divert His Majesty's attention. The Duke of Barry, a Lord Lieutenant of the 95th Rifle Regiment, stepped in, almost instantly altering his unsteady gait with expert precision. Only his white face and the sheen of perspiration on his forehead gave him away. Mutely, he stepped forward and laid a dueling pistol on the foot of the cashmere and silk royal bedclothing.

"Dare I ask?" His Majesty's voice took on an arctic edge.

Barry opened his mouth but no sound came out. He tried again. "I believe I shot a man. He's in your billiard room, Majesty."

The Duke of Abshire entered the royal chamber behind Barry with the hint of wickedness in his even, dark features marred by a massive black eye. Known as the cleverest of the bunch, good luck had clearly deserted him on this occasion.

"I thought you were leaving, Abshire. Or do you need me to show you out?" Candover's usually reserved expression turned thunderous.

Alex leaned toward Sussex, and almost fell over before righting himself. "What did I miss?"

"Trust me," Sussex whispered. "You do not want to know. You've got enough on your dish, old man."

Alex raised his eyebrows at Sussex and missed Abshire's dry retort directed at the premier duke, Candover. There was no love lost between those two. Then again, Candover's remote, holier-than-thou manner grated on just about everyone.

Middlesex, still on the floor, tugged on Alex's breeches and Alex bent down to catch the former's whisper. "I heard a lady shouting in chambers next to mine, then two doors slammed, and Candover came out rubbing his knuckles."

Alex shook his head. Could it get any worse?

The black-haired duke, Abshire, clapped a hand on the shoulder of the most respected and most quiet duke of the circle, Barry. "Is he dead?"

"Yes," Barry replied.

"Are you certain?" Sussex asked, eyes wide.

"I think I know when a man is breathing or not."

"But there are some whose breath cannot be detected," Middlesex croaked.

"Rigor. Mortis," Barry replied.

An inelegant sound came from the duchess's throat.

"Please forgive me, Isabelle," Barry said quietly. "Your Grace, I do not know the man."

"Just tell me you locked the chamber when you left it," the prince said dryly. When Barry nodded, the prince continued darkly. "I had thought better of you, Barry. What is this world coming to if I cannot count on one of England's best and brightest?" The prince, still in full shadow, sighed heavily. "Well, we shall see to the poor, unfortunate fellow, as soon as I am done with all of you."

"Yes, Your Majesty," Barry replied, attempting to maintain his ramrod posture.

"Now then," His Majesty said with more acidity than a broiled lemon. "Does not one of you remember what precisely happened last night?"

"I remember the Frenchified spirits Kress's man"— the Duke of Sussex looked toward Jack Farquhar with pity—"brought into His Majesty's chamber."

"I must be allowed to defend . . ." Farquhar began and then changed course. "Yes, well, since three of you locked me in a strong room when I voiced my concern, I cannot add any further observations."

"Is that the queen's coronation broach, Sussex?" the imperial voice demanded suddenly.

The Duke of Sussex, now pale as the underbelly of a swan, looked down and started. Hastily, he removed the offending article and laid the huge emerald-and-diamond broach on the end of the gold-leaf bed frame, beside the pistol.

Alex just made out Middlesex's whispered words below. "Very fetching. Matches his eyes to perfection."

Alex felt a grin trying to escape as he helped Middlesex to his feet.

"Just like the wet muck on your shoulder compliments your peepers, Middlesex," retorted Sussex.

Ah, friendship. Who knew English dukes could be so amusing when they dropped their lofty facades? Last night had probably almost been worth it. It was too bad none of them could remember it.

"Well, at least the columnist did not know about the unfortunate soul in the billiard room," Isabelle breathed. "Did you all really swim in the Serpentine? I declare, the lot of you are wetter than setters after a duck. I would not have ever done anything so—"

"You were not invited," the Duke of Candover gritted out.

"And whose fault was that?"

"Enough," the Prince Regent roared. The royal head emerged from the gloom and Alex's gasp blended with the rest of the occupants' shocked sounds in the room.

His Majesty's head was half shaved—the left side as smooth as a babe's bottom, the long brown and gray locks on the right undisturbed. None dared to utter a word.

Prinny raised his heavy jowls and lowered his eyelids in a sovereign show of condescension. "None of this is to the point. I hereby order each of you to make amends to me, and to your country. Indeed, I need not say all that is at stake." His Majesty chuckled darkly at them. "And we have not a moment to spare. Archbishop?"

A small fat man trundled forward, his head in his hands, his gait impaired.

The future king continued. "You shall immediately begin a formal answer to this absurd column—to be delivered to all the newspapers. And as for the rest of you—except you, my dear Isabelle—I order you all to cast aside your mistresses and your self-indulgent, outrageous ways to set a good example."

"Said the pot to the kettle," inserted Sussex under his breath.

"You shall each," His Majesty demanded, "be given your particular marching orders in one hour's time. While I should let all of you stew about your ultimate fate, I find . . . I cannot. I warn that exile from London, marriage, continuation of ducal lines, a newfound fellowship with sobriety, and a long list of additional duties await each of you."

"Temperance, marriage, and rutting. Well, at least one of the three is tolerable," the Duke of Abshire on Alex's other side opined darkly and discreetly.

Alex could not let this farce continue. "Majesty, I appreciate the invitation to join this noble circle of renegades but—"

"It's not an invitation, Kress," the Prince Regent interrupted. "And by the by, have you forgotten your return to straightened circumstances if this column is correct? You shall be the first to receive your task."

"An order is more like it," the Duke of Barry warned quietly. The solemn man wore a distinctive green military uniform that reminded Alex of his own dark past. A past that would infuriate the Prince Regent if he but knew of it.

Prinny glanced about the chamber in an old rogue's fit of pique. "Kress, you shall immediately retire to your principal seat—St. Michael's Mount in Cornwall. Since a large portion of the blame for last evening rests squarely on your shoulders, I hereby require you to undertake the restoration of that precious pile of rubble, for the public considers it a long neglected important outpost for England's security. Many have decried its unseemly state."

A departure from London was the very last thing he would do. He hated any hint of countrified living. The cool lick of an idea slid into his mind and he smiled. "But, according to that column, I've no fortune to do so, Your Majesty."

Prinny's face grew red with annoyance. "You are to use funds from my coffers for the time being. But you shall repay my indulgence when you take a bride from a list of impeccable young ladies of fine lineage and fine fortunes"—Prinny nodded to a page who delivered a document into Alex's hands—*"within a month's time."*

Candover made the mistake of showing a hint of teeth.

Alex Barclay, formerly Viscount Gaston, with pockets to let in simpler times, felt his contrarian nature rise like a dragon from its lair, but knew enough to say not a word. The ice of his English father's blood had never been very effective in cooling the boiling crimson inherited from his French mother.

"And you, my dear Candover," the prince continued, "shall have the pleasure of following him, along with Sussex and Barry, for a house party composed of all the eligibles. While you are exempt at the moment from choosing a new bride, as homage must be paid to your jilted fiancée, I shall count on you to keep the rest of these scallywags on course."

Candover's smile disappeared. "Have you nothing to say to His Majesty, Kress?" The richest of all the dukes coolly stepped forward to face Alex and tapped his fingers against a polished rosewood table in the opulent room seemingly dipped in gold, marble, and every precious material in between. The rarefied air positively reeked of royal architects gone amok.

When Alex's silence continued, all rustling around him eventually stopped. "Thank you," Alex murmured, "but . . . *no thank you*."

Candover's infernal tapping ceased. "*No?* Whatever do you mean?" A storm of disapproval, mixed with jaded humor erupted all around him.

Oh, Alex knew it was only a matter of time before he would capitulate to the demands, but he just hadn't been able to resist watching the charade play out to its full potential.

The Prince Regent's face darkened from pale green to dark purple. It was a sight to behold. "And let me add, Kress, one last incentive. Don't think I have not heard the whispers questioning your allegiance to England. If I learn there is one shred of truth to the notion that you may have worn a frog uniform, I won't shed a single tear if you are brought before the House of Lords and worse. Care to reconsider your answer?"

It had been amusing to think that life would improve with his elevation. But then, he habitually failed to remember that whenever he had trotted on happiness in the past, there had always, *always* been *de la merde*—or rather, manure—on his heels in the end.

The only question now was how soon he could extricate himself from a ramshackle island prison to return to the only world where he had ever found peace . . . London.